ASKING FOR TROUBLE

USA TODAY & WSJ BESTSELLING AUTHOR

giana darling

Copyright 2024 Giana Darling

Published by Giana Darling

Edited by Jenny Sims

Proofed by Sarah Plocher

Cover Design by Najla Qamber

Cover Photography by Lunden Hopen

Cover Model Lunden Hope

To the trouble seekers and daredevils.

Don't ever let anyone tell you to back down from adventure or to stop fighting for what you want.

"The trouble with trouble is that it usually starts out as fun."

—Anonymous

PLAYLIST

"Feel Alright"--Steve Earle
"Don't Take The Money"--Bleachers, Lorde
"Highway to Hell"--AC/DC
"3AM"--Matchbox Twenty
"Trouble"--Hamish Anderson
"Bad Karma"--Miley Cyrus, Joan Jett & The Blackhearts
"Getaway Car"--Taylor Swift
"Share Your Address"--Ben Platt
"Rollercoaster"--Bleachers
"Homemade Dynamite"--Lorde
"Trouble"--Bellstop
"Chasing Cars"--Tommee Profitt, Our Vinyl
"The Night We Met"--Lord Huron
"This Is Why We Can't Have Nice Things"--Taylor Swift
"Tempt My Trouble"--Bishop Briggs
"No Plan"--Hozier
"Wild Heart"--Bleachers
"Daddy Issues"--The Neighbourhood
"Gives You Hell"--The All-American Rejects
"Run To You - LoFi"--Ocie Elliott, Nathan Kawanishi
"Blue"--Billie Eilish
"How Deep Is Your Love"--Calvin Harris, Disciples
"Caged Bird"--Myles Cameron
"Free"--Ocie Elliott
"Love Like Ghosts"--Lord Huron

NOTE TO MY READERS

This is a dark romance. *Asking for Trouble* contains graphic violence, domestic abuse, violence against women, verbal abuse, mentions of poor mental health, and criminal activity.

If you have a problem with any of these topics, please do not proceed.

While *Asking for Trouble* is a standalone and a great entry point point to the series, I do suggest reading The Fallen Men in order for optimal reading enjoyment.

Aren't we all?
SINNERS

CHAPTER ONE

Blue

LOTS OF STUFF happens in convenience stores and at gas stations. Most of it bad.

Especially on the Sea to Sky Highway, miles away from civilization, where drug running and human trafficking were known occurrences.

A young, decently attractive woman working the night shift was asking for trouble, but I was the kinda girl born and raised in chaos, who walked the razor's edge of risk like it was my daily commute to work.

I could handle myself.

Once, when a tweaked-out meth head wandered into the store, knocking over a rack of potato chips on the way to the till, he took out his junk to pee on the glass partition separating us, and I'd handled it. A calm call to the cops dispatched of the pervert without much fuss or fanfare. Cleaning the piss off the glass was another thing entirely, but bleach worked wonders.

Another time, when two drunks had started a fight in the back next to the fridges, I'd called the cops, grabbed my baseball bat and hit one asshole in the knee when he didn't heed my warnings. The snap of a tendon in his leg was grimly satisfying.

I'd been taking care of myself long before I'd left my family home, and I refused to take anyone's shit since that day.

Few people took tiny me seriously. It was a little hard to blame them when I was five foot two with cobalt blue and black hair and massive blue eyes that lent me an expression of eternal innocence.

It's funny how biology can tell lies much more eloquently than our mouths.

I looked sweet and younger than my twenty-five years.

The truth was, I'd lived on my own since I was seventeen, including a stint on the streets for a year or so. I was intimately acquainted with all seven of the deadly sins. They were my dear friends, like Snow White and her merry band of dwarves.

Some drunk idiots, strung-out addicts, high school wannabe rebels, and rich jerks with too much money and zero manners couldn't put me off working at Evergreen Gas Station. Not when it was putting me through cosmetology school.

Besides, Grouch Pedersen was the kindest man I'd ever known.

When I was eighteen and he caught me stealing from the station, again and again, he didn't turn me in.

He gave me a job and paid for my room at the Purgatory Motel for a month.

Truthfully, I was set to graduate from my beauty program in three weeks, but I was anxious about quitting Evergreen Gas. The retro-looking gas station and convenience store had become my home more than anywhere else. Maybe it was sad that rows of junk food and the whirr of a Slurpee machine were as familiar to me as most people's backyards and living rooms, but it was the first place where I'd felt in control of my life in too many years to count. Even the dangers of working the graveyard shift at a highway gas station were oddly comforting, familiar from my childhood.

I was reminiscing about exactly that when the bells over the door jingled in greeting. My gaze immediately lifted to the newcomer, an instinct born of self-preservation after years of working there.

My breath caught in my throat like a stuck lozenge threatening to choke me.

He was beautiful.

Like something out of the magazines I studied for inspiration.

Like someone who was paid to look that way.

Only he was too rough for that. The bright tattoos on his neck under the shadow of a days-old beard as black as spilled ink across his jaw. The worn-in leather jacket opened over a white tee with a small Hephaestus Auto Garage logo stitched onto the breast. The tee was too tight, his muscles almost obscene beneath the thin fabric.

I choked a little, trying to cough without making a fool of myself.

Of course, it was just my luck that he noticed me then, as I was coughing quietly, desperate for air behind a shaky hand covering my flushed face.

Oh, boy.

Yeah.

This guy was perfection.

The swoop of thick black hair falling over a tanned forehead into eyes the colour of whiskey held over a flame. The wavy locks tangled in his long lashes, and when he reached up to brush them away, I noticed the bright tattoos on the back of his hand, the letters on the base of each knuckle, and what looked like an owl with its wings spread over the sides of his throat. There were thick silver rings on his fingers and a heavy silver chain around his throat. I wasn't a girl who usually went for jewelry on men, but something about the glint of metal against his warm olive skin made my throat dry and my thighs tingle.

He was the hottest man I'd ever seen in my life, and *of course*, he was seeing me like this, flushed from the effort to breathe without coughing up a lung, anything but cute in my black and blue Evergreen Gas polyester vest.

"You gonna survive, beautiful, or do you need a hand?" he asked, amusement rich in his tone as he swaggered up to the counter on a slow, unbalanced stride that should have been ridiculous but somehow seemed right.

I held up a shaky hand and gave in to the impulse to cough loudly into the crook of my other elbow. When I could finally breathe again, I flipped my thick blue hair over my shoulder and leveled him with a cool look.

"Can I help you with something?"

His full mouth twitched at the corners as he unabashedly checked me out. "Not a question you should ask a man like me without addin' some caveats."

"Does a man like you know what 'caveats' even means?" I retorted sweetly, batting my lashes.

He laughed and damn him because it was a gorgeous sound, rolling and low. When he finished, he wiped at his mouth as if he could erase his smile. "You aren't wearin' a name tag."

I blinked at him because he hadn't asked a question.

Another laugh, this one just a rumble through his throat. "What's your name?"

"What's yours?"

"Called Boner by my friends," he said, so straight-faced I wondered if he could actually be serious about it. "But pretty girls call me Aaron until they learn why I earned that nickname for themselves."

Despite myself, I chuckled. "You're not serious, are you? This schtick doesn't actually work on women."

He shrugged one shoulder, leather jacket creaking. "Whaddya think?"

"I don't know," I said honestly, enjoying his outrageousness and the perfect symmetry of his face more than I should.

I didn't have time for boys *or* trouble.

And this guy was the prettiest boy I'd ever met, so of course, he was trouble with a capital T.

"Tell me your name," he pressed, knocking his knuckles against the plastic countertop on his side of the partition. "Wanna know what to call you when I ask for your number."

"You're pushy."

Another one-shoulder shrug. "You see somethin' you like, why wouldn't you make an effort to make it yours?"

"'Make it' implies a lack of consent," I warned him, half-serious and half-flirting because I couldn't help it. He was too damn charming.

"Oh, trust me, you'll be askin' me to kiss you minutes into our first date. Beggin' me to make you come after an hour. Never taken anyone against their will in my life, never had to, and certainly never fuckin' would."

"Arrogance isn't attractive," I informed him, but really, it was a lie.

He didn't take himself too seriously despite his obvious confidence. His smile was more goofy than smug, his tone full of humour implied he was laughing at himself as much as he was enjoying our interlude.

"Let me prove you wrong," he suggested, leaning forward until he was so close to the slightly blurred plexiglass that I could see a faint scar cutting through the inky stubble on his chin. "The only thing I 'make' is trouble." He winked outrageously, a self-mocking smile curving one side of his mouth. "What's your name?"

I opened my mouth to tell him my name, my number, maybe even to demand he take me out on that first date at the end of my shift because I was curious about him, too curious, when his phone rang. The ringtone was AC/DC's "Highway to Hell".

Aaron cursed under his breath, excused himself reluctantly, and answered the call as he walked to the back of the shop. I couldn't see him beyond the shelves, but I listened to the low murmur of his voice and hated myself for finding even that attractive.

To remind myself that I didn't need the hassle of a man in my life, I hit a button on my phone to light up the home screen. The photo of a man appeared, heavily doctored by the edits I'd made with an app on my phone so that his eyes were crossed out and devil horns sprouted from his head.

Otto Granger, my ex-boyfriend, the man who stole all my savings six months ago.

We'd been dating for two years, living together in his basement suite in Whistler, on the track to spending the rest of our lives as a team.

And then one morning, I'd gone home to find the space cleared out, nothing but the dented metal lockbox I'd kept my savings in broke open on the kitchen counter. I didn't care about the money as much as I ached for the disappearance of my mother's sapphire ring. It was the only thing I had left of her, and I'd gone to dangerous lengths to take it with me when I'd fled home. To have my scumbag boyfriend steal it to pawn it off still made me prickly with rage.

After that, I promised myself that I wouldn't let anyone or anything else distract me from becoming a certified cosmetologist. It was the only thing I'd ever wanted for myself, to take part in making someone feel beautiful and special.

I wasn't built like the models all over social media, my curves softer and more exaggerated, but I knew how to work with what I had, and I fucking owned it. Over my years of sparse living, I'd learned that even a coat of nail polish could give a woman a reason to smile throughout the day. It might have seemed insignificant or trivial, but joy was joy in whatever amount or iteration it presented itself in.

So my dreams came first.

And this Aaron character, as beautiful as he was, as warm as I felt under the light of his regard, was a risk I wasn't willing to take.

If Otto had taught me anything, it was *not* to trust chemistry. I'd grown up with bad men all around me, and despite leaving that life behind a long time ago, it seemed I was still inexorably drawn to dangerous men.

I was uncharacteristically zoned out, so I didn't look up when the bells over the door chimed even though it was gone midnight and into the hours when I had to be hypervigilant.

"Hey, pretty girl," a rough voice rumbled, alerting me to the presence of a large man just to the left of the till.

Instantly, I took a step back from the partition between us, hand reaching for the panic button installed under the lip of the counter.

He grinned beneath the lady's stocking pulled down over his face, the shape of his smile obviously sinister even though the black nylon obscured it.

"Not so fast," he warned, whipping his arm from behind his back to lay a massive sawed-off shotgun on the counter. The barrel angled up into the window box designed in the partition, where customers and I could exchange coins and lottery tickets, cigarettes and receipts. It had to be opened on my side for the gun to get through, but even though the plastic barricade was thick, it wasn't bulletproof. Gun laws were strict in Canada, and there usually wasn't a need for it.

My throat went dry as fear thundered through me like a herd of stampeding bulls.

"I'm thinkin' you know what to do," he encouraged in that gravelly voice. It was artificially deepened in an attempt to obscure his true tone, but something about it seemed familiar. "Put the cash in a bag and slot it on through."

They'd hit at one in the morning, so there was a decent amount of money in the till.

I hesitated, my fingers so close to the button that would raise the alarm.

The bells jingled again, such an innocuous sound heralding three more alarming, gun-toting men with stockings over their heads. Two joined the original thief, but the other turned down the rows with a murmured, "No one needs a Good Samaritan fuckin' things up."

The man in front of me laughed harshly. The sound scored down my spine like sharp nails.

"Do what I tell ya, bitch, and maybe I won't shoot ya."

My heart lodged itself in my throat, making it hard to breathe as I opened the till and slowly collected the money for these thugs. Self-preservation and personal terror collided with fear for Aaron as I watched the thickset man with a gun wander down one row and up the next.

Where was he?

Had he left out the back when he heard the men enter?

It was hard to believe a man like him would cower in the face of these assholes, but anything was possible, and it wasn't like I knew Aaron from Adam.

I just thought he was beautiful.

I just thought something at the back of those large, thick-lashed eyes spoke of goodness despite his obvious counter-culture appearance.

"You're takin' too long," the man growled, cocking his shotgun with a *click-schtick* that chased chills down my spine. "Hurry the fuck up."

"All clea--" the man wandering the rows started to say.

But his words were interrupted by the unmistakable sound of a gasp and then a clatter as he fell to the ground in the far aisle to the left, dislodging a stand of beef jerky as he landed.

"The fuck?" their ringleader demanded. "What the fuck're you doin'?"

There was a slight pause that seemed to throb with tension, then a low masculine groan.

"Fuck," came a voice I recognized even in that single syllable, even though he'd only spoken a handful of words to me. "Tripped over a damn magazine."

The ringleader standing in front of me seemed to quiver with pent-up adrenaline. His head was cocked back toward the aisle, and I felt sure he would know his thief-in-arms had been taken out and replaced with Aaron. There was no air in my lungs and no hope in my heart.

Aaron was fucked.

While the ringleader was distracted, I pressed the panic button and prayed the cops would arrive before the handsome stranger ate a bullet.

"Fucking hell, asshole," he finally barked. "Stay on your goddamn feet. We clear back there?"

A man rose from behind the aisle, his head obscured by that nylon sock. He was wearing the original man's grey zip-up sweatshirt, the hood pulled up over his masked face. But I knew it was Aaron.

What kind of man took out an assailant with a gun and swapped places with him as easily as you please?

A shiver of dangerous arousal bit sharp teeth into the base of my back.

"Clear," Aaron said, raising the long-barreled shotgun as he adjusted it. I had to wonder if he did it for my benefit, to show me he had a weapon now too.

The ringleader turned back to me as his two other cronies pilfered packages of chips and peanuts from the store. "Hurry the fuck up, you fat bitch."

Heat rose at the back of my neck, the words igniting age-old embarrassment in me like a match to a strike strip. My ex and some of my old friends I'd met through him had always called me chubby or fat as if I didn't know I wasn't a size zero. It wasn't that I cared about my weight. I was happier with myself now as a woman than I had been as an underfed, terrified girl, but my ex liked to harp on me about the few extra pounds I wore well on my hips, thighs, and tummy. Even though I'd grown around the wounds from my past, it was hard to remain unmoved when someone really wanted to humiliate you, and the name-calling triggered old memories.

I could feel his leer as he watched me put the stacks of money––over three grand––in an Evergreen Gas Station paper bag.

"Nice tits, though," one of the other men murmured as if he was reluctantly impressed.

Immediately, my right hand flew to my neckline even though I was conservatively covered in a long-sleeved navy-blue tee beneath my polyester uniform vest. I never wore anything remotely revealing when I was working. When I looked up into his expression, it was feral with entitled, savage interest.

"Pretty thing stuck in a glass cage," the ringleader murmured as the other guys joined him in front of the counter. "Maybe I should break you out and take you with us, along with the cash. A little bonus for my crew."

"I'm locked in," I said, surprised by the levelness of my voice when inside, I felt seconds away from a panic attack. My chest was so tight, I couldn't force air into my compressed lungs.

"Good thing we know a thing or two about breaking in," he retorted, and I could see the faint impression of a smile beneath the dark nylon.

Fear clutched my heart with talon-tipped hands. I was suddenly a teenager again, stuck with men who wanted to break and bend me to their will, with no hope of escape. The edges of my vision crackled with static, the present colliding with the past in a way that short-circuited my brain and made me forget the difference between who I'd been and who I was.

"Not worth it," Aaron grunted. It was obvious he was trying to modulate his voice. "Let's get the cash and get out before the pigs come." There was a jingle as he fished through the pockets of the hoodie he'd taken from the thug he'd knocked out and produced a set of keys. "I'll start the car so we can get the fuck outta here."

The entire store seemed filled with static energy as the others waited for their leader to give the final verdict.

"No," he said slowly as if the word had flavour, and he relished it on his tongue. "Let's take the girl. I think I know someone who'd be happy to take her off our hands when we're done with her."

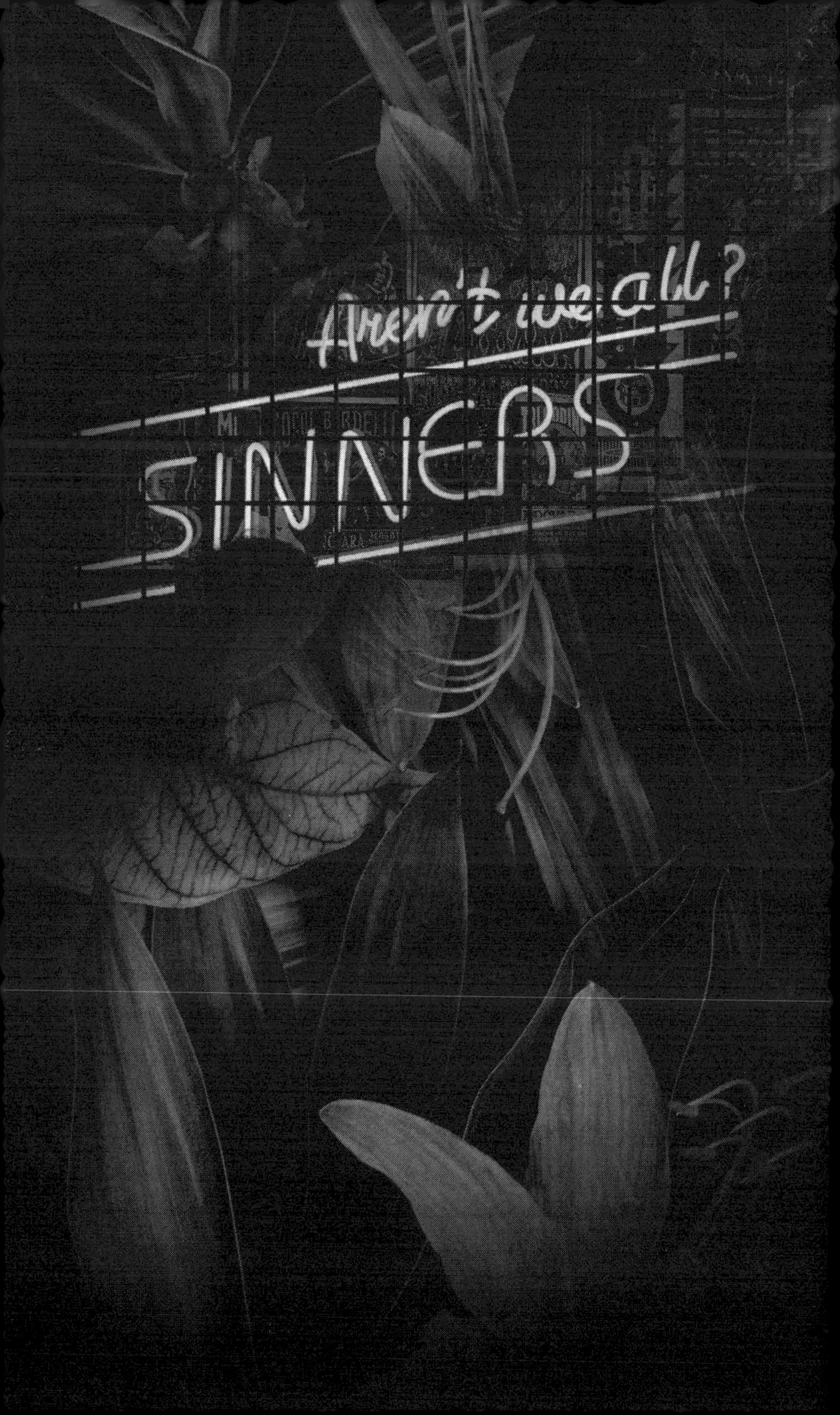
Aren't we all?
SINNERS

CHAPTER TWO

Blue

Three things happened immediately.

I opened the moving closure in the box where he'd wedged the shotgun and used his momentary shock to tug hard at the gun's barrel. He wasn't prepared for me to act offensively, and the weapon slid through his grip, wedging itself awkwardly in the opening until it was stuck. Behind him, the two other men raised their guns to target me, and I ducked to the ground, pressing my chest to the floor as if to hug it.

The ringleader cursed savagely as he tried to unstick the gun from the cage, and in his haste to retrieve it, a bullet discharged over my head, blasting through the open window box. Sharp bits of material rained over my head.

And Aaron, the stranger with the scarred chin and pretty smile, cursed savagely under his breath. "Well, fuck. Now, you haven't given me any fuckin' choice."

I squeezed my eyes shut as a cacophony of sounds erupted in the small space. The harsh exhalation of air as something thunked against flesh and then the heavy weight of something hitting the plexiglass door; male exclamations cut off by curses, then gurgling noises like someone trying to breathe underwater. Finally, the low *boom* of a shotgun discharging punched through the air, followed by the tinkling rattle of glass exploding, shards of it falling to the linoleum floor.

Meanwhile, I rolled over onto my back and scrambled back against the L-joint of the counter, secured in the corner. There was a bat Grouch kept on the bottom shelf, and I grabbed it with both hands, laying it across my lap in case worse came to worse, and I had to fight each asshole off myself.

I was thrown back to the worst moments of my life. The roots of my hair still stung as I remembered being dragged down the hall by strong hands fisted in my locks, my throat raw from screaming. No one had come to save me, then. Not even my own father.

I blinked away the cold horror when a gunshot ricocheted through the store. When my gaze lifted, it was just in time to see an unmasked face pressed to the plexiglass door. The man's cheek was cut open, the flesh distorted against the plastic, blood leaving a red smear behind as he slowly slid to the ground.

Behind him, breathing heavily, his nylon stocking discarded, nose bleeding, and jaw already bruising, stood Aaron.

We locked eyes through the bloody glass, both of us panting so powerfully that our shoulders rocked with the movement. There was righteous fury in those dark-as-soot eyes, but concern also bracketed his drawn mouth. When he moved forward slightly, I flinched. My nerves were drawn so tight I thought I'd break in two.

"Hey, hush, Blue baby," he murmured, holding his hands up in surrender. "Not gonna hurt you, okay? I just wanna get you outta here 'fore these motherfuckers come to again. You press the panic button?"

I nodded slightly, but even that felt like an effort.

The man lying on the ground pressed against the plexi wasn't moving.

"Hey, give me those pretty blues, yeah?" Aaron coaxed, dropping into a crouch so I didn't have to crank my neck up. His expression was utterly open, wide-eyed, and soft-featured with sincerity. It should have looked strange, such gentleness on a tattooed, gun-wielding badass, but it suited him somehow. "Ignore the blood. Those idiots deserved it and more for threatenin' ya. Just focus on me and take some deep breaths. Yeah...yeah, that's my girl. In and out. My mum used to say in for seven, hold for seven, out for seven. Can you do that?"

He watched me as I struggled to do what he said. A count of seven was long, though, and I sputtered through it, coughing and hiccuping on sobs that threatened to swell in the wake of each breath.

I'd seen a lot of shit in my life, but I'd never had three men make any sort of attempt to abduct and sexually assault me.

"Alright, I'm thinkin' I overestimated your lung capacity," Aaron corrected with a lopsided grin as I choked on my ragged breathing again. "Just breathe, Blue. When you feel up to it, you think you can open this door for me? I wanna get you outta here 'fore these brutes come to."

"T-The police," I protested weakly.

I hated cops, but I owed it to Grouch to stick around and give them a statement.

"I'll take you to the station myself when these fuckers have been processed and put in cuffs, yeah? Blue baby," he murmured, voice dipping into molten chocolate, sweet and so smooth, "you're shakin' alone in a bloody cage. I get I'm a stranger, but I'm dyin' to help you out here. Will you let me?"

Before I could even process an answer, I was nodding. My hands clutched at the bat across my lap, squeezing so hard around the metal I thought for a moment I might bend it. Then I looked back into Aaron's warm eyes, as chocolatey as his tone, and got to my feet.

The view from up there was different. I could see where the other two thugs lay on the ground like toys discarded by a psychopathic kid, clothes askew, limbs akimbo at angles that definitely meant they were broken.

Aaron had fucked them up.

Not just knocked them around a little or stood his ground in a fair fight.

No.

This man with the gentle eyes and cocky grin had dismantled the criminals the way a veteran dismantled a gun; as if it was muscle memory, as if it was almost boring it was that easy.

When my eyes flew back to him, he was standing too, palms to the sky in a frozen shrug of faux-innocence.

"Won't hurt you," he promised.

"I don't know you," I countered, but I took a step closer.

"No," he agreed, a flicker of that charming grin before he sobered entirely. "But there isn't a bone in my body capable'a exactin' violence against a woman. My sister..." A brief spasm of pain contorted his face. "She was kept in a cage for a long time. I don't like seein' ya in there, scared and alone."

"Put the gun down," I asked, mostly just to see if he'd do it. At this point, the guy had risked his own life to save me, a perfect stranger. If he was going to hurt me, he would have done it already or at least let the thieves do it themselves.

Aaron hesitated, gaze flicking to the prone bodies before he slowly dropped the shotgun to the ground. When he straightened, he surprised me by stepping closer to the plexiglass between us in order to press his large hand to the door. Blood was streaked across his broad palm, and silver rings adorned nearly every finger, but none of that was alarming for a girl who'd grown up around rough men.

"Empty," he murmured, "unless you open this door and take my hand."

On the ground, someone moaned.

It settled my uncertainty. My hand only shook slightly as I undid the lock and tried to push it open. The body of a passed-out thug blocked my way until Aaron wrenched the door so powerfully, it pushed the man across the floor. Blood followed like rust stains in his path.

Before I could dwell on it, Aaron took my hand in his surprisingly warm, calloused grip. I still had the bat in my other grasp, comforted by it like a child with a teddy bear.

"C'mon." He tugged me forward toward the front door.

On our way there, a hand lashed out and gripped my ankle like a vise.

I let out something like a squawk of alarm, kicking instinctively. The chunky heels of my blue platform combat boot hit the asshole square in the chin.

Despite the horror of the entire situation, Aaron, witnessing that, *laughed.*

He laughed like we were on a first date and I'd just told a good joke.

Like we were walking through a fucking meadow and not a vandalized gas station convenience store.

And somehow, that husky grind of vocal cords made me smile too.

He tugged on my hand again, breaking into a jog as we hit the door to the shop. We rocketed through it into the hot spring night. The scent of asphalt was rich in the air from being baked all day under the sun and then rained on during a brief spring shower. Under that, a faint whiff of Aaron's masculine cologne reminded me of cigarettes after sex.

We pulled up short at a massive black Harley Davidson motorcycle with blue flames painted onto the body. Seeing it doused me with cold water. It was a good reminder that the man holding my hand was just as dangerous, if not more so, than the guys he'd beaten into mincemeat back in the store.

This man was a weapon. The only question was whether he would attack or defend me.

Given what just happened, I was optimistically inclined toward the latter.

"Fucking mother*fuckers*," Aaron cursed savagely as he noted the slashed tires on his bike. "Fuck!"

He turned as if he planned to stalk back into Evergreen Gas and beat them *again* for daring to touch his ride. A part of me wanted to roll my eyes, *bikers and their fucking bikes.*

It was lucky that we turned back to look at the store though, because one of the nylon-masked men had dragged himself to his feet and was stumbling to the door.

"Fuck," Aaron cursed again, and I had the sense it was a well-used word in his lexicon.

"The van," I pointed out, jerking my chin at the rusty, dishwater-grey van parked at one of the pumps. "You have the keys in the pocket of the jacket you took from one of the guys, remember?"

Now that I wasn't being threatened with sexual assault, my natural calmness had kicked in. Sure, it was a fucked-up situation, but I'd been through enough like it, if not worse, to keep my head.

Aaron cocked a brow at me, then shook his head as if he wanted to piece me together like a puzzle, but he knew he didn't have the time. Instead, he led me again by the hand to the van and opened the driver's side door with a key on a Morton BBQ keychain. When I moved to go around to the passenger side, the door to the gas station exploded open.

"You're both fuckin' *dead*," the man screamed across the tarmac.

"Get in," Aaron barked, lifting me easily with both hands on my waist and thrusting me into the driver's seat before following in quickly after me. For a single moment, we were tangled in the seat, his big hand on my thigh, squeezing tightly in a way that shot sparks straight to my groin. And then I was scrambling over the console awkwardly with the bat in my hand, his shoulder pressing into me for momentum.

The first gunshot *crack*ed across the empty lot and pinged against the metal pillar beside the van.

"The fuckin' idiot," Aaron grumbled as he cranked the old engine to life and peeled the van into a half-donut to reverse out of the station. "Shootin' at a goddamn gas station."

On cue, our attacker fired again, the bullet lodging with a sharp *click* and *thud* into the side of the van. Aaron cursed again under his breath but otherwise seemed perfectly calm as he efficiently maneuvered the ungainly van around the pumps and out onto the street leading to the Sea to Sky Highway.

I sat there for a moment before I realized I clutched the bat to my chest like a shield. A little laugh expelled with my breath as I carefully lowered it into my lap.

"You got a thing for baseball?" Aaron asked so dryly that I wasn't certain he was joking at first.

A shocked smile tweaked the left side of my mouth. "Please, the Seattle Mariners are the only team to support over here and they suck."

I tried not to be too pleased when Aaron tipped his head back, strong throat working around a hearty laugh. When he was finished, he peered at me under a dislodged piece of dark hair falling across his forehead. I noticed his slight widow's peak and loved the slightly piratical look it gave him.

"You seem pretty damn calm after what just happened," he noted, but a question was buried there.

"Because I'm making quips about one of the world's most boring sports?" I returned with a shrug. "Some people use humour as a shield, you know?"

He snorted, checking the rearview mirror for pursuers. "Yeah, I know a little somethin' about that."

"You think they'll follow us?" I asked, turning in my own seat to train my eyes on the dark stretch of the highway behind us. The ocean glittered like navy velvet beneath diamanté moonlight on one side of the asphalt, and mountains rose on the other, steep and forebodingly black in the night.

"Depends on what they got in this piece'a shit," he muttered. "You wanna check it out?"

I hadn't buckled my belt yet, so I just turned in the seat and crawled over the console into the shadowy depths of the van. It only took me a moment to realize I wished I hadn't.

There was money, stacks of it, in an open duffel bag to one side and another that rattled when I unzipped it to reveal thousands of dollars worth of jewelry. My sparkly silver nail caught on the scalloped edge of a diamond necklace, lifting it from the tangled mess of expensive gems. It had to have been at least a hundred thousand dollars just for the one adornment hanging from my finger.

"Aaron," I said, but my shock and receding adrenaline made my voice a harsh rasp. "Aaron," I tried again. "I think we stumbled on a serious jewelry theft."

I raised the diamond necklace higher for him to see in the rearview mirror and wasn't surprised when I received a muttered curse in response.

"Hold on, Blue. Let me call a buddy'a mine." He lifted his hips to fish a phone out of his back pocket, then left it on his thigh to order voice command to call a person by the name of Lion.

"Hey, man. Just on a run, but I got a little situation here I'm wonderin' if you can shed some light on. Anythin' goin' 'round about a jewelry store robbery?"

"You got your head buried in the sand? Twelve stores have been hit in the past two months from downtown Vancouver to Whistler. You got a lead?"

Whoever Lion was, he had a rough, slow drawl like a Canadian cowboy. It was almost sinfully hot.

Aaron looked at me crouched in the back, his eyes dark pits in the shadowed interior of the van. I wondered what he would do. He was clearly an outlaw, and in my generous experience with outlaws, they didn't have much respect for the law. Would he turn over the evidence or keep the treasure for himself?

A tiny part of me I was afraid to listen to also wondered if he factored me into his mental math. Would a man nicknamed Boner give a shit about what some random girl thought about the situation?

I ripped my gaze away from his, unable to bear the intensity of his scrutiny.

And that was when I saw it.

The jean jacket.

I would have recognized it anywhere, even half folded and crumpled between two boxes in the shadowed recess of the back seat. It was distressed in a natural way, born of wear, and not fabricated to look that way. The left sleeve had been barely hanging on until I'd sewn it back together myself with vivid blue thread.

My heart beat a vicious tattoo in my throat, choking me as I leaned forward to pull the jacket into my lap. I must have made some kind of distressed noise because I was vaguely aware of Aaron calling my name.

But I couldn't focus on him.

Only on the vivid blue thread I was tracing with my thumbnail.

"It was him," I breathed the words as if they were punched out of me.

"Who?" Aaron's voice was a sharp exclamation point of sound, but I still couldn't answer.

The man I'd spent years with. The man I'd told my secrets to.

This was the same man who had stood across from me in Evergreen Gas Station with a gun leveled at my belly. The same man who had suggested he knew someone who might think I was worth something. I knew it with a certainty that chilled me through to the bone.

A vicious, full-body shiver rocked through me so hard my thumbnail cut through the blue thread on the shoulder of the jacket owned by Otto Granger, my thieving, scumbag ex-boyfriend.

"Blue!" Aaron growled, swerving to the side of the highway even though the road barely had a shoulder. He clicked his seat belt free and twisted to lean between the front seats to reach me. The touch of his hand on my thigh grounded me like a lightning rod, that electric hatred receding until my head was clear enough to think again.

When I looked up at him, his tanned face was tense with worry, those night-dark eyes scouring my face and body as if searching for visible wounds. I wasn't sure how to tell him they were so far beneath the surface there was no hope of excavating them.

"Who was it?" he asked, softer this time, as gentle as the thumb rubbing over my denim-clad thigh.

"Otto," I whispered on a defeated exhale, twisting the jean jacket while I imagined it was Otto's neck. "My ex-boyfriend."

Aaron's brow climbed into his broad forehead. "Your ex-boyfriend just robbed the gas station you work at? You a new employee, or did he know you worked there?"

I didn't have to answer. He read the truth in the toxic tangle of humiliation and rage stamped like a brand I was afraid would never fade on my face.

The stranger with the absurdly pretty features rocked back to run a hand through his thick mess of dark hair and blew a raspberry between his lips before surmising, "What a motherfuckin' bastard."

A short bark of laughter erupted from my throat. "Yeah, pretty much."

He peered at me from under that errant lock of hair that seemed to perpetually flop across his forehead. "You got bad blood with him? Before now, that is."

"I came home from work one day, and he'd cleaned out my savings." It hurt to admit to this beautiful man that I'd been such a fool, but I wasn't a proud person. I'd never had much to be proud of, not my family, my prospects, or even my looks or personality. I was a pretty average girl with a pleasant face and body who was lucky to be left alone in life. "The night before, we fell asleep talking about our future--you know, marriage, puppies, babies in bassinets--but..." I shrugged, my heart beating loudly in a chest that felt mostly hollow. "Men do that."

"What?"

"Say things they don't mean."

Aaron's thick lashes swept his cheekbones as he closed his eyes as if in pain. Close to him like this, all the markers of a bad boy—the tattoos, the heavy silver jewelry, and the slight menace in his continence—seemed so insignificant. He looked romantic, leaning toward me in the dim yellow glow from the front seat overhead lights, his Byronic features etched in pure gold and liquid shadow. I wanted to trace the line of his nose with my fingertip and test the texture of his plush lower lip with my teeth.

Then his eyes opened, and all that softness was erased by the heated intent of that stare.

He moved closer so quickly I flinched, but he wasn't perturbed by it. If anything, his brows knotted with further resolve, and he slowly but deliberately crawled into the back seat so he was facing me on his knees. When he took my face between his big, rough hands, I found I could barely breathe through the tension that seemed to smoke between us.

I trembled, but he stilled me within the frame of his palms and rounded his spine to bring his eyes directly in line with mine.

"I'm a stranger. You're a stranger. We part ways in a minute, and I'll just be a crazy memory for you. You'll be that girl with the blue hair stuck in my mind like a question mark I'll always wish I'd answered. But no matter what happens, I want this night to change somethin' for ya."

"My predilection for scumbags?" I joked weakly.

Aaron wasn't moved. "I want you to get that you're worth somethin'. First moment I saw you, I lost my fuckin' breath to the sight'a you. Not 'cause you're damn pretty, Blue, but 'cause a man like me knows pretty girls. Nah, the sight'a you knocked the air straight from my chest 'cause a pretty girl with a sweet smile was mannin' a gas station in the middle'a the night on a dangerous stretch'a highway, and I thought, this girl doesn't have anyone in her life to tell her not to risk herself like this. She's fightin' and clawin' for everythin' she's got, and what she's got is no one. And, Blue baby, that sucker punched me. A girl like you should have a whole army'a family at your back keepin' ya safe and makin' ya promises they *always* intend to fuckin' keep."

That hollowness in my chest was suddenly filled with warmth, with a sloshing, overwhelming fullness that threatened to drown me. The wet of it leaked out the corners of my eyes and trailed down my cheeks. Aaron caught the dampness on his thumbs.

"Gonna hug you now, that's alright with you," Aaron said, a question buried in his confident tone.

Warning bells should have been ringing, alone with a stranger on the side of an empty highway in the middle of the night in a sketchy-ass van, but they weren't. Instead, I felt a connection, tentative but tangible, building between us.

So I hugged him.

I threw my arms around his neck and pressed my chest into his. He caught me with a little chuckle but held me with a tenderness that felt somber, almost sacred. I knew he mostly felt sad for me, but I didn't really care. I hadn't even had someone to pity me in so long, and even that was nice.

"You gonna tell me your name now?" he asked into my hair.

One of his big hands cupped the entire back of my skull, making me feel almost nauseated with pleasure.

"No." I pulled away and pretended to preoccupy myself with Otto's mangey jacket. "Blue sounds nice enough in your mouth."

"Tastes good too. You wanna kiss it off my lips?"

I rolled my eyes so hard they hurt, but keeping the wild giggle at bay in my throat was a struggle. Aaron gave me that crooked grin, eyes dancing like he knew he was full of shit, but he didn't give a fuck because it was fun.

He was fun.

Somehow, after being held at gunpoint, I was enjoying myself.

Our moment was shattered by the telltale rumble of thunder climbing up the mountain road.

The distant murmur of motorcycles.

"Friends of yours?" I asked on a breath as adrenaline sluiced through me again.

Aaron cocked his head as if he could discern the exact notes of the cacophony. "Better not risk it. C'mon. I was headed to Whistler on business. I'll get shit settled there, and it'll give those bastards time to get arrested or get gone."

"And then?" I couldn't help but ask as I followed him back into the front seat.

I didn't have to look at him as I buckled my seat belt to know he was smiling that impish, sexy grin.

"And then, I take you out."

"I don't date bikers."

"Who said anythin' about datin'?" he countered with a roguish grin.

"Fine, I don't *sleep* with bikers."

"Blue baby, the way I do it, there's no sleepin' involved at all."

I rolled my eyes while I angled my body to look out the window as Aaron pulled the van back onto the highway, but when he started chuckling, I thought it was safe to let a smile break through. The reflection of my curved mouth in the dark mirrored window was a welcome one. I'd always looked prettiest when I smiled, and that didn't happen so much anymore.

Even then, I couldn't count the number of times Aaron had made me smile in a single night. That might have been the moment I realized he was more dangerous than the tatts and experienced fighting already made him seem. Because a man who could make a woman smile on demand was a special kind of magic, one I wasn't sure I was strong enough to resist even though I'd vowed to stay out of trouble.

CHAPTER THREE

Boner

The minute I saw her, I KNEW.

I'd always ribbed King and Cyclops for goin' on about how it only took one look for them to know their Old Ladies were the ones meant for them. It seemed fuckin' ridiculous and, honest to fuck, pretty damn shallow. You like the look'a someone enough, you fall for them straight off?

No, thank you.

I'd been fucked by good looks in the past, and I was wiser now.

No pretty face was gonna rock my world straight off its axis.

I liked it just as it was, thank you very fuckin' much.

But then, I walked into Evergreen Gas Station just like I had a hundred other times over the course'a my life in Entrance, BC. Only this time, I'd seen the girl workin' the night shift.

She was just a little thing behind that plexiglass box, but the light had hit her blue hair in a way that made it shine like the inside of a flame.

It drew my gaze to the rest'a her, the rounded figure beneath the black and blue vest, the unfiltered shade'a blue in those huge eyes the very same intensity as her dyed hair. There was a silver Medusa piercin' in the divot above her top lip, a ring through the center'a her nostrils, and the blue ink of some tattoo curlin' over the bottom curve of her neck under her tee. She looked like somethin' outta a comic book, all exaggerated features and curves, a dream brought to life by a vividly coloured pen.

Pretty, fuck *yeah*.

But also different. Unlike the hordes'a hot biker bitches that flooded club parties lookin' to hook up with one'a the brothers 'cause they were addicted to dangerous men like tweakers to meth.

And then she'd opened that little pink mouth and sassed me.

Trust me when I say that wasn't the normal reaction women have to a man like me.

Usually, they scream at the sight'a me and run the other way or somethin' kindles in their bellies, the roughness'a me like a strike pad lightin' their lust into flames, and they're all over me.

But little Miss Blue acted like I was only a mild irritant, a slightly amusin' pest.

I'd always been a contrary fucker, and her dismissal'a my charms was heady.

Maybe, if those motherfuckers hadn't come into Evergreen, we woulda flirted a bit, and then I'd've been on my way. Later, I might've made a point to go back in to press my luck again, but female attention wasn't exactly hard to come by, and I was a busy guy. More than that, I didn't do emotions. My heart was already preoccupied enough with my club, the family I'd made through it, and the sister I'd had to leave behind years ago who still haunted my thoughts every fuckin' day.

But they did arrive, and they did threaten the blue-haired, blue-eyed girl.

When they did, all that chemistry and curiosity that lay like kindlin' in my belly caught fire, and viciously protective rage filled me to the fuckin' brim. I'd always been a fighter. Growin' up in foster care with a pretty sister made me a fighter before I was a fuckin' preteen. But this violence was different.

The snap'a one asshole's radial bone beneath my hands and the howl'a pain when I crushed in the cheek of another roared through me in tandem with that primal fury.

It felt satisfyin'.

Right.

What kinda men threatened a woman like Blue, so pretty, so sweet and vulnerable behind that flimsy fuckin' plastic screen?

The kinda men who deserved to *die*.

Only the thought'a Blue watchin' with those wide eyes curbed my wild anger. She was an innocent, no doubt in my mind about that, and she didn't need to see me snap any necks.

I could also get Curtains to hunt the fuckers down later and do it then.

Lookin' at her huddled on the ground in that cage, fear in her eyes but resolve in the set of her chin as she clutched a baseball bat in her lap, somethin' subtle but profound shifted inside'a me. Somethin' I'd always had inside me to give meetin' a reason to give it.

It was a no-brainer to take her outta that hellhole even though involvin' myself in theft and assault was fuckin' stupid. I was a known associate of The Fallen MC, and the cops were always lookin' for reasons to put us behind bars.

Somehow, in ways I didn't know and didn't wanna think too hard about, savin' this blue-haired girl was worth the trouble it might've bought me.

Which was really the only explanation for why she was curled up, knees tucked to her chest and arms wrapped around them, on the passenger seat in a stolen van filled with contraband jewels on the way to Whistler with me. I'd been on my way up the mountain on club business to meet with one'a our dealers who was havin' a sudden change'a heart about his involvement with the MC.

I was gonna have a little friendly chat and remind him that our friendship was unbreakable.

Blue would wait at Bob's Diner while I did business, and then I'd pick her up on the way back down the Sea to Sky.

After that, I wasn't sure.

All I knew was, I didn't want to let her outta my sight and the scope'a my protection 'til I was sure those thievin' assholes, especially her fuckin' ex-boyfriend, were safely behind bars. Somethin' in my gut told me they weren't done with Blue, and I wanted to be there if they came for her again.

"We'll leave the van parked here," I told her as I swung the cage into the deserted lot across from the diner. "Got a buddy who'll lend us a car to get back down the mountain. Don't need to get caught drivin' a stolen vehicle associated with jewelry theft."

"What if someone finds it?"

"I'll send someone to deal with it."

"And the jewelry?" Blue asked in that surprisingly low, buttery voice. "Are we just going to wear it beneath our clothes?"

I laughed, startled yet again at her ability to make humour outta shitty situations. Maybe she wasn't as innocent as I'd assumed if she was unfazed by most'a the events'a our fucked-up night.

"I was thinkin' we'd just take the duffels, transfer the loot, and figure out what we do with it when we get back to Entrance."

Somethin' about her demeanor changed then, a bristlin' energy that cloaked her like a shield.

"You live in Entrance?" she asked carefully as if she was defusin' a bomb.

"You gotta problem with Entrance?" My tone was incredulous if only 'cause my town was the prettiest damn place on the West Coast.

Nestled in the belly of a wide bay tucked up against sheer cliff faces and towerin' mountain ranges clothed in thick forest, it was a natural wonderland. The town itself was what King's Old Lady, Cressida, called "quaint", with old-style buildings on Main Street and all things associated with small-town charm.

It was also, and this was most'a the reason for my pride in it, the home'a The Fallen MC.

One'a the biggest, most profitable motorcycle clubs in North America with chapters all the way to Europe. The club originated in Entrance decades ago and still housed its mother chapter.

My chapter.

Blue peered at me from under a lock'a electric blue hair. "No. But anyone who reads the news knows some shady stuff goes down in Entrance."

This was true.

Human traffickin', pornography operations, drug makin' and dealin', police corruption, and plenty'a violent events marred its history.

"Most of it seems tied up with The Fallen MC," she continued, her mouth movin' over the words too judiciously, as if she was strugglin' not to speak her truth. "You know anything about them?"

"Some."

Her gaze was hot on my face as I parked the van behind the veil'a two dumpsters and swung outta the car. The back door rattled as I slid it open to grab the bags, securin' them crosswise over my shoulders. Blue appeared beside me, worryin' her lip with her teeth as she watched me.

"You think schlepping around town with contraband strapped to your chest is the best idea?" she questioned when I finally turned to look at her. One'a her full hips was jutted to the side, sassy in tone and body.

It made me smile to see her like that, so full'a verve in the face of an unknown situation. I wondered if she'd spit in the eye'a death when he came for her one day.

My hand found that cocked hip and curved around it while the other went to the van on the opposite side'a her head, cagin' her in with my body. When I dipped closer, the smell'a somethin' sweet like sugared plums swarmed my senses and made warmth coil low in my gut.

"I'm not known for my good ideas," I whispered hoarsely, caught off guard by the visceral reaction my body seemed to have to her. My blood practically fuckin' hummed with desire, a song I could hear beatin' against my rib cage like a drum.

"I'm not surprised," came her breathy return, those huge eyes lookin' up at me without fear. "I knew the moment I saw you that you were trouble."

"The best kind," I agreed. "What's reward without a little risk?"

As if in answer to my own question, I found myself leanin' forward, transfixed by the plump shape'a her mouth and the tiny dimple in the middle'a her bottom lip. My tongue snuck out to tap the indent 'cause I was sure it would taste sweet as sin.

And it did.

I hesitated for only a second, my body a question mark hoverin' over hers.

And then she sighed, a little puff of warm air against my heat-seekin' lips.

The next moment, she kissed me.

Fuck me, but I hadn't been kissed since I was a boy. Girls didn't often grab me by the chin, jerk to their tiptoes, and land a hot, wet kiss on my waitin' lips. My aura didn't allow for it. I was the one doin' the huntin', the sweet-talkin', the kissin'.

But holy shit, bein' kissed had its own kinda glory.

She quivered on her tiptoes in an effort to reach my mouth, to part my lips with her small, hot tongue.

I was tempted to let her orchestrate it all, just to watch how she'd come at me, struggle to have all'a me, but my blood was roarin' too loudly in my ears, urgin' me to *take, take, take.*

So I did.

My body slammed hers against the metal with a bang. Her groan exploded into my mouth, a spark I swallowed that flared brightly in my belly. When I hiked her higher with the hand on her hip, anglin' it down over her sweet, round ass, she moaned and squirmed like makin' out against a shitty van was the carnal delight'a her fuckin' life.

It took my mind to a darker place, imaginin' all the noises she'd make if I had my proper way with her. If she had her way with me. Somethin' told me she'd be a goddamn wildcat.

I rocked my hips into her denim-covered groin and ate her gasp off her pretty pink tongue.

"Oh my God," she said, pullin' away with panic in her eyes, a flush painted high and bright on her cheeks.

"What?" I growled, unable to pull back on the animal desire surgin' through me. How was it possible for a girl to taste like sugar and rum all at once?

"Your, uh, your..." She struggled with the words, her blush flarin' higher.

It only took me a second. A grin slid across my damp mouth, and masculine triumph swelled inside my chest.

"Yeah," I murmured against her mouth, nippin' at her lower lip and pressin' the length'a me she was commentin' on a little harder against her belly. "Told ya they call me Boner for a reason."

"Oh my God," she said as her head thudded back against the metal so she could look at the sky as if actually talkin' to the Big Man himself. "Why is your ridiculousness so charming?"

One shoulder lifted in a shrug as I pressed my smile like a stamp into her cheek. Fuck, she smelled so good, felt so good all soft and warm against my hard edges. "People usually don't expect men who look like me to have a sense'a humour."

"Why?"

It was a good question but a hard one to answer. Why was a man riddled with tattoos and scars, a man who lived by a code of honor not written in law books and bibles but in blood and leather, judged to be a certain way?

"'Cause it's safer to look scary and be scary than it is to be vulnerable. Humour is its own kinda vulnerability. What if you don't laugh?" I murmured, lookin' down into those brilliant-cut sapphire eyes and unable to stop the thought that I'd found more treasure that night than I had secured to my back. "We all choose our masks, yeah? It's safer that way."

"You don't get so wise without living through some shit first." Her small fingers were in my hair, tuggin' and twirlin' the long ends floppin' over my forehead. It was a small intimacy, but it seemed profound in our dark corner'a the abandoned parkin' lot. As contraband as the stolen jewels.

"Yeah," I agreed easily. "You don't."

We stared at each other from inches apart, our passion coolin' but intrigue burnin' up in its wake. I couldn't shake this rabid curiosity I had about her. There were questions I wanted answered and moments I wanted to witness with her. It wasn't just sex, and that was usually more than enough to freak me out and send me runnin'.

So what was it about this girl with blue hair that hooked my soul like a caught fish?

"Don't you have shit to do?" she asked, still twirlin' my hair, still holdin' me close like she wasn't keen to let me outta her sight.

"Yeah."

A tiny smile. "Are you going to do it?"

"Pretty comfortable as I am," I noted, flexin' my hips forward, smoothin' my palm over her lush ass.

Her eyes danced, dark like the night sky filled with stars. "The sooner you get done, the sooner we can get back to kissing."

I stepped away abruptly and hiked the straps of the duffels back into proper place on my shoulders, already walkin' backwards away from her.

"In that case," I called out as I put space between us. "I better hurry the fuck up."

Her laughter followed me outta the lot, warmin' my back as I turned down the street toward my destination. I waited 'round the corner just outta sight for her to reach the warm glow'a Bob's Diner 'fore I headed out to Beaker's place.

BEAKER WAS one'a many cogs in the wheel'a The Fallen Men MC. He wasn't a member, but we used guys like him as dealers and informants. They always had their ear to the ground 'cause they were down there in the gutters doin' shit none'a the brothers would ever be caught dead doin'.

Case in point, I found the bastard inside his trailer in a pair of loose, stained briefs that belonged in a toxic waste pile and a dishwater-grey wife beater that hung off his skinny frame. He was bent over the stove where an array of glassware you'd find in a high school chemistry lab was bubblin' away. An acrid odour filled the entire trailer with fumes that had stained the walls brown over time.

Beaker was—unsurprisingly, given his name—a big-time drug user and producer.

The club didn't use him for any'a his own product. We didn't deal in hard-core drugs that ruined lives like meth and heroin, but a lotta other criminals sure as fuck did.

That was why I was payin' him a visit today.

"Yo," I called to him 'cause he still hadn't noticed me. My knuckles rapped hard against the open door 'fore I shut it behind me and dropped the duffels filled with stolen shit to the ground by a wobbly table. "Beaker."

He twirled so fast, he upset his balance and crashed into the laminate counter across from the stove. A howl cut through the air as he rubbed hard at the sore spot on his hip. He leveled a glare at me 'fore he discerned exactly who I was.

Then he smiled real pretty.

Or as pretty as a meth head with half his teeth rotted out could smile.

I cocked a brow at him and watched that smile slip, then fall off his face like a mis-hung paintin'.

"B-Boner, man!" he crowed, lurchin' forward to offer me his hand. When I didn't take it––there was mysterious brown gunk caught beneath ragged fingernails and some kind of infection on a cut across his palm–– he shifted from foot to foot and tried to grin again. "What brings ya to my humble abode?"

"You know why I'm here."

He blinked rapidly. *Click, click, click* of dry lids over bloodshot eyes. "Yeah, yeah, maybe Zeus mentioned somethin' about it. Can't seem to remember now."

Normally, I was a patient man, but that night I had a pretty girl waitin' for me in a diner a few blocks down the road, and I was already tired'a Beaker's bullshit. So I took one step forward, right hand lashin' out to grab him by his skinny neck.

He squawked, flailin' dramatically even though the hold was a threat instead'a an attack.

"You know why I'm here," I reiterated. "You've been dealin' weed that doesn't come from the club. You know our agreement, don't ya, Beak? Or do you need me to remind you that the only green product you sell is Fallen product?"

Tremblin' like a leaf, it was no surprise he bit his tongue in his haste to answer me. When he spoke, blood was smeared across what remained of his yellowed front teeth. "You know all I got is loyalty to the club, man! But some shit came into play, and I got no choice, you see?"

"There's always a choice," I murmured, pulsin' my grip on his neck a little tighter. His hands flew to my hand, scramblin' to lessen my hold. "You made the wrong one."

"I-I'm fuckin' sorry, man," he croaked weakly. "What can I say? I'll never do it again."

"You're damn right. But you know how we are about loyalty. It's our way or the highway, huh? So you want me to leave here with a smile on my fuckin' face and not your blood all over my hands, you start talkin'. Who the fuck approached you about dealin' weed for them?"

Beaker's eyes rolled in his head like loose marbles as he scrambled to decide who was the worse threat: the unknown supplier or the man holdin' his neck in a vise-like grip.

"Name's Rooster," he finally gasped. "President of the White Raiders MC."

Now, that was fuckin' interestin'.

The White Raiders were a white supremacist club outta southern Alberta that dealt with toxic street drugs like heroin, meth, fentanyl, and stolen prescription drugs. They were still small-time criminals, but they'd been in the papers a time or two for beatin' up people'a colour at bars from Medicine Hat to Lethbridge.

I hated them the first time I heard about them.

Racist pieces'a shit who deserved to die fiery fuckin' deaths.

Lotta biker clubs were white-bred, but The Fallen family didn't discriminate by skin tone but by the quality'a a man's heart. It burned in me somethin' fuckin' fierce to think'a these lowlifes encroachin' on Fallen territory.

Without warnin', I cocked my left fist and sent it crashin' into Beaker's drug-ruined face. My right hand on his throat kept him from reelin' back, but his legs went limp, so I was the only thing holdin' him up.

"What the fuck?" he gargled through the blood pourin' into his mouth from his broken nose. "What the *fuck*, man! I told you what you wanted!"

"Yeah," I agreed easily. "The hit was for workin' with assholes like the Raiders." Then again. The second punch landed on Beaker's left cheekbone. He wailed like a fuckin' baby. "That was for betrayin' the club. You don't want more'a the same, you tell me everythin' there is to know about that club. Startin' with what the *fuck* they're doin' in BC."

Beaker kept cryin', holdin' his bloody face as if he was afraid pieces'a it were gonna fall off. I sighed heavily, then shoved him into a chair and started to root through the drawers in his tiny kitchen.

"You know," I said conversationally as I rummaged. "I get it. Lotsa people think Wrath and Priest, or Zeus, Axe-Man, and Bat are the scary motherfuckers. It's the pretty face," I explained, gesturin' to my features. "That trips people up. Same thing happens to Nova and King. People take one look and think *shit,* but those pretty boys don't know pain or misery, let alone how to dole it out."

Beaker watched me with blood drippin' from his nose to his stained briefs, his hands twistin' on top'a the Formica table. He was already jonesin' for another hit, but he was too afraid'a me to ask for it.

"It's funny," I continued, shootin' him a consolin' smile as my hand finally encountered somethin' worth usin' in one of the dirty drawers. "People always assume bein' pretty means bein' *good* as if beauty can't be evil."

My laughter echoed through the cramped trailer as I stalked over to Beaker and crouched in front'a his cowerin' form. When I brandished the pliers, his sickly yellow flesh went white.

Even though he clambered to get away, I pinned his left hand against the table with my forearms and brought the pliers to his index fingernail.

"I'm evidence to the contrary," I finished with a wide, wicked grin as I pinched the nail between the metal teeth and *pulled*.

Beaker screamed as the nail peeled away from his flesh. Blood spilled to the table, bright and metallic-scented.

"I'll do anythin' to protect my family and my club, Beak," I told him earnestly as I flicked the discarded nail onto the floor and pinched the next one. "Even if it ain't pretty. Now, tell me what you know about the Raiders."

Aren't we all?
SINNERS

CHAPTER FOUR

Blue

I WAS STARVED, so I ordered French toast.

It was indulgent, something I never would have ordered when I dated Otto because he would have shamed me about my body. I drowned the powder-sugared mountain of carbs in a lake of maple syrup and shoved a stacked mouthful between my lips, eating with angry relish. It wasn't enough that Otto had made me feel shitty when we dated and that he'd stolen my mother's ring, but now he'd actually had the audacity to hold up Evergreen Gas Station? The one place he knew meant everything to me because it had been my soft place to land when I ran away from my old life.

Fuck. Him.

What was it about men wreaking havoc on my life like it meant nothing to them?

Like I meant nothing to them.

I sat there in the diner's bright white light, staring at my reflection in the dark window overlooking the street, wondering if it was the angle of my jaw or the plumpness in my cheeks that they took umbrage with. If it was the fact that I liked make-up, skincare, and clothes more than dude stuff or if it was my penchant to smother every real thing in humour until true emotion suffocated and died.

Whatever it was, life had taught me that I couldn't rely on anyone to look out for me but *me*.

Except there was Aaron last-name-unknown.

Really, everything about him was a mystery besides what I could see with my eyes: his beauty, his crooked smile, and his silly sense of humour. The fact that he put himself at risk to help a random girl when she needed it. That he kissed like the devil luring innocents to sin.

Yeah, so I didn't know much, but what I knew was heady.

Because it painted a picture of a man who *should* have been all the things I'd vowed to stay away from but who was actually proving to be the kind of man I'd assumed only existed in my fantasies.

I was musing over this as I dragged my last piece of French toast through the sticky remnants of syrup, bobbing my head to the strains of Hamish Anderson's "Trouble", when I noticed the increasing roar of noise in the distance.

Immediately, my fork dropped to the plate with a clatter as I leaned over the table for a better angle to look out the window down the street.

Sure enough, seconds later, five bright, circular lights like flashing moons crested the hill and descended the street toward the diner.

"Holy shit," I whispered as they drew closer.

Because I recognized the man on the first bike, sitting astride the giant hog awkwardly like he was hanging on to the powerful beast for dear life. His dark, shaved head gleamed under the yellow lamplight. Without the jacket currently in the back of the van we'd parked across the street, he wore only the long black tee he'd been in at Evergreen Gas.

I should have recognized him even beneath the nylon sock back then, but it wasn't like I expected Otto, idiot though he was, to hold me at gunpoint for some cash in the till.

Now, though, I recognized him right away.

I lurched to my feet, the chair screeching loudly across the chipped, checkered linoleum. The diner was mostly empty, but the trucker in the corner and the female server both looked over at me in concern.

I ignored them.

My gaze was pinned on Otto and the group of thugs trailing him.

How the hell had they found us?

Unless...

The duffel bags filled with money and jewels.

If those assholes were smarter than they seemed, they might have put a tracker in the bags. It irritated me that I knew enough about the criminal mind to make such a guess, but it was also helpful.

If I was right, they were looking for Aaron, and he had no idea.

They'd picked up another man who'd probably been the one to deliver the motorcycles in lieu of the van we'd stolen, and I didn't like the odds of five against Aaron's one even though he'd proven himself an incredible brawler.

I tossed a handful of bills on the counter, downed my now-cold coffee, wiped my mouth on my sleeve, and walked toward the back of the restaurant.

"Is there a back exit?"

The server pursed her painted bubble gum-pink lips at me, then nodded curtly. "Past the bathrooms on the right. You okay, girl?"

"I will be," I promised opaquely as I turned down the hall.

I ducked into the break room to grab a black ball cap and hoodie off the employee hooks and then jogged out the back, exploding into the muggy night with my heart racing.

The little parking lot behind the diner was occupied by an old Honda and a fairly nice Audi. I made a beeline for the Honda because it was a model without modern security. There was a rock by the fender that would do nicely, and after wrapping my hand in my Evergreen Gas vest, I used it to knock out the back seat window on the driver's side. Carefully avoiding the jagged edges, I reached inside to undo the lock and slipped into the front seat.

Hot-wiring the car was easy. Anyone could do it after watching a few videos. I'd been taught by the best on the streets of Calgary, so the Honda Civic was a piece of cake. The engine groaned to life like a sleepy beast and protested with a sputtering exhale when I peeled into reverse and out of the lot.

At that point, the motorcycles had already progressed down the street, but I could still see them up ahead. They were driving slowly, in case, I figured, they ran into Aaron or me.

I followed them.

I'd promised myself I would stay out of trouble after Otto left me, but the truth was, I'd been drawn to trouble my whole damn life. I was born into it. So how was I supposed to stay impartial when the most handsome man I'd ever met, who had saved me from my own predicament just an hour earlier, was in danger?

When I was younger, I'd known a man named Cedar who had taught me all there was to know about stalking someone without being seen. It wasn't about melting into the shadows and not making a noise so much as it was about acting like you belonged somewhere and were preoccupied with anything but the person you were tailing.

I hadn't tailed anyone in years, but it seemed I was still good at it, even in a noisy old car, because the bikers didn't turn around once on their way out of town and farther up the mountain.

They stopped at the base of a gravel driveway curving out of sight beyond a bend framed with scraggly trees. A couple of them got off their bikes to deliberate.

It was my only chance to get to Aaron before they did.

I parked the car in a random driveway and then got out to slink through the shadows. I curved far into the brush, moving as quietly as I could over the dry, crackling sticks and grass in order to avoid the group of bikers. Only a dim spot of light through the trees served as a kind of North star, leading me to a small, dilapidated trailer set on concrete blocks.

The window to the kitchen was held open by a wooden chopstick. The screen behind it had been warped with time and punctured in a few places. Voices drifted out of the gaps like smoke.

"They're fuckin' scary, man," a weak, warbling voice whined. "I mean it. You guys've been good to me, and I know Z's a shit crazy motherfucker when he wants to be, but these guys..." There was a sharp inhalation of breath and then a little whimper. "Man showed up and made me shit my pants."

"He threatened to take away your drug stash?" Aaron asked dryly.

His voice deepening to cruel, dark tones shouldn't have sent a vibration of energy zipping like an electrical current to my sex, but it did. I shivered in the warm spring air and carefully moved closer.

"My b-brother Davey, he's in Ford Correctional Prison. Roo-Rooster threatened to have him killed. I know the guy from when I lived in Calgary. He ain't someone you fuck with!"

The air disappeared from my lungs as if they were vacuum sealed. I struggled to drag new oxygen into my chest but choked. Black spots reeled across my vision, and I had to catch myself with a hand on the trailer.

I hadn't heard that name in years.

A part of me had honestly started to believe I never would again.

"What was that?" the strange voice asked nervously.

A hushing sound from Aaron.

I moved to the door, knocking as I pushed it open and stepped into the rank interior.

A man sat at a small yellow table. His skin hung off his bones like an old T-shirt, and what little hair he had was greased back from his forehead. Blood caked around his misshapen nose and pooled beneath the skin of his left cheek, but it was the red pool of blood on the tabletop dripping over the edge with a faint *splat* to the floor that was most compelling. In the lake of red, fingernails floated like macabre boats.

And standing beside it all was Aaron with a gun in his bloody hands trained at my chest.

I arched a brow at him. "You're the second man today to level a gun at me. If you think it'll turn me on, you're wrong."

Only, he wasn't really.

The sight of him so tall, dark, and dangerous was mouth-watering in the extreme.

But it was impossible to ignore the fact that he'd been pulling off this man's fingernails.

I winced in sympathy. "What did he ever do to you?"

"He fucked with my family," Aaron said, more serious than I'd seen him. "You gotta problem with violence, Blue?"

"I was raised in the thick of it," I quipped. "But this isn't the time for ghost stories. Otto and his crew are at the base of the hill trying to decide how best to take you out."

Aaron blinked at me, then swore viciously, dropping the gun to his side and dragging a tattooed hand through his mess of hair. "A tracker in the bags."

"That's what I assumed," I agreed as if none of this had fazed me. As if I wasn't reeling from the sound of Rooster's name and the knowledge that he was involved somehow in British Columbia.

Aaron spun to face the cowering man at the table, who whimpered when Aaron grabbed him by the stained tank. "The next time Rooster makes contact, what do you do?"

"C-C-Call you," he promised, eyes wide and blown black with fear.

"The second," Aaron insisted. "You remember, they might threaten your brother, Beaker. But I'll threaten your entire goddamn family and every person you've ever known if you fuck with my family, you hear me?"

Before the man named Beaker could answer, Aaron was twirling around, tagging my hand and the duffels on the ground by his feet, and dragging me to the back of the trailer to the tiny bedroom that smelled like mold. The bed was so stained with mysterious colours that I couldn't look at it without wanting to gag. There was a window over it facing the back of the mountain that Aaron popped out with one fierce hit from his elbow.

"I don't think you can fit through that," I mused as the sound of voices drifted up the mountain to our ears.

"I better," he said, totally unfazed as he moved me into position and helped push me through.

I was almost out the other side when his hand landed on my ass, and despite myself, I snorted. Only Aaron would cop a feel while we were running from outlaws.

My landing was hard against the packed, cracked earth, but I rolled to absorb the brunt of the impact. The thud of the two duffels sounded in quick succession behind me. By the time I righted myself, Boner was squeezing his big body out the window with surprising grace, landing on booted feet.

At the front of the trailer, there was a crash as someone kicked the door in.

"C'mon," Aaron murmured, grabbing the bags and my hand again as he ran hunched over to the cover of trees I'd climbed through on the left side of the lot. We raced through the growth, heedless of how much noise we made. Behind us, there were shouts and an errant gunshot that echoed through the hills.

"You think they killed him?" I asked, alarmed that Otto had turned into a violent criminal when he'd only ever been a slightly lazy ne'er do well with me.

Aaron didn't answer.

We burst through the evergreens, our shoes slapping against the asphalt as we met the sidewalk.

"I got a car," I panted as a stitch stabbed into my side under my ribs.

Jesus, I needed to do more cardio.

Aaron flashed me a glance over his shoulder but slowed enough for me to lead us to where I'd parked the muted green Honda. He shucked off the duffel bags, unzipped them both to root around until he found square black monitors in each, and then shoved the bags in the back seat. I watched as he tossed the trackers into the bushes before getting into the front seat. After I raced around to the passenger side, he laughed at the evidence of my hot-wiring abilities.

"You're gonna explain this skill on the way down to Entrance," he warned as he started the car and executed a half-donut that spun us the right way down the road.

I was too preoccupied with catching my breath to answer.

Aaron gave me a few minutes of silence as he expertly navigated through the dark streets of Whistler and back onto the Sea to Sky Highway. Still, he looked at me often, his gaze a tangible caress on my sweat-damp cheek.

"Never met a girl like you," he finally mused, almost to himself. "And I know a lotta girls."

I snorted. "Way to make me feel special."

His grin flashed white in the dark interior. "Got a lotta brothers shacked up with some pretty kick-ass women."

Ah, okay. Well, that was cute and not misogynistic like I'd assumed.

"How many siblings do you have?"

"You wanna have a heart-to-heart, Blue, you start by tellin' me how you cottoned on to Otto's crew findin' where I was at."

I looked out the window at the dull metallic sheen of the ocean beside the cliffside road and wondered what to say. It had been so long since I'd explained my history to anyone, and I wasn't anxious to do so now.

It was better to let sleeping dogs lie.

Only, Rooster wasn't some far-off threat. He had a connection with the man in that trailer, potentially a connection to the man beside me now.

"I grew up with criminals," I explained slowly, carving out the easiest words to explain a complicated history.

"They taught you," he surmised.

My laughter was as hollow as a spent gun casing. "Taught me? Ha! I was a girl, Aaron. A waste of space if no one was allowed to fuck me. No one taught me shit." Except for Cedar and, briefly, a brother named Axe who'd helped get me on birth control despite Rooster forbidding it. "I learned, though. I was invisible, mostly, so they did a lot of their worst kind of shit in front of me."

Aaron's hands squeaked on the wheel, and I realized his knuckles were white with strain. "They hurt you?"

I shrugged a shoulder. "Only once. I left a few days later."

It took me a moment to realize that grinding sound came from Aaron. He was *growling*.

Something about that warmed my belly like good whiskey. I'd told Grouch my story when he'd caught me that last time stealing from his shop. But that was years ago. Since then, I hadn't made any good enough friends to confide in or commiserate with me.

To care.

It felt absurd and beautiful that this essential stranger cared enough now to be enraged for me.

"It was a long time ago," I placated.

"Time's got nothin' on the depth of a wound," he snapped, then rolled his shoulders to release some of the tension. "Didn't mean to bite your head off. Never reacted well to women gettin' hurt."

I didn't curb the impulse to reach over and squeeze his hard, denim-clad thigh. "Mr. Wise Guy, eh?"

A tiny smirk. "People usually don't accuse me'a bein' wise. More like stupid."

"Was it stupid of you to pry off that guy Beaker's fingernails?" I asked. "He could press charges."

A deep, smug chuckle. "Beaker wouldn't know how to press charges against someone if he was hit in the head with a law book. Besides, he fucked with family, I fuck with him."

Hearing the vehemence of his loyalty caused something to pang in my chest. What would it be like to have Aaron at my back? Safe, I thought.

And God, I yearned to feel safe.

"You don't seem real fazed by my show'a violence." He dropped a hand to cover mine on his thigh and tangled our fingers in a casual way that belied how intimate it felt. His heavy rings were warm from his skin.

"Criminals, remember? I'm not as innocent as I look."

"You look like a wet dream," he murmured, bringing our joined hands to his mouth to plant an open-mouthed kiss on the back of my hand.

"Stop." I tried to tug my hand out of his grip, but he wouldn't release me. "You don't need to say things like that to me."

He shot me an incredulous look. "Does anyone ever hafta say somethin' nice about anyone? It's not 'cause I feel you're owed the words,

Blue. It's 'cause I feel moved to say them."

His words prompted something to squirm uncomfortably in my belly. I wanted to tell him he was stupid or crazy, that his flattery was false, but how could I when he seemed so sincere?

"Blue," he said, tone heavy so the word dropped in my lap. "You're so goddamn gorgeous I've been hard since we kissed in the parkin' lot. You know how difficult it is to run with a fuckin' boner?"

Laughter exploded from me, rich and warm spilling out of my lips into the car. I was aware of him grinning at me, shooting little glances my way as if he just *had* to watch me. As if I was beautiful doing it.

And oh God, how did I resist a man like this?

Why would I want to?

When I finished, the smile still wouldn't leave my face, and our joined hands were back on his thigh, his thumb rubbing back and forth on my palm.

"Well, aren't you gonna say somethin' nice about me?" he quipped with a goofy grin.

I rolled my eyes, but there was too much humour in my tone to curb. "I thought you said people should only compliment others if they feel moved to do it."

"Damn," he groused, then grinned when I giggled. "Love the sound'a that laugh."

"What now?" I asked because I felt giddy with lingering adrenaline and warmed through with vivid attraction for this man with the roguish grin and soft, dark eyes.

"We take this loot to a friend'a mine and get it off our fuckin' hands."

"You seem to have a lot of friends willing to do a lot of favours for you," I noticed.

Another smile, this one slow and wide. "Yeah. Yeah, I do. And now, you're gonna know them too."

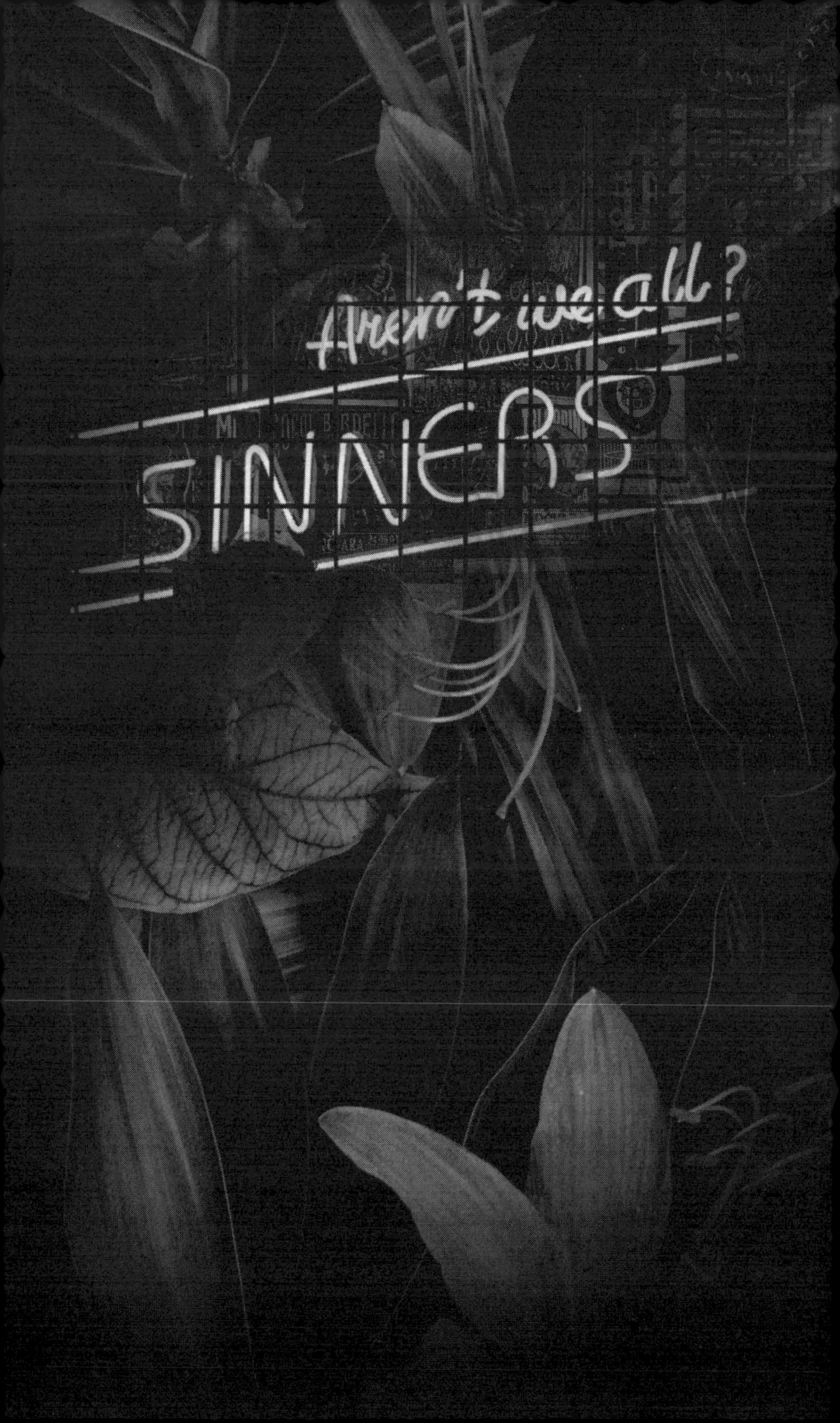
Aren't we all?
SINNERS

CHAPTER FIVE

Blue

WHEN WE PULLED up in front of The Fallen MC headquarters in Entrance, my heart plummeted to the pit of my stomach and anchored there, a heavy, pinching weight.

It was obvious now that I thought about it.

Aaron might not have been wearing a leather jacket with club patches when he entered Evergreen Gas at the beginning of our night, but the rest of it—the tatts, the swagger, the way he'd systematically disarmed and beaten down the robbers, and that tangible charge of erotic danger surrounding him—all lent itself to an outlaw biker.

I should have known 'cause I'd grown up with them.

"I can't go in there," I told him as he parked the car. "I mean, I won't."

Aaron turned to me with an open, curious expression, resting one forearm on the wheel in a way that was strangely sexy as hell. "You wanna tell me why?"

I gestured to the mural of a skull and tattered, flaming wings painted on the brick wall of the low structure in front of us. A floodlight lit the massive mural like a spotlight from the heavens, highlighting a den of iniquity.

"This is The Fallen MC clubhouse," I stated flatly, trying to ignore the surge of bile threatening the back of my throat.

One thick brow arched. "You know the club?"

"Doesn't everyone in BC?" I asked.

"You afraid?" Something gentled at the back of those coffee-coloured eyes, and he reached forward to brush a tattooed thumb along the edge of my jaw before gripping my chin lightly. "You got nothin' to fear when I'm with ya, Blue. Don't you get that?"

"I don't *get* anything. I don't know you," I protested, but the words were like ash on my tongue.

Could you know a person without having their details?

I didn't know Aaron's last name, his favourite colour, or where he was born, but I felt like I had a sense of his soul, a blurry outline coming into focus.

And the truth was, I wanted to see more of it.

More of him.

But I couldn't, not if he was one of them.

"I told you, I was raised by criminals. It took a lot for me to get away from them. I won't risk everything again on another criminal," I said, mostly honest because I couldn't seem to keep from confiding in him. Not when he was staring at me like I was a movie star or a model—as if he could spend years looking at me and never get bored of what he saw.

He was silent for a long moment, but I didn't press. I liked the feel of his rough-tipped fingers on my chin too much to force this exchange to its inevitable conclusion.

"You wanna call me a criminal, I can't stop ya, but I wish you'd think'a me like somethin' less defined. Like twilight between day and night. I got darkness in me, Blue. Don't have to tell ya that after what you saw in Beaker's trailer. But I got light too, a fuck ton'a it. Maybe the ratio's too close for comfort, but I thought for a second you were the kinda girl who found more comfort in chaos than in what others think is right."

He paused, and I realized, somehow, he'd drawn closer without me realizing. I could taste his breath on my lips and see the detailed ink of the inked owl wings spread over his throat. He was so beautiful, it seemed unthinkable he could be as ugly inside as the other criminals I'd known, but I wasn't naive enough to think the face of evil had to be as grotesque as its heart.

"You might see me and this place as dangerous. As criminal. Maybe you're right. But I'm also the same guy who took your hand when you needed help, and I learned that from the people in that clubhouse, Blue. I learned how to love like the best'a them 'cause my brothers and their families taught me what it means to be a man who protects his kin, who fights to the death for what he feels is right, and who won't change for anyone. Even pretty girls with lake water eyes he could drown in."

His thumb traveled from the dip above my chin to the swell of my lower lip, pressing lightly into the indent there to open my mouth. The pad of that finger dipped just slightly over the edge, past my teeth onto my tongue.

He tasted like salt and metal and man.

Electric lust sparked over my taste buds and charged down through my belly to my groin.

"Yeah," he murmured in a voice so low it seemed like more of a purr. "I may be a dangerous man, but I'm the one in danger here. You walk out on me, that'll ache in a way I've never ached 'fore. C'mon, Blue baby, what's reward without a little risk?"

Those words echoed back at me from earlier in the night. The taste of him on my tongue, like one single bite of forbidden fruit, tempted me overwhelmingly to screw all the wisdom and lessons I'd learned in my life and follow trouble wherever he led.

I opened my mouth to say something even though my mind hadn't yet landed on the right words because my heart was muddling up my thought process. But I didn't get the chance because Aaron kissed me then.

He pressed his warm lips to my mouth, his thumb still pressing my lower lip down so his tongue was free to slide inside and claim every inch of me. He kissed me like a reverent scholar learning an ancient text, testing the texture of my tongue against his, mapping the edge of my teeth and the vibration of the moans that seeped unbidden from my throat. His other hand dipped into the hair at the side of my head and traveled to the back of my skull, cupping me like I was precious. A treasure he'd found and would never voluntarily part with.

There was passion and lust, but also something that kicked at the door of my heart, demanding entry.

Tenderness.

That was what it was.

The word floated into my brain when he crowded closer, tipping my head back to plunder me further.

This big brute of an outlaw was seducing me. Not taking. Not even owning. Just luring me deeper into his thrall. I was utterly defenceless against it because I'd thought he was the kind of man to force and push and bruise, and there he was, kissing me breathless while holding me carefully close.

How was I supposed to walk away from the only man who'd ever held me like that?

From a man who'd save a defenceless stranger.

From someone who said things like 'lake water eyes'.

I didn't want to.

God, I didn't want to.

How cruel of God to dangle such beauty before my eyes, knowing it would be ripped away.

"Stop thinkin'. You're woundin' my pride," Aaron murmured against my swollen lips before he angled his head and licked a wet trail up my throat to my ear, where he nipped and sucked at my lobe. "I won't stop you, you want to walk away from me. But, Blue baby, kiss me now and give me somethin' good to think about at night when I'm wishin' you were here with me."

Something like a whimper and a moan tangled in my throat a second before I arched up into his embrace, sank my hands in his overlong hair, and kissed him back. He fed me his own groan before clamping his wide hands over my thighs, fingers curling beneath the edge of each leg, then tugging sharply. I gasped as I fell back against the passenger door, but Aaron caught me with one hand to the back of my head while the other travelled down the inside of one thigh. Splayed over the console, my jean-clad groin was totally accessible to him, and he took full advantage by cupping me hard through the denim.

"So hot," he murmured as he bent to nip at my mouth. "Fuck, I bet I tease this zipper open and slide my fingers inside, I'd find a pool'a wet waitin' for me."

"Do it," I urged him, throwing my own rulebook out the window.

I'd pick it up later when I'd had my fill of this man and this moment.

Something dark and dangerous sparked in those brown eyes. When he spoke, his words were all gravel. "Yeah? You wanna taste'a me 'fore headin' for the hills?"

"You got a problem with being used, Aaron?" I taunted, scratching at his chest through his tee. My nail hit something metallic on his left pec, and when I pinched, I discovered it was a hooped piercing through his nipple.

Any reservations I had evaporated in the flames of lust licking up from my core.

"A girl as pretty as you wants to use me, I won't say no," he agreed, but there was something a little sad, I thought, lurking in those flippant words.

It made my heart pang.

I ignored it, instead focusing on pulling his shirt up over his head. He lifted his arms for me and off it went, revealing tight, warm olive-brown skin with vividly inked tattoos across his shoulders and down his strong, flexing arms. Moisture pooled in my mouth as I traced a finger over the ridged boxes carved into his abdomen down to the rough path of hair leading into his jeans. The massive bulge down the length of one thigh was so obviously thick and long that a spark of worry actually made me pull back.

He chuckled huskily. "Don't worry, Blue baby, I'll get you nice and ready."

"Even so," I murmured incredulously as my questing fingers tentatively tried to wrap around that iron length. "I think this is a matter of physics, and you just won't fit."

Aaron's laughter was so dark, it moved like smoke between us. In the low light creeping in the heavily tinted windows from the clubhouse exterior lights, I could see the joy and desire dancing in his eyes as he bent his head to my belly. When he went to lift my shirt, I batted his hand away. He tried again, this time with his eyes locked on mine.

When I blocked him, a sexy growl worked loose from his throat.

"You gotta let me touch you, Blue," he groaned, voice wrecked by lust. "I'm dyin' here."

Feminine power surged through me, giving me confidence I'd never felt so acutely. I lay back and threaded my fingers through his, curling them both around the hem of my tee so we could lift it together. Aaron's eyes were hot and bright on every inch of my skin as it was revealed, his Adam's apple bobbing as he swallowed roughly. There was no cruelty in his expression at the soft convex curve of my belly or the tracks of silvery stretch marks near my naval. Only a burning need so acute, it seared my skin and made me tremble.

"Fuckin' gorgeous," he groaned roughly, dipping to press his mouth to my stomach. He rubbed his stubble-rough cheek against me as he peppered my torso with kisses, following the path of the tee as we raised it up to my breasts and over the twin mounds. My nipples pebbled in my bra, and Aaron found them immediately, sucking one into his mouth through the thin cotton. I arched into the hot, sucking friction of his mouth, clenching my hands in his hair to keep him still as he feasted on my tits. One and then the other, back and forth like a pendulum luring me into a trance. Distantly, I was aware that I was murmuring his name over and over, less coherent words as he worked me slowly and patiently into a frenzy using just his mouth on my breasts.

His teeth rasped against a swollen nipple in a way that made me rut up against him, searching for contact where I really needed it, between my thighs.

He laughed, husky and cruel. "You want more, Blue?"

I nodded, eyes closed, head tipped back as I focused on the lingering heat in each peak of my breast.

"Wanna hear you tell me what you want," he ordered me, fingers flexing around my breasts, plumping the full weight of them in his big hands. "You want me to take off your bra and fuck these gorgeous tits? You want my tongue lower? Lickin' up all that sweet honey you got leakin' between your pretty thighs? You tell me what you want, I'll give it to you, baby."

"God," I moaned, almost scared by the level of heat burning low in my belly. "Can I choose all of the above?"

"Be careful what ya wish for," came his throaty response a moment before he pulled away.

I murmured a protest, but he was only gone for a moment, cranking the front seat back so he had space to kneel on the ground before the wheel. His new position brought him low enough to kiss the inside of my denim-covered thigh. His eyes burned like banked coals as he slowly popped the button, then bent to drag the zipper tab down with his teeth.

"Oh my God," I breathed, hypnotized by the sight of his broad shoulders between my thighs, of his mouth so close to my shamefully wet sex. My hands tightened in his hair when he kissed the flat of my groin covered by the simple blue panties he'd uncovered through the opening in my jeans.

"Lift," he ordered as he started to peel the fabric from my legs, his big body coiling as he pulled them down to my ankles, then off along with my blue boots.

Finally, I was naked but for my underwear, sprawled indelicately across the passenger seat and the center console, my legs pushed wide by the breadth of his body between them. I squirmed, too exposed, doubt creeping in along old pathways.

Aaron stilled me by sliding his arms beneath my legs and wrapping his hands around my thighs to frame the inside of my groin where the fabric of my underwear was soaked through with desire. He dipped to press his nose to the top of my pussy and inhaled deeply, a shudder rocking through his spine.

"Fuckin' gorgeous," he growled, pulling back just enough to show me the desire carved brutally into his features. "Smell like goddamn heaven. Now, be a good girl, Blue, and lay still while I take my fill. This is as close to heaven as a man like me's ever likely to get."

I opened my mouth to say something that ended with a ragged groan when he sealed his lips around my clit through the thin cotton and sucked me into the hot cavern of his mouth. The friction of his lashing tongue against the fabric was like a match to strike paper, igniting a heat so high inside me I thought it would burn me from the inside out. When he trailed two thick, rough-tipped fingers down the crease of my thigh and groin, then hooked my panties to the side so he could sink a finger inside my aching pussy, my bones turned to ash, and I collapsed limply against the passenger door, unable to hold myself up anymore.

He ate me like that, ruthlessly, ceaselessly. Tongue, teeth, fingers, the hot clasp of his lips all over every inch of my pussy, over the cotton and under it.

The first time I came, it crashed over my head like a wave, submerging me in pleasure so blue and bright it seemed like I'd fallen into the summer sea at noon. Heat blazed through me and left me a shaking, quivering mess in his strong hands.

He laughed, a soft, triumphant sound that gave way to a groan when he licked a path from the bottom of my crease to the top. "So fuckin' delicious. All that cum just for me."

A shiver rattled through me. "Come here, now. I want you."

"Nah, not yet. You're not nearly ready. Trust me." He winked, one of his hands disappearing to wrench open his own jeans and pull out his cock. It slapped hard against his belly, a thick column of flesh wrapped with veins throbbing in time with his heartbeat. There were five silver bars through the underside of that wide shaft that glinted in the low light. A Jacob's ladder.

My mouth watered, and my stomach flipped at the sight of it.

"Oh my God," I whispered from deep in my throat. "I have a thing for piercings and that..." My hand fluttered uselessly. "Oh my God."

But I had to agree with him.

I was not ready for that monster.

Aaron chuckled again at the expression on my face. His voice was a hot caress against my inner thigh as he nuzzled it and whispered, "Don't worry, by the time I'm slidin' inside this hot little pussy, you'll be so ready, you'll be beggin' to feel the stretch and burn'a me. But I'm glad you like the look'a me 'cause I sure as fuck love the look and taste'a you."

"Get to work then," I said, trying for haughtiness, for a joke when all I wanted to do was stay in this steaming car forever being worked over like a fine instrument by a musical genius.

Aaron didn't laugh. Instead, he looked up at me as he lay his cheek on the inside of my soft thigh and wrapped his hand firmly in the soaked-through placket of my underwear. With a sharp, sudden tug that cut into my hips, he wrenched the thong apart in his grip. I watched without breathing as he lifted the ruined panties to his nose, breathed deeply, then shoved them into his pocket for later.

His grin was wicked as he brought his hands around my hips to cup my ass and lifted me high to bring my leaking pussy to his mouth again.

"Feel free to scream if ya need to," he allowed before sealing his mouth to me.

My spine bowed as he sucked my tender clit and slid two twisting fingers into the silken clutch of my body.

This time, he didn't work me up slowly. He attacked me, nipping at the swell of my pubic mound, whipping my clit with hard tongue lashes and sucking so firmly I felt he was about to turn me inside out into his mouth. When I came, I screamed around the sound of his name in my mouth and shattered into pieces, knowing he would catch every single jagged edge of me.

I floated so high on my climax that, at first, I wasn't aware of the tear of foil, then the hiss as Aaron rolled a condom onto his length. I blinked once, twice, clearing the fog and the sheen of pleasure-bought tears. Aaron's gaze was fixed on the sight of his large sheathed cock parting my folds, sliding through the wet over my entrance but not actually entering me.

I whimpered as I canted my hips, too far gone to be embarrassed.

"I need to feel you," I said, but I didn't beg. My voice was strong, unwavering. I needed this man inside me like I needed my next breath. Electricity sparked along my skin as I thought of being connected to him, of having someone worthy for the first time in my life between my thighs. "I don't care if it hurts. I want it to, so I remember you for days after this."

Aaron moaned, and his hands lashed on to my hips, hauling me over the console so I settled suddenly in his lap. My cum-slick thighs slid against the rough fabric of his jeans as he moved me up and over his cock.

"Look at me when I spread you open," he barked gruffly, one hand curling into the back of my hair to clench tightly and the other slowly pressing me down onto his erection. "I wanna watch you struggle to take me."

"Fuck," I hissed, fisting both hands in his shirt so tightly there was a *rip*. Even though I was loose and ready, slick as spilled oil between my thighs, it was a struggle to work myself down onto his thickness. He held me close, panting raggedly as he watched me wriggle and rock onto him.

"That's it," he coaxed thickly. "Yeah, Blue baby, work that cock into your snug little cunt. Wanna see you work for it."

God, I was working for it. My head fell back between my shoulders as he released his grip on my hair and trailed a hand down the center of my chest, spreading his fingers over my thundering heart. I shuddered as the last of my resistance snapped like an elastic band, and I finally impaled myself on him. The metal bars through his frenum warmed instantly against the heat of me and felt utterly erotic rubbing into my sensitized flesh.

We both groaned, the sounds tangling together like our sweat-dampened bodies. Aaron wrapped his strong arms around me and hugged me close, grinding me down onto him in a way that made feverish shivers break out across my body.

It was intimate.

Not fucking, not quite.

He held me so close I could feel his heartbeat against my own chest. I could taste the salt of his neck against my tongue and hear the way his breath stuttered and filtered through his laboring lungs. He held me in that way I was discovering he had that made me feel like more than a stranger.

Like more than the past I was ashamed of and the future I was scared for.

Like I was just a girl and he was just a boy.

"Ride me," he ordered on a hot exhale in my ear before leaning back to prop his hands behind his head in an arrogant, insanely sexy posture that made his arms bulge and his abs contract. "Wanna watch you take me."

Confidence like I'd never felt buoyed me. I rose, cresting his tip like a wave I rode all the way down to the end of his length, then back again.

"Touch your gorgeous tits for me."

My fingers trembled as I reached up to tweak my nipples through my thin bra.

"Take them out over the cups." His voice was like a hand at my throat, almost threatening and dangerously alluring.

I pulled the cups down so my heavy breasts were plumped up over the fabric and Aaron responded with a groan that rumbled through him into me.

"You're fuckin' gorgeous," he told me, then when I shied away from his gaze, he clasped my chin and forced me to look into his heavy-lidded eyes. "Gorgeous. A fuckin' dream."

Tears seared the back of my eyes even when I tried to blink them back. "Why are you ruining this?"

"This?" he asked, with a raised brow, grinding me down on him so my clit caught fire at the impact of his short, coarse pubic hair against my tender flesh. "The only way I'm ruinin' this is by tryin' to ruin you for other men. I'm thinkin' you should be mine alone."

"You don't know me," I panted as he dipped to suck my left breast into his mouth, one hand palming the entire thing and lifting it to his lips. "You don't know enough to want me."

"Know enough to wanna know you more," he countered, nipping hard at my flesh in a way that had me tightening like a vise around his cock as I churned over it. "Know enough to wanna mark your neck with hickeys and fill your tight cunt with so much cum I leak outta ya for days. So any man who gets too close can smell me on you and know, even though you walked away, I had you here, and I wanted you bad."

"Stop," I begged, but my hips were pumping hard, my fingers spasming in his hair as I held him close to my breasts, to my heart. Dreams and desires spun a mad dance together in my blood, heating it until I felt I would burst.

"Only if you make me," he growled, pulling back with a snarl to glare at me with flashing eyes. His hands found my hips in a punishing grip that somehow made the pleasure coil tighter in my belly. "Until then, you're fuckin' *mine*."

He fucked up into me then, fast, hard strokes that dragged across my raw nerves and lit them all on fire. He fucked me until I couldn't breathe, every single muscle in my body clenched around the monstrous girth of him inside me.

"Ohmygod, ohmygod," I chanted, a desperate edge to my voice as pleasure clawed at my insides and threatened to tear me in two. "Fuck, fuck, Aaron, I c-can't."

"You can," he growled, and as if to prove it, he wedged a hand between our bodies where we were joined and carefully worked one of his fingers into my stretched pussy beside his pounding dick. I shuddered and made a keening animal noise I couldn't control as I struggled and surged against him, so close to breaking I almost couldn't bear it. "You will," he ordered and then bit down hard at the junction of my neck and shoulder.

I burst apart.

Like waves against the rock or fireworks shattering into bright pieces in a dark night sky, every particle of my body separated and reformed around him. Around Aaron. I sobbed from the sheer power of the climax and the swift aftermath of realization that reality was still outside this car and would inevitably call me back home.

I clutched my midnight stranger close, pouring my tears over his shoulder and pressing kisses on top of his pounding pulse as he groaned and arched and seated himself at the very end of me as he came inside me.

Recklessly, I wished I could feel the heat of him at the entrance of my womb without the barrier of a condom.

I squeezed my eyes shut as we held each other in the quiet, warm afterglow. Aaron's hand mapped a lazy trail down my right side, tracing my curves like he planned to sculpt me later out of clay.

A tear escaped the tight compression of my lids and rolled down my cheek.

In all the years I was with Otto, and the man before him, I'd never been cradled in the bowl of a big man's arms and held like he'd shield me through anything.

And fuck, it was a powerful moment, one I felt sear itself into my soul in a way I'd never, ever forget.

"What'd that motherfucker do to you?" Aaron asked, rough voice low like he was afraid to startle me.

"A scumbag who stole my savings and the sapphire and diamond ring my mum gave me. Otto was nothing," I admitted. "It's what happened before."

What might be happening again, I thought but didn't say. If Rooster was in the area, I was as good as fucked. And if he thought for one second I'd taken up with a new man, and worse, that the new man was affiliated with The Fallen...well, he'd kill him.

I couldn't--*wouldn't*--let that happen to a man who could hold me like this.

Like I was precious.

"Stay," Aaron said suddenly, and the hand cupping the back of my skull pulled at my hair so I was forced to look at his pleasure-softened face. "Stay with me. After we get this shit sorted, gimme your name, gimme your number. Let me know you."

I was already shaking my head before he'd finished. "You don't want to know me. I'm trouble."

A sharp-edged grin flashed across his inky stubble-stained cheeks. "I'm a fan'a trouble."

"Yeah and you're too much of it for me to handle."

"You handled me just fine right now," he quipped.

"Aaron," I said, leveling him with a somber gaze. "Trust me, you don't want to get involved with me. There's trouble, and then there's more trouble than I'm worth."

"Never had anythin' good come to me I didn't hafta work for first," he rebutted with a stubborn jut of his scarred chin. "You think you aren't worth that? Even knowin' ya for five hours, I can tell havin' you is worth a lifetime'a trouble."

My heart twisted and flopped like a slippery fish as I tried to get a grip on it and force it back into its net.

"Blue," he whispered, moving a big, ringed hand over my hair to push it back from my face. "Take a chance on me."

"I want to," I admitted as I pressed my forehead to his. "But it's better for both of us that I don't."

He stared at me, but we were too close for me to read the expression in those dramatic eyes. After a long moment, he pulled away and gently lifted me off him into the passenger seat. He avoided my eyes as he tucked his still-large but softening cock into his jeans and tied off the used condom.

"Fine," he said gruffly. "But there's no way I'm lettin' ya outta my sight until we get this shit sorted with your ex. He could come for you thinkin' you have his loot."

"I can handle Otto."

He shot me a withering look that made me feel guilt like a spear through my side. "Yeah, well, you're not gonna. At least not alone. You wanna moment to get cleaned up, I'll wait outside. But you're goin' in that clubhouse with me so we can sort out a plan to keep you safe. I don't care if I gotta drag you inside kickin' and screamin' to do it. You get me, Blue?"

He slid out of the car before I could say another word.

A massive sigh nearly choked me on its way out of my mouth. I wanted to meet The Fallen MC almost as much as I wanted Rooster to discover me again, but I couldn't deny that I...trusted Aaron. If he thought they were good people, and I knew he was a good person, how far off base could he be? Truth be told, I didn't really have any other choice. We had two duffels of contraband goods and a criminal gang after us, after me. I was fucked if I did and fucked if I didn't. At least if I went inside with Aaron, the danger was targeted more at my heart than my life.

With another heavy sigh, I flipped the visor down to check my appearance and nearly laughed at the sight that greeted me.

Because despite knowing no matter what happened for the rest of the night, I had to leave Aaron behind forever, mussed from his grip and his kiss, flushed from the pleasure he'd coaxed from my body, I looked prettier and happier than I'd ever looked before.

CHAPTER SIX

Boner

THREE IN THE MORNIN' and the clubhouse was still filled with people. It was a Saturday, which meant partyin', and a club party didn't ever really end until the light had come up and some Old Lady or biker groupie started to make breakfast for the men still drunk enough to be wakeful and the poor bastards woken by their hangovers.

It wasn't about the partyin' though; the booze and the weed and the constant thrum'a bass through the worn floorboards.

It was about family.

About celebratin' the fact we were alive and safe and so fuckin' loved you could feel it like somethin' in the air.

It seemed Blue could smell it too, ski-jump nose tipped high as she dragged a breath of smoky air into her little lungs. Her eyes were wide but unsurprised as she took in the bikers loungin' 'round the large room, hangin' at the bar draped over stools or slouched into deep leather couches. Nova and Lila swayed on a makeshift dance floor, tangled together almost indecently, makin' out as they ground their hips together in a lush, slow-kinda tango. Axe-Man, Mei, Harleigh Rose and Lion were usin' the dart board for knife throwin' target practice with Bea cheering them on and Priest lookin' on impassively, probably 'cause none'a them were as good as him. Bat, Dane, Curtains, and Buck played pool in the back corner, but the red-headed fuck I called my best friend noticed me instantly and made his way over with a curious frown.

Zeus tagged me too, his eyes sharp and alert despite the fact it was three in the mornin' and he had a set'a twin toddlers that kept him up most nights. He unfolded from the couch where he'd been shootin' the shit with his son, King.

He and Curtains hit me at the same time.

"You pick up a stowaway at Beaker's?" Zeus asked, towerin' over Blue by more than ten inches. His fierce, craggy face was fixed in a scowl that coulda seemed furious if you didn't know him well.

"What's in the bags?" Curtains asked next, eyes narrowed at the duffels Blue and I carried. "See, Z, this is why I shoulda gone with him. Boner never does things right."

I rolled my eyes. "I get things done. Who the fuck cares if they're right?"

Beside me, Blue smiled. Even outta the corner'a my eye, that shit was gorgeous.

"You deal with business 'fore you picked up a pretty girl?" Z asked.

"A little more business than I was expectin', but yeah," I agreed, then handed the duffel to Curtains. "There were trackers in the bags, but they were hot on our tail, so I had to get rid'a them."

"Dude, I could'a done a reverse––" Curtains started, geeky excitement lightin' up his eyes.

I held up a hand. "Not sure this is related to Beak, but I came across some thugs robbin' Evergreen Gas Station tonight." I winced at the look on both Curtains' and Z's faces 'cause they were right, it was fuckin' dumb to get involved, but... "They tried to fuck up Blue here, and I stepped in. Wasn't gonna let them hurt or take her, and that's what they had planned after robbin' the place. The motherfuckers fucked up my bike, so we took off in their van and found these."

Lion approached then, his cop instincts probably goin' off like an alarm after the call I put in to him. "What've you got here, Boner?"

I jerked my chin at Blue, who unzipped the top'a one bag to show the glitterin' hoard within. "Think we might've stumbled on the stolen loot from the jewelry robberies you mentioned."

"Fuck," Lion and Zeus said at the same time for different reasons.

"That's about the extent'a it, yeah," I agreed. "They came after us, but I threw the trackers out and lost them on the Sea to Sky. Figured we could talk next moves here."

"Good thinkin'," Lion agreed.

"You're not gonna call the cops?" I tested 'cause Lion was a private dick now, but old instincts die hard sometimes.

He crossed his arms and glared at me in response.

I grinned.

"We'll talk 'bout this in private," Z asserted with a frownin' nod at Blue, but there was a wealth'a thought behind that gunmetal gaze.

"You got no fear in those eyes lookin' at me and mine," he said, slow and deep in a voice rough as gravel under tires. When I was a prospect, just the sound'a that voice used to scare the shit outta me. Now it was as familiar and soothin' as the hum'a Harley pipes.

Blue shrugged one shoulder but subtly shifted her body into mine. The little move set flame to my lungs and made it kinda difficult to breathe. It was probably my wistful imagination, but I thought she smelled like me. Like us. The sweet-salt of satisfaction. I could still feel the wet phantom clutch of her around my spent cock, and it gave a twitch at the thought of takin' her again.

"I didn't know Aaron was a brother in a club." Her voice was sharp-edged, cutting at me even as she leaned into me, like she resented me for the omission, and herself for not carin' enough to cut me out for it. "But I should've. It makes sense."

"You didn't ask," I pointed out, bumpin' her with my shoulder. "I did tell ya about my brothers."

"You weren't wearing one of those." She gestured to Zeus and Curtains' leather cuts covered in a variety'a patches that denoted their rank and chapter in The Fallen MC. "Maybe I was being deliberately obtuse. I don't usually like to associate with criminals."

Zeus raised a brow at her, then cut his gaze to me.

You vouchin' for her? *the look asked.*

I jerked my chin slightly without hesitation.

Hell yeah.

Maybe I'd only known her a couple'a hours, but that's the way it'd happened for all the important relationships in my life. Met Curtains when I was on the hunt to save my sister years ago and knew by the end'a the night I'd forged a bond'a brotherhood with the skinny, freckled kid. The story'a how I met Z was more complicated but followed those same lines.

I knew.

Not with my eyes, just seein' them like love at first sight or some fairy-tale kinda shit.

I knew it in the way certain birds know to migrate south, as if the impulse to love them was programmed in me, layin' latent 'til the right trigger ignited it inside'a my soul.

That was how I felt about Curtains and Zeus.

And now, I had that feelin' about Blue.

Like I'd been waitin' for her.

Zeus read it all in me as easy as a fuckin' picture book. A grin edged the corner'a his mouth in his dark beard as he reached forward to clap a hand on my shoulder and squeeze hard.

"You might not do shit the traditional way, Boner, my man, but you gotta way'a goin' above and beyond for those lucky enough to have your loyalty."

His words hit my gut like expensive rum, warmin' me through to the bone. I reached up, slightly over Blue, to clamp my own hand on his shoulder too. It closed the loop'a energy between us so I could feel the tangible electric current'a our bond prickle along my skin.

"You give a man a good home, he'll fight to keep it," I reminded him 'cause he'd once said those very words to me when I was young and heartbroken with loss and so alone I thought I'd rather die than go on.

In answer, he shook me slightly, movin' his hand up to cup the side'a my neck 'fore releasin' me. When he stepped back, he dipped his head to grin at Blue.

"You're welcome here." He extended his hand and waited patiently for Blue to take it. Her fingers were engulfed in a big, tatted palm that had killed more men than I knew, but his touch was all gentleness. "You'll find good people, you're open to lookin' beyond the surface."

'Fore Blue could respond, the door opened behind us, and a blur of blonde hair streaked between us and Zeus. Loulou crashed into her man without care, knowin' he'd catch her exactly the way he did, hands to her ass, liftin' her into the air so she could wrap her legs 'round his waist. They kissed then, long and wet and totally uncarin'a the audience 'fore them 'cause they were totally caught up in each other.

Blue blinked at them, then looked up at me. "I forgot how, uh, affectionate bikers can be."

I chuckled, taggin' her hip to drag her back against me. She was so tiny the top'a her electric blue head only met the middle'a my sternum, but those sweet, soft curves pressed into me like a fuckin' dream. When I ducked down to whisper in her ear, the scent'a sweetness like bubble gum met my nose and hardened my dick.

"You feelin' neglected, Blue, I have a mind to show you just how affectionate I can be."

"I think you just did," she teased with a charmin' kinda reluctance.

I grinned wolfishly. "I don't mind givin' you another reminder."

She squirmed but didn't move away. "You're a slut, Aaron."

"If bein' a slut means I like sex and I'm talented in the sack, I'll have to agree with ya." My teeth found the lobe of her ear and nibbled at the edge in a way that set her hips cantin' back into the bowl'a my groin. "You got a problem with that?"

"No." The word was breathy, sweet as sin. "But that doesn't mean I want any part of it again."

"Ah, but I think you do, liar," I countered, vaguely aware that Zeus and Loulou were pullin' apart finally, and Curtains and Lion were discussin' what to do about the stolen loot. "How about I play you for the right to seduce ya again? Take your pick: darts, pool, or cards."

She peered back up at me, strands of blue hair stickin' in her dark lashes, as vivid as those wide eyes. "And if I win?"

"You win, I drive you home like a gentleman and never bother you again," I promised, just hopin' to see a trickle'a disappointment in her gaze.

I was rewarded with a flash'a it, lightnin' quick and bright across her face.

Masculine satisfaction rumbled through me.

She bit her lip as her gaze slid fearfully to the pool table 'fore dartin' back to my face. "I don't know, I'm not really good at any of them. Maybe you pick?"

My wicked heart rejoiced. The idea of watchin' her bend over a pool table was too good to pass up, and if her shaky look at the table was any indication, it would be an easy win.

As desperate as I already was to feel her around me again, I took the easy road.

"Pool it is, then."

"We'll play with you," Loulou proclaimed, havin' finally unattached her mouth from her man's. She beamed at Blue, and my heart gave a little pang 'cause it was just like her to roll out the welcome mat when one'a her boys brought a woman home to meet the family. "I'm Loulou, but the brothers call me Foxy, and you can feel free to do the same. I have to say your hair is incredible. I wonder if I could pull off blue like that."

Z growled, fistin' his big hand in the back of her white-blonde hair. "You could pull off a sack over your fuckin' head, little Lou, doesn't mean you should."

She laughed up at him, blindingly bright.

Fuck, but I wanted Blue to look at me like that. Like I'd hung the damn moon in the sky just for her enjoyment.

"Thanks," Blue murmured, a little shy and a whole lotta cute. "Your hair is gorgeous, though. No matter what I try in the salon, I could never mix such a pretty blonde."

Loulou's eyes sparkled, and she stepped forward to slot her arm through my new woman's, bendin' to chatter in her ear as she dragged her off to the empty pool table.

"We'll get a head start on this," Lion proclaimed as he and Curtains took up the duffels and started to move through the clubhouse on their way to Curtains' office. I didn't have a clue what kinda shit those two got up to most'a the time, especially when Axe-Man and King got involved talkin' numbers and codes and shit. So I was happy to take a load off for a second and enjoy the high of my family meetin' this blue-hearted girl who'd already left an ink stain on the skin over my heart.

"Sweet as fuck, brother," Zeus decreed, clampin' a hand over my shoulder as we moved to follow them. "She a keeper?"

"Known her like five hours and I'm already picturin' a thousand more nights like this, so yeah, I'm thinkin', she lets me keep her, it's a done deal."

Zeus shook his head, bitin' off the edge'a his smile. "Fallin' like flies these days."

"Flies to honey," I agreed 'cause there was no way to look at Mei perched on Axe-Man's back about to throw a knife from her perch, both'a them laughin' or Nova spinnin' Lila around the floor like they were alone in a dark room, or Priest pinnin' a smilin' Bea to his side and not see the joy the women brought my brothers.

I'd never wanted that, never even thought about that for myself, and now, lookin' at Blue as she stood by Lou rackin' up the pool balls, laughin' a little at somethin' she said, I wanted it more than anythin'.

And I wanted it with her.

"Uh-oh," King said, appearin' beside me with his crooked grin. "I know that look."

"What look?"

"The look'a a man who's been enchanted and never wants to break the fuckin' spell," he said with a laugh, squeezin' my neck in comradery. "Welcome to the club, man."

"Happy for you, but we still got business to discuss," Z reminded me before handin' me a pool cue. "We wipe the floor with 'em, then talk in the chapel, yeah?"

"Shouldn't take long," I promised, grinnin' at Blue as she awkwardly took a cue from Loulou and stared at it skeptically. "I'm countin' on an easy win."

TWENTY MINUTES LATER, I WAS STARIN' gobsmacked as Blue folded her curves over the felt, lined up an almost impossible bank shot, and sank the eight ball without blinkin' a goddamn eye.

"You fuckin' hoodwinked me," I accused her, stalkin' over to pin her against the table. "You little hustler!"

She shrugged one shoulder but couldn't contain the triumphant grin splittin' her rosy lips. "It was just so easy, Aaron. Like taking candy from a baby."

I pressed my groin tight to hers, bendin' my head to nip at her ear, and whispered, "Do I need to remind ya just how much of a man I am? Just how *hard* I can be?"

She giggled, and fuck me, that sound was gold, silver, and bronze wrapped up in her soft little package. "Maybe you should, but you didn't win this little bet. *I* did, so maybe I should show *you* some things this time."

"Oh, fuck yeah," I agreed heartily, droppin' my cue to the floor so I could cup the generous swell of her fine ass in my hands. "Givin' sore loser a new meanin' if you're talkin' about ridin' me 'til I can't feel my legs."

She rocked to her tiptoes, nipped my chin, and grinned. "I am."

"Definitely a keeper." I was vaguely aware of Z sayin' from the other side'a the table 'fore I bent my head to take Blue's hot mouth with mine.

A keeper. Kissin' her there after shootin' the shit with my family, Blue fittin' in just right like she'd been born to be at my side, it wasn't hard to imagine more nights like this. Plantin' her sweet ass on the back'a my bike, wakin' up to her soft body pressed to mine, her smile a gift I got every single fuckin' day...

Yeah.

Yeah, that sounded about right.

She thought she wasn't worth the trouble, but she didn't get yet that I was the kinda man who thrived on gettin' into messes and gettin' out (relatively) unscathed. Whatever trouble she'd bought, I'd take care'a it 'cause even after a single night, I knew in my bones she was worth it.

I was just easin' into the heat buildin' between the two'a us when there was commotion outside the clubhouse and a sound that made me go cold.

Bang.

A gunshot.

I was twirlin', pushin' Blue behind me as I faced the door 'fore I could even think about it. Z was already sprintin' across the room, faster than he shoulda been able to at his age with his bulk, his gun in one hand.

"Get the Old Ladies and women to the back right *fuckin' now*," he roared before pryin' open the door and disappearin' outside.

Axe-Man and Priest were on his heels, a gun and knife in their hands, respectively. They slithered out the front door behind him like shadows, soft and deadly.

I took a breath then, knowin' Z had backup.

"Get to the back, yeah?" I told Blue, facin' her to find worry etched into her white-washed face. "Stick with Mei and Harleigh Rose. They're about as deadly as the rest'a the men in the club."

"Aaron," she whispered, clutching at my wrist. "Be safe, too. Okay? I had a feeling Otto wouldn't give up, and…well, if I brought trouble to this doorstep, I'm so sorry."

"Don't worry about that. Just go," I ordered, punchin' a kiss to her lips so she'd feel me even after I followed the rest'a the brothers out the door.

Curtains caught up to me 'fore we muscled through it, shovin' me in the shoulder in a silent show'a partnership.

The Fallen MC Compound took up two acres'a land beside the West River that cut through Entrance and delineated the posh fuckers from the normal folk. Our main front, Hephaestus Auto, set back from the road behind an eleven-foot chain-link fence, took up most'a the front lot, but the clubhouse was tucked just behind and to the right'a it. Obviously, the motherfuckers had climbed the damn fence to get inside the locked gates.

They were idiots for thinkin' that was our first and only line'a security.

Our prospect, Carson, had been keepin' an eye on the monitors from behind the bar inside the clubhouse, but it was Wrath who'd been skulkin' outside to brood and first seen the intruders. He stood head and shoulders above the one he held in a chokehold lookin' like he could'a taken a nap even though the man struggled in his arms.

Dude was built like a brick shit house, and nothin' ever got to him.

Not even four men with guns in our front parkin' lot.

Another man lay on the ground moanin', clutchin' his right shoulder. Bat loomed over him, boot planted in the middle of the man's chest, and his gun trained right between his eyes. Dane stood behind him like his shadow, mouth curled into a sneer as he trained his two Smith & Wesson pistols at Bat's captive.

I wondered what the two of them had been doin' outside when they came over the fence, but even brothers were entitled to their secrets.

Besides, the second my eyes caught on the bastard locked in a stand-off with Zeus, I lost my motherfuckin' mind.

It was Otto.

I swung over the railin' on the clubhouse landin' and stood easily, already springin' across the lot in a jog 'til I reached Z's side.

"Stand the *fuck* down, or I'll gun you down right here," Zeus was growlin'.

Otto didn't say a word, but even in the low light, I could see his hand tremble.

"I'd do what he goddamn says, Otto," I said pleasantly enough, but my grin felt feral on my face, and I was one second away from foamin' at the damn mouth. "He's not the kind to fuck around with threats."

"I'm just here for the girl."

The three other men were standin' free with their guns trained on our semi-circle'a Fallen brothers, but it was obvious they were takin' their lead from Otto.

So I made a split-second decision from the gut 'cause instinct had driven me my whole damn life and rarely led me astray.

I stalked forward, ignorin' the three guns suddenly aimed at me, knowin' my brothers would have my back, and I didn't stop 'til Otto was within my reach. The gun shook in his grip but steadied when I pressed my chest into the barrel.

"Watch your––" he started to demand.

But the only authority I listened to my whole damn life was Zeus's, so I didn't heed his order.

Instead, I cocked my fist back and hammered it down on his weak motherfuckin' chin.

He crumpled to his knees with a whine that deepened into a guttural groan. While he was vulnerable, I kicked him in the sternum and then pinned him there with my boot when he fell onto his back on the asphalt.

Someone cocked their gun to my left, but I heard Nova growl, "You're dead before you pull that trigger."

Silence and stillness reigned.

Only then did I crouch, still half-raised by Otto's body beneath my right boot and waved my gun in his face. "What's this about a girl?"

"I-I need the girl, man," he stuttered. "It was part of my deal with the Raiders."

Tension rose behind me like a tsunami wave bearin' down on my back. The White Raiders were an Albertan gang with no ties to British Columbia that any'a us knew about. Why the fuck would they be enroachin' on our territory?

Occupyin' the Sea to Sky Highway leadin' tip to toe along the province and then deep into the States all the way to Mexico meant we were used to protectin' our territory. But the Raiders were small fish suddenly swimmin' in our shark-infested waters. There was zero fuckin' reason they should think they could take down our crew.

"What's a BC boy got to do with Alberta bikers?" I asked, grateful Z was lettin' me take the lead, 'cause I wasn't capable'a backin' down when this asshole was a direct threat to Blue.

"I tried to blackmail the prez," Otto admitted pitifully. "I knew he'd been looking for his daughter, and when I figured out I'd found her, I reached out."

I laughed, the sound meaner than I'd ever heard it. "Let me guess, that didn't go to fuckin' plan?"

"He told me if I wanted to live, I'd do a job for him."

"The robberies," I guessed.

He nodded, eyes rollin' wild as loose marbles in his skull, then fixin' on somethin' behind me.

Someone.

Zeus squeezed my shoulder but didn't say a word, just lendin' his intimidatin' as fuck presence to scare the man outta his mind.

"Why?" I asked, lowerin' my gun 'til it was pressed between his eyes.

He swallowed hard but didn't answer, so I pulled back and drilled a round into the concrete beside his ear. He writhed, his hands flyin' up to cup his ears.

"Why?" I roared, leanin' down into his face.

"He needed money to fund the move!"

"The move?"

"Fuck," Otto cried out when Zeus handed me his wicked curved knife, and I pressed it to his throat. "Fuck! The move to BC. They're here, forty fuckin' minutes south in Newstone."

Fury emanated from Zeus like heat waves buffetin' my back.

A rival club movin' forty minutes from Entrance was as good a declaration'a war as them showin' up with guns at our doorstep like these idiots. And based on the rage I felt from Zeus, this was more than just a mistake.

This was a deliberate insult, a personal vendetta.

They were gunnin' for us.

And, it seemed, they wanted Blue.

"Why do you want the girl?" I demanded.

He blinked at me like I was the dumbass pinned to the ground by a boot heel and at knife point. "She's the president's kid. Rooster Cavendish's daughter, Faith."

I almost reeled back, but Z was there, clampin' his hand over my shoulder to steady me.

"And she's married," he continued, spittin' the words. "To their VP, Hazard."

Rooster's daughter.

Married.

The fuck?

"Where're they stayin'?" Zeus demanded, takin' over 'cause suddenly I was mute and struck dumb. "I'd'a heard if they were stayin' close by."

"They're still moving. Rooster's in town with some'a the others stayin' above Morton BBQ."

"Fuck," Curtains said from somewhere over my shoulder.

He loved their smoked beef ribs.

"Rooster should be dead," Axe-Man declared, movin' forward with a glower to step slowly down on one'a Otto's prone hands.

He let out a squeal of pain. "*Fuck*. Well, he isn't! Man kept a low profile in Alberta, people just called him Whitey. But h-he's alive and he wants his fuckin' kid back."

"You're sober enough to drive. You're on your bike," Zeus called out. "Bat, Dane, you round up these motherfuckers and remind 'em what it's like to operate in Fallen territory without our go-ahead. When you're done with 'em, hand the lot over to Lion, and let 'im get the cops involved." He looked down at me, then at Otto. "Rooster go to war to get his kid back?"

He asked 'cause that was what Zeus would do.

He'd battle the whole goddamn world if someone took one'a his kids from 'im.

Hell, he'd battle the whole goddamn world if someone took one'a his brothers in the club from him, too.

"Fuck yeah," Otto agreed with a wince. "He's been searching for her since she ran away years ago."

Z cut his gaze to me, but I could only grind my teeth.

I was too stuck on the fact the girl I was already fallin' for was fuckin' married.

Cyclops appeared beside us, movin' to take control'a Otto, so I got up and let Z steer me toward the clubhouse. Axe-Man followed us, mouth twisted with hatred. Rooster'd been the one to betray him years ago when he was prez'a The Fallen's Calgary chapter. Been the one to turn him over to the triad when he'd fucked up and caused beef with them. Been the one to get Axe-Man sent down to prison for three years, leavin' his daughter, Cleo, without a parent.

He was basically the definition of my brother's arch-nemesis and it couldn't feel anythin' but wrong to know he'd survived the ambush all those years ago.

Probably felt somethin' like the feelin' turnin' rancid in my gut as I thought about turnin' Blue over to someone as evil as Rooster.

"She's a good kid," Axe-Man told me, watchin' me warily. "Didn't recognize her across the room with the blue hair and the tatts and the curves. She was fuckin' emaciated back then, skinny and bruised and livin' in hell. She ran the night shit went down at Turner Farm and I asked Cedar to help her out. Always wondered what happened to her."

"She's been workin' at Evergreen Gas Station for a minute," I divulged. "She was fucked over by this fuckin' moron."

"And before that she was basically given to Rooster's VP as a fucked-up gift for his loyalty," Axe-Man told me, clampin' a hand on my shoulder briefly when I unleashed a growl of rage at the thought. "You gotta get this. Rooster won't stop 'til he gets her back. He's not the type'a man who suffers loss well and he always felt he owned her. Blood and bone. That she was his to do whatever he fuckin' wanted with."

"Well, she's not his anymore," I grunted, and almost finished with *'cause she's damn well mine.*

"You've got five minutes to talk to her, then we're ridin' out," Zeus muttered, movin' his grip from my shoulder to my neck. The weight'a his huge hand should'a felt like a threat. Instead, it settled somethin' in me like a stroke to the side'a a startled horse. "You want her, she wants you, we'll fight to keep her, yeah?"

Just that simple.

Just that easy.

This was the reason every single man in the club would fight and die for Zeus Garro. 'Cause he'd do and had done the same for every one'a us without blinkin' a motherfuckin' eye. We were his, and he was ours.

"Yeah," I grunted 'cause otherwise I might'a done somethin' a helluva lot less manly. "Five minutes."

A smile flickered in his beard 'fore he turned around, already barkin' out orders to our crew. We were ridin' out to deal with the Raiders before they could get a foothold in our territory.

But 'fore I could do that, I had to decide if Blue was my territory to defend too.

Everythin' was muffled in my ears as I walked up the stairs into the clubhouse. Only Ransom, Pigeon, and Carson, our prospects, stood in the main area, standin' guard if things went to shit. I clapped Ransom on the shoulder as I walked by. He'd taken a bullet for the club a couple'a months back when I'd taken a knife to the gut protectin' Mei and the Old Ladies. It was only a matter of findin' the time to fully patch him in 'fore he'd be a true member of The Fallen.

The Old Ladies and other women were in a room down the hall leadin' to the bunkrooms. Zeus had a fuckin' steel framed door put in to protect our vulnerable in case'a emergency, so I had to punch in a code 'fore I opened it.

Soon as I did, Mei was there, a martial arts-ready stance, a knife held in one hand, and a snarl on her pretty as fuck face. It'd taken a while to get used to the fact that such a small, delicate-lookin' woman could land me on my ass, but I'd learned the hard way.

"Easy," I told her, holdin' up my hands. "It's all good."

She studied me. "You've got blood splatter on your face."

"It's old," I assured her.

She lowered the weapon, and Loulou, Bea, Harleigh Rose and Lila immediately surged past me to go to their men. The rest were slower to move, but I spotted Blue right away lookin' uncomfortable in the back corner. I tilted my chin at her, and she pushed off the wall to make her way to my side. I tagged her hand without a word, pullin' her into the hall and down to the room I kept at the clubhouse.

The second I pushed her inside, I closed the door and turned to yell at her. Only, she was lookin' around the room like it was a foreign land, and she couldn't wait to study the culture. Her fingers trailed lightly over the signed baseball in its stand on a shelf beside the door.

"Yankees? I wouldn't have guessed," she murmured.

"Are you married?"

The words fell between us like a defunct bomb, the threat alive but unpredictable. She froze, her fingertips still hoverin' over the ball.

"Blue," I growled, lungin' forward to pull her hard against me. "You married?"

"Yes," she breathed, fingers spasmin' against my chest like she didn't know whether to cling to me or push me away.

I held her tighter. "You always cheat on your husband?"

My anger seemed to spark somethin' in her. "I haven't seen that asshole for years. I wasn't even sure he was still breathing."

"Great, so let's add desertion to infidelity."

"Fuck you, Aaron." She struggled against me, but I didn't relinquish an inch. "I was a goddamn kid, okay? My dad married me to his vice president when I was sixteen years old because he was worried about Hazard making a move for his presidency. I was married for thirteen months before I got away successfully. I've been *hiding* from both of them ever since. If you want to call that desertion, so fucking be it."

"Jesus Christ." I pressed my forehead against hers, fingers clamped over her hips to keep her from headbuttin' me. "Blue baby, I'm so damn sorry."

"Yeah, well," she grumbled, glarin' at me with those huge, gumball blue eyes. "So am I. Otto threatened to take me to them when he robbed Evergreen Gas. I think the money was just a cover to kidnap me for Rooster. I never doubted he'd keep looking for me. He was always territorial."

"Yeah, well, so am I," I growled. "You don't owe them shit."

"Try telling that to them. The second time I tried to get away, one of their men found me, beat me, and delivered me to Rooster's and Hazard's feet. I couldn't walk for a week after they were done with me."

A roar built in my throat. "You're not goin' back to those bastards. You don't wanna stay with me, fine. But no way in hell are you gettin' within fifty fuckin' kilometres of those fucks."

Blue stopped breathin' then, lookin' up into my snarlin' face like she'd never seen me 'fore. Her hands flexed against my pecs, then slowly curled into the fabric'a my stolen hoodie. "You mean that?"

"Fuck, yeah."

The very thought of those motherfuckers even lookin' at Blue again made rage blacken the edges'a my vision.

She swayed into me, soft breasts flattenin' against my chest. "You're a good kinda man, Aaron."

"The best kinda trouble," I promised. "Stay and let me show you. I swear to God or whatever the fuck power you believe in that I'll keep you safe."

She bit that plush lower lip, eyes searchin' my face, but she didn't answer.

I shook her a little. "Blue, I gotta ride out with the club to deal with some shit right now. Tell me 'fore I leave you'll be here when I get back. You'll give this thing between us a chance."

"What thing?"

I cocked a brow. "That thing that's tellin' *both*'a us we're meant to be together."

"Romantic," she snarked, but I shook her again.

"Nah, no jokes this time, Blue." I bent my knees so I was closer to eye level with her, needin' her to see my sincerity. "Already lost one woman I cared about in this life, I won't lose another if she doesn't want to go. You get me?"

"Yeah, Aaron, I get you," she whispered breathlessly. "Kiss me, okay? Kiss me before you go. I wanna feel like I'm yours."

The words seared through me, scarrin' me, brandin' me. I knew as I bent my head to claim her succulent mouth that I'd never be the same after this night. Blue'd transferred some'a herself to me, and I'd guard it and whatever else she'd give me preciously 'til the day death took us.

"Be mine," I murmured against her lips before lickin' into her mouth. "Stay."

"I'm yours," she agreed before rockin' to her toes to deepen our kiss.

I still felt the impact'a it minutes later when I was stalkin' through the clubhouse and out into the front lot to borrow Wiseguy's Harley 'cause those fuckers had slashed the tires on mine back at Evergreen Gas. Pigeon was already on the way with the tow truck to pick it up.

Maybe 'cause I was so hooked on the phantom taste'a her kiss, I didn't realize she hadn't promised to stay 'til I was starin' into the flamin' remnants of Morton BBQ with the rest'a the men.

And even though I raced home ahead'a the group without askin', by the time I stormed back into the clubhouse, Blue was nowhere to be seen.

Aren't we all?

SINNERS

CHAPTER SEVEN

Blue

I WONDERED if it was the right thing even as I snuck out of the clubhouse and into the night. Either option was upsetting, but at least if I went back to what I knew, where my blood said I belonged, but my heart hated, I knew what to expect. The awful grim reality of life in an MC with a prez who hated my guts as much as he loved me.

My dad.

I didn't go to him right away, but I knew I didn't need to. He'd found me through Otto, and he'd find me again. I had two weeks left of class at cosmetology school. I refused to let him run me out of my education again, so I stayed around the area, sleeping in my old Mazda I recovered from my apartment. I didn't contact Grouch even though I knew I was leaving him in the lurch at the gas station and, even more, that he'd be worried sick about me.

I should have known that was how Rooster would come for me.

When Grouch called me two weeks into my self-imposed exile,

Rooster spoke through the phone and threatened to maim my friend if I didn't meet him in Carrick, a small town forty-five minutes away from Entrance.

When I arrived at the truck stop, he was waiting alone.

It had been eight years since I last saw him. Nearly a decade even though it felt both longer and shorter than that in my head. I'd lived an entire other life since Axe and Cedar helped me run away, but the memories of my youth were branded so deeply into my brain I knew no length of time would fade them.

Rooster wore the time poorly, though.

While I'd come into myself, he seemed to have faded out. His once firm features were softened by extra weight and folded wrinkles that draped over the edge of his eyes and jaw. Years of exposure to sun and wind had turned his skin to creased leather and yellowed his white streaked hair like aged lace. Still, he was a big man, thick in the neck and wide in the shoulders like a minotaur. Like something trapped with me in an endless maze to harass me for the rest of my days.

I'd been foolish to ever think that wasn't my fate.

The true psychopathy of my father revealed itself the moment he caught sight of me walking in my wedges across the dusty asphalt to his side.

He smiled.

A great breaking open of his craggy features to reveal radiant smile lines and square, white teeth. He looked thrilled and relieved to see me.

And when he stepped forward to drag me into his embrace, his arms were gentle as they enclosed me against his chest.

He smelled the same and something about that nostalgia poured vinegar into my wounds and made tears spring to my eyes. How strange to find comfort in the arms of your abuser. How contrary to want to hug him back because my instincts as a daughter always interfered and cried out for love from the same man who loved to hurt me.

I didn't hug him back.

I even tried to stop breathing so that rich cigarette, leather, and Old Spice scent of him wouldn't make this any more confusing than it had to be.

"Faith," he breathed into my hair as if all his prayers had been answered, when I knew he'd never prayed in his life. "Thank fuck, I found you."

"I wasn't stolen," I said, forgetting myself because it had been so long. "I ran. I wasn't for you to find and you know that, otherwise you wouldn't have taken Grouch and forced my hand."

The shift in his frame was so infinitesimal it was barely noticeable. But I'd spent years learning to read his body language so I recognized the blow before it came. I tried to duck the ham-sized hand that swung toward my left ear, but he used his other hand to grip my shoulder too hard to move. It was a move he'd used before, clapping the meaty palm over my ear so pain and dizziness erupted in my head.

I stumbled away when he released me, but my vision was swimming and I couldn't find a straight line to walk.

Vaguely, I heard the distorted sound of his chuckle.

"Never too bright, were you, Faith?" he taunted me as he watched me reel from his hit. "Dumb bitch just like your mother was."

I had been too young when she left to remember her clearly, but Rooster liked to tell me about her whenever I acted in ways he disapproved of. *You're so much like your mother.*

As if the only way to express my worthlessness was to equate it to the woman who'd given birth to me and promptly became a drug addict and then eventually run away.

Probably to get away from Rooster.

I knew he wanted me to blame her, but how could I?

I'd run away myself and I'd do it again as soon as I could be certain

Grouch and Aaron were safe.

"What do you want from me?" I asked Rooster, straightening even though my entire head felt like a throbbing wound. "Why were you looking for me?"

"You're my daughter," he said the way someone would say 'because I said so' as if it was a good argument when it wasn't any at all.

"I'm a grown woman now." I moved my hand away from my aching ear to fist it on one hip. "I don't need your help or protection, anymore."

He guffawed, all smiles again, the edges rusty with old cruelty like blood stains. "You're never too old to listen to your father. Family is the most important thing, Faith. Didn't I teach you that?"

Unbidden, I thought of the family I'd witnessed at The Fallen MC clubhouse. The way the group had embraced me as soon as Aaron vouched for me. The way they interacted, like they'd known each other forever and through thick and thin. Like nothing and no one would ever come between them.

A sharp ache slid between my ribs like a blade, so visceral I had to look down to be sure Rooster hadn't stabbed me.

"You did, which is why I'm here. Let Grouch go and promise me you won't threaten or hurt him again," I demanded, trying to stare him down when there were still stars bursting through my vision from his hit. "I won't come back with you unless you swear it, Rooster. And I know how people in your club swear on things."

My father peered at me through those eyes that haunted my nightmares like the red orbs of some monster under my bed. "I don't have to promise you shit, girl. You'll do as I say because if you don't, I'll kill him."

Fear and anger twisted my insides into a knot. I wanted to be brave so badly but my knees shook and I had to lock them to stay standing. It was one thing to pump myself up when I knew I was safely away from my abuser and another thing entirely to be within striking distance of him. But I would be brave for those I loved.

And Grouch had only ever stood up for me in that quiet, stalwart way he had that made me feel protected but also gave me room to grow by myself for the first time in my life.

"If you let him go, I won't run again," I told him solemnly, reaching for the blade attached to his belt. He watched me with wary eyes as I unclipped the leather and slid the blade into my palm. Even with a weapon in my grip, Rooster knew I was no threat to him. "I'll swear it."

The blade quivered slightly as I hovered it above my palm, waiting for his acknowledgement.

"You'll live with Hazard as his wife as you're meant to," he demanded. "And you'll contribute to the damn club this time. Zeus Garro's fuckers burned down the one fuckin' foothold we'd managed to make in this godforsaken province and handed over our thieves to the fuckin' pigs so we're short on cash temporarily. I want you workin'."

Hope almost choked me, a great, shining bubble of it perched delicately on my tongue.

"I can do that," I said slowly, so that I wouldn't give away my excitement.

"No fuckin' hassles, Faith, or I'll lock you in your room for a month." His gaze split me open like one long slice from a scalpel.

I'd been on the edge of emaciation in my youth under Rooster's care. Mostly because he forgot to feed Red and me more often than not, our house an empty cage compared to the rowdy, excess-filled clubhouse where our father spent most of his time. We mostly subsisted on canned pasta and pop tarts. When Red turn thirteen, he was deemed old enough to 'hang around' the club, but I was only granted that permission as Hazard's wife and I quickly found out the clubhouse had food aplenty, but never enough to satisfy the hunger of the kind of men in Rooster's company.

I'd been too skinny, too malnourished and pale, an impression of a girl instead of a real life woman to draw too much salacious attention from the men. And Hazard had intimidated them enough to curb the rest.

But Hazard wasn't in British Columbia.

And whatever Rooster said, he wanted me back at home as a tool of service, not because he missed me by his side.

It was up to me to fend for myself.

For myself and Grouch.

And Aaron, even if he never knew how much I longed to help him.

Rooster took my silence for obedience and slid the knife from my hand to cut into his own palm. When we pressed our wounds together, the truth I'd been trying to flee from for eight years finally hit me like a slap to the other side of my face.

I'd never be able to outrun the blood that flowed through my veins and connected me to this monster. And it was silly of me to have tried.

I was proven right the moment Rooster got me to the apartment he was renting thirty minutes outside of Entrance. He didn't take me to the clubhouse right away, because he didn't want anyone else to see how he would punish me for staying away for eight years.

It was astounding really, how easy it was to fall through the looking glass into Rooster's version of the world again. Where what he said went and what he said about me was toxic sludge he forced down my mouth every other moment to remind me just how worthless I was without him to guide me.

All those years of independence dissolved in seconds.

But I stared at the photo of Grouch and me I kept in my wallet and told myself it was worth it.

And when I closed my eyes at night, desperate for sleep to take me away, it took me straight into Aaron's arms.

Two weeks later, when I was well enough to walk again, Rooster took me to the White Raiders MC hideout at an abandoned farmhouse they'd turned into their new headquarters. Hazard was still in Calgary, but it was a small mercy because he planned to move to BC with a fresh batch of recruits after training the new president there.

It was hell.

Pure and simple.

A life filled with humiliation and criminal neglect, but I knew what to expect. Red and Cedar, the only two men in the club I had a hope of finding refuge in, were back in Alberta with Hazard and wouldn't ride out for weeks.

I comforted myself by remembering that this way, I could look out for Aaron. Because I knew there was only one reason Rooster Cavendish had come to British Columbia, and it was to take over the drug and illegal arms dealing trade The Fallen MC had monopolized for so long. There would be gang warfare in the sleepy streets of Entrance before too long, and I was the only one on this side of the line looking out for Aaron. So I'd be miserable, but he'd be safe. And at the time, it seemed like a good enough trade-off.

It was easy to talk myself out of longing for him after a while. There was no way a perfect night existed, that somehow, despite the violence and the running for our lives, we'd had exactly that. No way a man like Aaron, leather wrapped around a core of golden goodness, would ever have lived up to the pedestal I'd placed him on by the early hours of that night.

And then, weeks after that night, when I was just getting into the rhythm of club life and degradation, Grouch dropped off a package for me at the clubhouse. Rooster wouldn't let him see me, but just the sight of him through the curtains made my aching heart unclench.

III

The prospect, Jerky, tossed the parcel to me recklessly so that it crashed into the wall above my head and then dropped into my lap.

I winced as I looked at the torn brown paper, but the moment my eye caught on the blocky script, something in my chest turned over.

Faith Cavendish, it read above the address for the clubhouse and then in small letters tucked under the larger script, *Blue*.

My heart beat so loudly in my chest that I felt sure the men in the room would notice and call me out on it, but I managed to slowly get to my feet and casually walk down the hall to my room without detection. As soon as I closed the door, I dragged my desk chair over to the knob and fitted it beneath as a makeshift lock. The bed squeaked in protest as I jumped on the mattress. The paper gave way easily under my sparkly blue nails, and then, when I couldn't open the box quickly enough, the cardboard ripped at the seams as I tore it open.

Within the mess of discarded wrapping lay a small blue box with a smiley face drawn in felt tip pen on the top.

I stopped breathing as I gently worked the lid off, and then my heart stopped beating when I saw the gift Aaron had taken pains to send me.

My mother's sapphire ring.

The large round gem winked at me from the three diamond bands it was nestled between. It was even more beautiful than I'd remembered, so precious to me that tears started streaming untamed down my face, soaking the collar of my shirt. I lifted the ring with shaking fingers and fit it onto my right ring finger even though I'd never be able to wear it publicly without Dad beating the shit out of me.

Folded in the bottom of the box was a note.

Blue,

Got one more thing outta Otto 'fore Lion turned his crew into the cops. He sold the ring to some pawn shop in Nanaimo. Had a friend'a mine look for it. He's good at that kinda shit, and it still took him an age. Then it took a minute to find you. Couldn't exactly look up 'blue-eyed, blue-haired beauty who left me broken-hearted' in my Google search. Hurt like a son'a a bitch to go back to the clubhouse and find you gone, but I shoulda known you wouldn't stay. You think you're trouble for a guy like me, and there I was spendin' the whole night we spent together thinkin' you'd leave 'cause I was too much'a that for you. I gotta say it, or I'll hate myself for never takin' the chance but, Blue baby, you're exactly the kinda trouble a man looks for his whole damn life. The kinda trouble I'd fight an entire fucked-in-the-head club for the chance to call my own. So you ever need me, you ever want me, you know where to find me.

Never been a patient man, but I'll be waitin',

ABC.

CHAPTER EIGHT

Boner

THE WHOLE CLUB helped with the search. Curtains worked his technological wizardry, Zeus put out feelers with dealers and smaller allied clubs in the province, the prospects did rounds of our territory, and I went out every day for two weeks searchin' the cold trail of our one night together for any sign'a Blue.

We didn't find her.

But Curtains wasn't a well-known hacker for nothin'.

We found out Blue was Faith Felicity Cavendish, born to 'Rooster' Thomas Cavendish and Davina Wood in Calgary. Married to 'Hazard' Rick Elsher.

She was twenty-five. Same as Mei and Cleo.

Only three years younger than Curtains and me.

And married.

Curtains had tried to talk me down from my feelings as if I was on the ledge of a buildin' about to plummet to my death.

"She's *married*, man," he'd said like I didn't know. Like those words weren't branded on the inside'a my skull. "And you told her to wait for you, but she didn't. I know you think you had somethin', but maybe...I mean maybe she just wanted independence, or hell, wanted to go back home?"

Home.

I'd known the woman for less than twenty-four hours and we'd barely talked about our pasts, our traumas, but I knew in my bones that Blue was a girl who'd never known a home.

It was in the way she seemed shocked by my kindness and praise. In the way she seemed stunned by the club, not 'cause of our outlawed nature but 'cause we got along, shot the shit and supported each other like a family.

Even though I was the one who didn't have any family left, save the sister I'd lost years ago, it was Blue who was alone in this world.

And I couldn't stand the thought'a that.

It haunted me almost more than her absence. This idea that wherever she was, she was alone, and she'd probably stay that way outta fear for a long fuckin' time.

A girl like Blue deserved the world, and I wanted to be the one to give it to her so bad it ached in my fuckin' teeth.

So no, I didn't think she went back to that motherfucker Rooster and that limp dick Hazard 'cause she missed her family. I had to hope she'd left me to flee from them and find some kinda freedom for herself again. I liked the idea of her livin' free and bold, blue hair shinin', smile beamin' as she went through her day without worryin' about the men who'd tried to cage her for so long.

I wished she'd given me the chance to prove I could take care'a her myself, especially 'cause I refused to believe the connection between us was one-sided, but I got rationally that a lifetime'a fear had a lot more weight than one night'a heaven.

If she had found some peace somewhere far away, I could live with that. I just needed to *know*, or my mind would take me to dark places I knew all about 'cause my sister had disappeared once 'fore too and ended up in exactly those kinds'a places.

"She's not Swan," Curtains had reminded me softly as we sat side by side on the couch playin' *Call of Duty* one night. "You don't know she needs savin'."

The sound'a my sister's nickname burned through my brain and tangled with the synapses worryin' about Blue.

I knew they weren't the same.

Elsa was lost to me forever. I got that. We'd saved her from the triad years ago only to lose her in a way we knew she didn't want to be found.

But...

"I gotta know she's okay, man," I'd murmured, lettin' the ache in my soul saturate the words on my tongue. "You think I can get outta bed every day knowin' I'll never see my sister again without those emails she sends once a year checkin' in? If I didn't know she was alive, that she didn't *want* us to find her, you think I wouldn't tear the world apart searchin'?"

Curtains was quiet after that. He got it 'cause it'd been years, but he still loved Elsa more than he'd ever loved anyone probably.

It was the thing that'd brought us together. The thing that brought us to this club.

"I gotta know," I'd finished, unpausin' our game. "If she needs help, I gotta be there to give it."

So we searched for weeks, and Z even pulled Lion in on it. I offered to pay him 'cause he was one'a the most sought-after private investigators in the province now, but he'd tossed my wallet in the trash and told me not to be a fuckin' idiot.

I'd always liked that guy.

We didn't find Blue, but I did find her mother's ring. Or really, Lion found it and paid a buddy to pick it up for me on Vancouver Island and drive it up to Entrance for me. Like hell I was trustin' the postal service with somethin' like that.

With nowhere to send it, I'd decided to give it to Grouch Pederson at Evergreen Gas. He hadn't seemed surprised when I showed up with the package, and he'd made no promises she'd get it, but he promised to try.

At that point, it was all I could ask for. Even if I never saw her again, Blue deserved to have that piece'a her mother back, and I wanted to be the one to give it to her after so many other men had fucked her over.

In the end, King said somethin' that eased the sharp bite'a longin' in my chest.

He was good with words like that.

"The kinda love that redefines what it means to be alive is the kinda love that doesn't come cheap. You gotta earn it, man, and sometimes that means bein' patient, and sometimes that means fightin' for it. If you really think Blue's that woman for you, you gotta trust that you'll see her again and 'til then gotta live life knowin' she'd want you to be happy. Maybe that's why she left in the first place."

Twenty-four-year-old emotional savant.

So I had no answers, but the club had its own shitstorm to weather, and in a way, it was a welcome fuckin' distraction.

The White Raiders were tryin' to set up shop on our turf.

It wasn't the first time another MC had encroached on our territory, but this was different.

The Raiders were here solely 'cause'a bad blood.

Rooster'd got Axe-Man sent down to prison.

Hazard and Cedar, both men in their crew, had gone to war with Axe-Man and Bat. Cedar had helped us with the Seven Song triad, but it only opened up more questions. What the fuck were the Raiders, known racists, doin' with the Chinese gang? Why the fuck had Cedar helped us when he was flyin' Raiders colours and Bat had admitted things didn't end so smooth between them when their second tour ended.

We'd burned down their rathole in Newstone, but now, a month later, Kodiak was tellin' us in church that he'd caught sight'a Cedar in town and followed him out to a rural farm out near Furry Creek.

"Burn it to the ground," Zeus declared, almost dispassionately. "Don't care if they keep croppin' up, we'll burn 'em down each time. These motherfuckers will not dig roots in our soil."

"I gotta ask, why the fuck does Rooster hate you so much?" Shadow asked, and I was glad he did 'cause I'd been wonderin' the same thing.

Z shared a look with Bat in that secret language they had I'd never been able to crack. It was the same kinda code Curtains and I shared, that I'd seen between Mute and King. The secret language'a soulmates writtin' on each other's bones.

"He was one'a the brothers we kicked out after takin' down Crux," Zeus admitted, and the silence that followed was toxic with old memories.

It'd been before my time, but lookin' at the faces'a Buck, Bat, Skell, Smoke and King around the chapel table, it wasn't hard to imagine the horror'a that takedown.

Zeus had killed his own uncle, the prez'a the MC in Entrance, 'cause he'd gone so crooked that he started to target his own brothers in the club.

Includin' Bat.

"Rooster wasn't excommunicated like some'a the others 'cause we couldn't find evidence he was involved in Crux's betrayal," Bat added, lookin' down at his scarred hands, the words Hell Bent on each set'a knuckles. "He left himself when Zeus took over."

"Sore loser," Z added with a grim smile. "Wanted the seat for himself. Said he deserved it 'cause he'd been Sergeant At Arms to Crux."

"If anythin', it means he was probably involved in takin' out his own club members, too," King muttered darkly.

"I didn't know shit, and I was his fuckin' nephew," Zeus pointed out with a long look at his son. "Eugene knew even less, and he still cut himself off from this club from the shame'a it. This wound these fuckers are pickin' at? It´s old, and it's gnarly as fuck. I want Rooster dead in the fuckin' ground, and I wanna be the one to put 'im there."

Axe-Man snarled, an animal expression that made the hairs on the backs'a my hands stand on end.

Zeus inclined his head like the magnanimous biker king he was and allowed, "If Axe-Man doesn't get there first."

"I can make him suffer," Priest offered in that cold, hollow monotone that made most grown men crap their pants. "Better than any'a you."

Wrath rolled his eyes and shoved Priest with an elbow, braver than any'a the rest'a us who stared at him like he was fuckin' insane. "You're not the only one here who knows how to deliver pain."

Faster than I could track, Priest had his Karambit knife outta the holster, flipped through his fingers, and then sunk with a dull *thud* into the table.

Right in the sliver'a space between Wrath's index and middle fingers.

Our second enforcer only blinked at the still vibratin' knife and then slowly lifted his hand, deliberately slicin' into the webbin' between his fingers as he did so. He glared at Priest as he brought his bleedin' hand to his mouth and smeared the blood over his teeth so that when he smiled, he did it bloody.

"If Priest hadn't knocked up Bea, I'd be readin' some serious sexual tension between you two," I drawled to break the frisson'a tension runnin' along the table.

Nova was the first to laugh, tippin' his chin at me in camaraderie.

"I'm just sayin', I get a shot at that asshole, I'm takin' it, too," I tossed out mildly even though the thought'a anyone else puttin' Blue's abusive fuckin' father in the ground made my blood curdle.

"We gotta find 'im 'fore anyone can damn well kill 'im," Z grunted. "Boner, King, Curtains, go with Kodiak and scout the farm. Take the prospects with ya. I wanna know how many brothers they got and what kinda heat they're packin'. You can, you torch it then. We need to regroup, we do it tomorrow in church at eleven in the a.m."

There was a chorus of "yeah, boss," 'fore the twenty or so men in attendance started for the door. The prospects were on the other side standin' guard, Carson handin' back everyone's phone as they piled out.

I waited for a beat 'til everyone was gone but my Prez.

"We're still lookin', brother," Zeus said the minute we were alone, standin' up to clap a hand around my shoulder. "We won't stop, yeah?"

"Curtains thinks I'm bein' an idiot. I can tell some'a the other guys think so, too." I didn't give a fuck what the other brothers thought about it.

I cared what Z thought, though.

Never had a mother or father, and Z was the closest I'd ever come to havin' a parent.

Someone coulda said I was unlucky to never know my parents, but only if they didn't know Zeus Garro.

No one was better than him, and he proved it every fuckin' day.

And he did it again then by sayin', "Men like us don't fall in love the way they do in storybooks. We see a woman, and somethin' hits us like a bullet through the chest. We get this sense in our blood and bones, through the center'a our bein' that this person is meant for us. It might take a while to get there." His grin was a small, secret thing in his beard, the one carved there by the hand'a his wife, Loulou. "Sometimes we gotta get our heads outta our asses to realize that no obstacle between us is worthy'a keepin' us apart. But you already got that clarity. You've always been clear-sighted like that even when you came to me, just a kid and hurtin'. You've always known what you want and who you are right down to your bones. And now, they're tellin' you to find this woman and make sure she's safe. Maybe even make her yours."

Zeus's rough palm moved to my neck, coverin' the entire width and shakin' me lightly the way I'd seen him do to King sometimes. Like I was his kid.

That ache in my chest I'd lived with since I lost Elsa eased at that touch and that look in his eye that said I was his brother, his son, his family.

"You picked a fiery one, though," he joked. "Tellin' you from experience, they don't mellow over time."

I laughed 'cause Loulou was a spitfire through and through.

It was what we all loved about her.

"Yeah, I'm more than fuckin' fine with that."

Z shoved me away then reeled me in to rub a hand into my perfectly done hair 'cause he knew I fuckin' hated it. I swallowed my smile and glared at him.

He chuckled, takin' his seat at the head'a the carved wooden table again and pullin' out his phone in clear dismissal. The lit screen showed an image'a Loulou and his daughter, Harleigh Rose, holdin' his twin kids, Angel and Monster.

And for the first time in my life, I was greedy enough to want somethin' like that for myself.

Not just the club but a family I could call my own with a woman who'd carve her name into my bones and make me hers forever.

Since I'd been stabbed in the spring, Zeus had me in charge'a the prospects. It was both a demotion and a promotion. The first was only in my head 'cause I wanted to be on the front lines of the action with my Prez, Bat, Priest, Wrath, Axe-Man, King and Nova. But I also got that takin' care of the prospects, teachin' them our ways like an anthropologist introducin' a new culture, was almost as sacrosanct as bikers got. This way'a life wasn't for the faint'a heart. It took an inexplicable kinda courage to be a man who could look society in the eye and tell it to fuck right off. A certain kinda guy to stitch into the patchwork quilt'a The Fallen and make it more whole than it was before.

And there I was, the man to induct them and judge them and hopefully, find them worthy of wearin' that flamin' skull and wing patch'a The Fallen MC.

So I decided to be honoured. There was no point in bitchin' about it the way Skell had done when he was in charge'a Curtains and me as prospects. I refused to take my bitterness about the way life could punch a guy in the throat out on the young men who'd already suffered at life's hands and found us for our unusual brand'a solace. We were a band'a outcasts and rebels, and there was no such thing as too much bad or weird in our crew.

Some clubs were ripe with racist, homophobic, misogynistic pigs, but not The Fallen.

So of course, I had to give Carson shit just like I woulda done with any'a my other brothers.

"Shit, you two don't quit it soon, it'll be turnin' me on, and trust me, ridin' with a boner is *not* comfortable."

Carson's Old Man, Benny, unlocked lips long enough to blush and duck his head in his man's shoulder. Carson just leveled me with a cool glare.

He was gettin' better at those.

And the fact he didn't immediately drop Benny's ass to the ground was good.

Progress.

Kid was raised by a piece'a shit father who taught him to be ashamed of where he liked to dip his wick. But he was learnin' there was no shame to be had here.

Sure, I'd surprised them makin' out against the side wall'a the clubhouse, but this was *our* space, so it was their space. They wanted to suck face anywhere on Fallen MC property, they were sure as shit welcome.

God knew Nova and Lila did it enough for the lot of us.

"Really, I'm doin' ya a public service by stoppin' this 'fore you pop wood, kid," I continued as I felt Curtains join my side.

"He's right," Curtains said, and I could hear his grin even though I didn't turn to face him. "Heckler actually crashed his bike once after starin' too long at this pretty girl in these little shorts."

"Fuck off, Curtains," Heckler hollered from inside the clubhouse.

We sniggered.

Carson sighed as if he was sixty years old and severely imposed upon and not a twenty-three-year-old prospect. "You two are the worst."

Curtains raised his hand for a fist bump that I was only too happy to oblige. We exploded the gesture, then turned with matchin' grins to see Benny hidin' a giggle behind his hand.

"I think they're pretty hilarious," he admitted to Carson. "I'll let you go. I just wanted to swing by to say hi on my way home from the bookstore."

Benny worked at Cressida's store, Paradise Found.

"Nice hello," I muttered.

"Tell me about it," Curtains quipped.

Carson raised his hand to flip us the bird.

Benny laughed, his big brown eyes sparklin' like somethin' from a comic book.

Unbidden, the image of Blue's anime blue eyes flashed across my vision.

Fuck.

How was it possible to miss someone you'd only known for a single night?

It was more than missin', though. Everythin' felt...off. Like gravity had shifted and I was constantly off-balance, overcorrectin' to fight the strain.

I thought about her when I went home at night and when I lay in bed alone. Again in the mornin' when I woke up with my arms empty and my nose bereft'a the scent of that lush blue hair.

When I saw my brothers hold their women, or in Carson's case, their man, and knew that I'd missed out on my chance for somethin' like that.

"You ready?" Curtains asked, bangin' his shoulder into mine.

I pulled my mind away from the sinkhole Blue'd left at the center'a my mind and clapped my brother on the back. "Let's do it. It's gonna be a drive."

"Nice night for it," Carson said, joinin' us as we moved toward the line'a bikes shinin' chrome bright under the hot sun.

Benny stood on the stairs to the clubhouse, watchin' us like someone sendin' their sailor off to sea.

It made somethin' in my gut twist and ache.

Longin', I thought.

King came out around the back'a the clubhouse with a backpack on and another in his hand that he tossed to me as soon as he got close. "In case we need to light it up tonight."

I unzipped the bag to see Firestarter sticks, flash torches, and good old-fashioned rags with bottles'a liquor.

Kodiak snorted from behind me, scarin' me shitless so I nearly dropped the bag.

"Jesus, Ko, make a noise once in a while, would ya?" I groused. "Fuckin' silent as the dead."

His answerin' smile was small and dark. He didn't say a word as he pulled his bike outta line and swung a leg over it, not even glancin' over his shoulder as he peeled outta the lot.

"Fucker," I grumbled as we all scrambled to get after him.

Everythin' fell away as soon as the purr of my Harley vibrated beneath me and the road opened up outside'a Entrance on the windin' ribbon'a the Sea to Sky Highway.

This was peace.

Sun blurrin' into one golden smear behind the dusky silhouette'a the mountains, gemstone colours streakin' across the sky like a child's finger paintin'. The purity'a this kinda beauty stole my breath, but I didn't need it as I streaked across the road just like those colours, only I was flyin' the green and black'a my club. Curtains rode beside me in formation, and it felt like home, like comfort, like brotherhood to have him at my side and King at my back with Kodiak leadin' us.

Whenever I felt small and alone, that kid who just lost his sister and the only family he'd ever known, I came to this place in my mind or rode out with any'a the brothers who'd keep me company.

Because *this*––this place, this club, this version'a myself––would always be my haven.

And I'd die fightin' to protect it, smilin' 'til the last moment.

So when we finally took the exit off'a Furry Creek headin' into the wild, the only thing I felt was excitement that we might crush an enemy 'fore they could hurt us. That I might stomp out the light'a someone who had taken the peace from a woman I cared about.

We parked the bikes one click out from the farm and continued on foot, stickin' to the high grass at the side'a the road even though dusk was settlin' a dark cloak over the landscape. By the time the black rectangle punctuated with yellow boxes'a light appeared before us, stars were startin' to dot the night's sky.

Still, two men were outside the house near a barn, the lit end of a cigarette like a firefly, and the low murmur'a their voices indistinguishable from where we hid, crouched in the dark. Kodiak turned to face us, usin' hand gestures to order us to spread out.

I crept around the left side'a the property, behind the two smokers, behind the barn and back up the side'a the house. Gravel crunched almost imperceptibly under the careful tread'a my boots, mostly drowned out by the buzz and click of crickets in the grass. Through the lit window, I could see a dingy kitchen with an older, heavyset woman sittin' at a peelin' Formica table scrubbin' potatoes with muddied hands.

And across from her, a flash'a blue caught my eye.

My heart crashed into my rib cage and lost power.

A second later, Blue herself appeared in the square frame.

Fuck, the sight'a her moved through me like a blade.

My imagination hadn't done justice to her beauty, the thick thighs and heart-shaped face, the glint'a metal in her upper lip and nose matchin' the way the light shone in those azure-blue eyes. She was wearin' somethin' that covered her from wrists to ankles to throat and she was still the sexiest woman I'd ever seen.

But my mind only had a moment to catalogue the joy'a seein' her 'fore I noted the blue'a the bruise tattooed on the skin'a her cheek as she turned her head to speak to the other woman.

She was here in the den'a the enemy, and she was *hurt*.

Rage possessed me, a demon wearin' my face.

My gun was in my hand in a heartbeat.

My feet takin' me to the back door in the next.

She must'a heard me comin' 'cause she was there lookin' at me through the closed screen door a beat after that.

And everythin' in me arrested as if in doin' so I could extend that single moment into many.

"Aaron," she mouthed without sound, those gorgeous eyes wide with shock.

Her gaze dropped to the gun, then back to my face, notin' the fury vibratin' every molecule in me.

"No," she mouthed then in an actual whisper, "No. There are nine men in this house with guns. Another few near the barn. Rooster is due back any minute with more."

I could barely digest the words. Rage was rushin' in my ears, drownin' her out and whisperin' its own devilish song: *kill them all, kill them all.*

Kill. Them. All.

What was a dozen men against the weight'a my wrath?

"Please," she said, steppin' closer to press her hand to the thin wire screen separatin' us. "I can't see you hurt."

"You're fuckin' hurt," I hissed quietly between my teeth.

"Not as much as I would be if you got yourself killed," she promised, before checkin' over her shoulder as someone hollered within the house. "You've gotta go."

"Promise to meet me," I pushed, placin' my hand over hers, the warmth'a her skin seepin' through the screen door. "And I'll go."

"It's too dangerous."

"I like livin' on the edge," I reminded her as thuds sounded inside and Blue tried to pull away. My fingers punched through the flimsy screen, tearin' holes so I could curl my fingers around hers.

She bit into that plush bottom lip, and I noticed a healin' split in one corner. My fingers curled tighter over hers.

When she whispered a series'a numbers before slippin' her hand from mine and turnin' back into the kitchen, I didn't get it at first.

It was only after I dissolved into the shadows to find my brothers to call off the fire that I realized what they were.

Her phone number.

Aren't we all?
SINNERS

CHAPTER NINE

Blue

AARON

Tell me you're okay.

Won't stop textin' 'til you respond.

Can't sleep not knowin' if you're hurtin' or safe.

Can't breathe either.

WHAT HAD POSSESSED me to give Aaron my number? I'd known he would abuse the connection, and honestly, I'd wanted him to. The phone was a burner, one I hid in the lining of my mattress and only checked before bed and after waking up every day. But the idea of having a connection with him again, a tangible lifeline to tug at when I felt like I was drowning, was too good to pass up.

distance, I fell victim to his charm within days.

Blue: I'm alive. I'm not exactly safe because the Raiders are assholes, and I'm hurting, but it's mostly inside my chest.

Aaron: You miss me.

I laughed under my breath as I sat cross-legged in my little twin bed at the farmhouse.

Blue: I missed my ring. Thank you for finding it.

Aaron: Ask me anythin' and you shall receive.

Aaron: Speakin' of askin' for somethin', meet me.

God, I wanted to see him again.

The brief sight of him outside the back door had been too terrifying to process properly. I could still feel the rough texture of his calloused hand against mine through the screen door, the jagged edges of wire digging into my skin when he broke through the partition to reach for me.

It was such a little gesture, but it made my throat ache because I thought Aaron might not let anything get between us if I'd let him come for me. That he might really take on all the horrors of my reality to get to me again.

He'd seemed more than willing to go on a suicide mission through the house after seeing the bruises on my face.

But it was so much more complicated than wanting each other.

Whatever connection we'd forged, he didn't know me, not really.

More than that, he didn't know how cruel and ruthless Rooster, Hazard and this lot could be.

Just last night, they'd returned home from a ride with a man in the back of a grey van. I could hear them torturing him in the barn through my open bedroom window late into the night.

When I woke up at dawn and looked outside, Jerky was sagging under the weight of a canvas-wrapped body slung over his shoulder.

I wanted to help Aaron and his club, but asking Aaron to get involved with me in secret, giving him leeway to insert himself in my life in a dangerous way, was not the way to do it.

So...

Blue: No. This is all we can have, and even then...we should keep our distance. I'm not joking around. Talking to me is dangerous.

Aaron: Your husband wouldn't like it? Good. I don't give a fuck.

Blue: Hazard is still in Calgary for now. But Rooster would kill you for touching me, and the rest of them would too, just to follow his orders.

Aaron: Some things are worth dyin' for, Blue.

Blue: Yeah, trust me, I'm not one of them.

I put the phone back in my hiding place after triple-checking it was on silent.

Not a moment too soon either because the door crashed open without ceremony, and Rooster was there, chewing tobacco and staring at me as if he couldn't understand why I was still in my pajamas at seven in the morning.

"You're lookin' good enough to start workin'," he declared finally.

"Okay," I agreed, too quickly because I'd been waiting for the go-ahead. Rooster didn't like me out in public after a beating because people were 'nosy cunts who ask too many damn questions.'

I'd already looked up nearby salons, and I still had a copy of my résumé saved in my inbox.

"Want you workin' at Eugene's Bar out off the Sea to Sky beyond Entrance," he grunted, moving to my little closet to check out my clothes.

He'd moved me in the moment I could get out of bed without groaning. He could probably keep better track of me when I was surrounded by the eyes of the club instead of just his own.

"I'm a certified cosmetologist now. I can make good money working in a salon," I said, trying to keep my tone light so it didn't seem like I was arguing with him.

He snorted, gaze skirting over me like I was discarded trash. It made me shiver and hug my arms over my heavy, braless breasts. "What the fuck is that? Some kinda beautician?"

"Yeah, kinda. I can do hair, make-up, and nails really well. I want to get into giving facials too――" I was cut off by fabric hitting me in the face as Rooster threw something at me.

"No. Eugene's is a well-known biker bar and outlaw hotspot in the area. We could use a girl like you keepin' her ears open there. We got a sponsor willin' to back our takeover of The Fallen, but they want it done quick."

"Who?" I asked before I curbed my curiosity.

Rooster was on me in a second, thick hand wrapped around my throat, squeezing so hard the pressure ached behind my eyes and my voice box felt crushed. His eyes, the same shade of blue as mine but bloodshot and filled with malice, were an inch from mine as he sneered into my face.

"You forget yourself already, kid?" he asked. "Do not question me."

My hands raised to his, scrambling to peel them off as I fought for air. I tried to nod, but his hold was too tight.

He stared into my eyes for a long moment until I was sure I was turning blue, and then released me so I fell back to the bed with a gasp. My throat ached so badly I honestly wondered if he'd broken something.

"You do as you're told without askin' dumb questions. Get a job at Eugene's and make yourself useful until Hazard gets here. He might decide then to keep you home and get you makin' some kids like you shoulda been doin' the last eight years."

He tossed another garment at me――a denim skirt――and then left as abruptly as he'd come in.

I lay there for a few minutes, struggling to breathe through the twin clutch of pain and panic still collared around my neck.

But eventually, I got up, pulled on the cropped shirt and little jean skirt Rooster had pulled out for me, and dragged myself to the bathroom. My reflection showed a woman I hadn't seen in years, if ever. My usually healthy complexion was sallow, tinted green and yellow from fading bruises on the left side of my face. I needed to refresh the blue dye and resolved to find somewhere to have it done in town. Until then, I could do something about the ugly, unhappy face staring back at me.

As I opened my glittery blue toolkit and assembled the tools of my trade, I tried to focus on one task at a time so the tears trembling in the lower troughs of my lids wouldn't ruin my canvas. Primer for staying power, foundation to even out my pale complexion, and concealer to hide the lingering bruises. Bronzer, blush, and highlighter made my features come back to life, if only artificially, and the addition of smoky eye shadow and a pink lipstick made my best features pop.

When I was finished, you couldn't even tell the girl looking back at me was a shell of her former self.

She looked...beautiful.

Tears trembled, and I caught one on my thumb carefully so it wouldn't ruin the illusion.

"You're beautiful," I told myself, my voice temporarily roughened by Rooster's abuse.

Ugly, stupid bitch! Rooster's voice yelled in my mind's ear.

"You're beautiful," I said again, and this time, I let myself imagine Aaron.

The way he'd looked at me, a little shocked and awed, the way he'd touched me in that stolen car, like I was more precious than the stolen jewels in the back.

Not 'cause you're damn pretty, Blue, 'cause a man like me knows pretty girls. Nah, the sight'a you knocked the air straight from my chest 'cause a pretty girl with a sweet smile was mannin' a gas station in the middle'a the night on a dangerous stretch'a highway, and I thought, this girl doesn't have anyone in her life to tell her not to risk herself like this. She's fightin' and clawin' for everythin' she's got, and what she's got is no one. And, Blue baby, that sucker punched me. A girl like you should have a whole army'a family at your back keepin' ya safe and makin' ya promises they always intend to fuckin' keep.

I closed my eyes as I recited those words back to myself, forever carved into my bones in a way I'd never forget.

When I opened them, I recognized the girl in the mirror again. She was the confidant, plucky woman I'd cultivated for eight years. The girl who wasn't ashamed to love girly things and my soft curves. The girl who used make-up and hair and clothes like both an armour and a canvas to show the world exactly who I wanted to be.

Brave, bold, beautiful.

The kind of woman who could hook a man like Aaron Clare through the heart in one miraculous night.

Before leaving the house, I didn't resist the urge to grab my hidden phone and stick it into the back of my short blue cowboy boot. Even if I didn't text him again that day, knowing he was within reach made me feel like I could get through my day.

"Why?"

I blinked at the huge, rough-hewn man looming over the counter from behind the bar, his massive arms bulging beneath the plaid shirt, his dark grey eyes narrowed on me.

For a barkeep, he wasn't very friendly.

"Um, because I need a job?" I suggested with a little shrug and what

I hoped was a pretty grin. "And I've got experience serving, so I figured, why not ask here."

"You figured," he repeated dryly, his expression entirely unimpressed. When I'd asked a pretty server to speak to the manager, I hadn't expected this man. He hadn't even introduced himself.

He was rude, but honestly, I'd fallen in love with *Eugene's* the second I stepped foot in the long, low building on the side of the Sea to Sky Highway. It was retro in a way that wasn't trying to be cool or hipster. Dark wood everywhere, neon signs and old biker paraphernalia on the walls, a small stage to the right of the huge U-shaped bar with some space for dancing before high-top tables. The right corner was made up of booths and short tables, the tops scarred by time and a few choice etchings from visitors. A jukebox was lit up against one wall, the sounds of old-school rock crackling over the speakers. It smelled like spilled beer and maraschino cherries, like leather and seasoned wood.

I could have spent the rest of my life inside those four walls and been happy.

It was cool as shit, and the people drinking there at eleven in the morning were cool too—a handful of bikers who probably hadn't gone to bed yet from the night before and a collection of pretty women crowded around two tables in the far corner.

"Listen," I said because I had the feeling this grumpy barkeep was a straight shooter. "I need the work. You don't want to give me a job, fine, but don't play dumb here. This place is the tits, and if you don't think I'd fit in, just say so, okay? I've had a long day, and it's only eleven."

The manager stared at me implacably for another moment before a tiny hairline fracture appeared around his mouth. A facsimile of a smile.

"Well," he grunted, straightening those tree trunk arms so his palms lay flat on the counter, the tattoos on the back of his hands clear to see. "Let me get you the paperwork, then."

I huffed out an incredulous laugh. "Are you serious?"

He cocked a brow. "Don't lose your gumption now. A girl pretty as you wants to work here, she's gotta have mettle."

"So you being a dick was a test?" I asked, shocked into sincerity.

He chuckled, a short, sharp bark of humour. "Nah, I'm a dick all the time. But it's good to know you can handle it 'cause the clientele here can be vicious. This isn't some Denny's, you get me? We get serious shit in here."

I rolled my eyes. "I'm not Little Red, and you're hardly the first big bad wolf I've ever met. I can handle some rude or grumpy bikers."

He pursed his full lips, pale pink framed by a dark beard, and if I hadn't met Aaron first, I might have found him wildly attractive.

"Eugene," he said finally, sticking out a huge hand for me to shake. His grip was cool and calloused against mine.

"I would've taken you for a Bullet or Hammer," I said, taking a stab that he was either former military or an ex-con, two sects of men who always had absurd, oddly fitting monikers.

His smile flattened into a sharp line, gaze glazing over as if looking into the past. "Had another name a long time ago. Doesn't suit anymore so, I'm Eugene."

"I get that," I said, my voice softening as I recognized the familiar stamp of tragedy on his features. "My name was Faith, but now..." I thought of Aaron calling me his Blue baby. "Now, I like to be called Blue."

Something sharpened in Eugene's gaze, but he nodded, and I realized when he dropped my hand that we had been holding each other's grip a little too long.

"Blue," he said the word like it had a taste and it was sweet. "I'll get you that paperwork."

He knocked his knuckles against the bar top and disappeared.

A moment later, someone slid onto the stool beside me, and when

I turned to face them, I found a gorgeous Asian woman staring at me contemplatively.

"Um, hello?" I asked when she didn't say anything for a moment.

Her grin was a quick flash of small, sharp teeth, almost vulpine. "Hey. I'm Mei."

"Blue," I indicated myself, then let my hand fall to the bar a little self-consciously.

Across the room in the corner with the group of beautiful women, someone laughed and then was abruptly hushed.

"You're stunning," Mei said, almost matter-of-factly, kind of bored by it. "Did you do your own hair and make-up?"

I fingered the curled ends of my hair at my collarbone and nodded. "I don't colour it myself, and it needs a refresh, but yeah. I actually do make-up, hair and nails for a living."

"No shit," Mei exclaimed, dark eyes sparkling. I was surprised she was so into it, given that she didn't look like she was wearing more than mascara and had that kind of fabulous sleek, straight hair that didn't require much maintenance.

"Shit," I said with a little grin and listened to her laughter.

"Well, my man's stepmum runs one of the best beauty salons nearby. Lin's Beauty Emporium, have you heard of it?"

I blinked because, yes, I had. It was one of the places I wanted to apply before Rooster forced me to work here.

"Yeah, I-I have. I was actually going to take a peek at it later today."

Mei clapped her hands, but her grin was too calculated for true surprise. "What a coincidence, I was going to head over there, too. You're new around here, right? Why don't we go together?"

Eugene's bark of laughter caught me by surprise and made me jump. He'd appeared silently in front of me, slapping the paperwork on the wood for me while he shot Mei a bemused look.

"What's with the voice?" he asked.

Mei narrowed her eyes at him, and the expression seemed to suit her features more than the saccharine smile she'd leveled my way. "Why don't you mind your own business, Eugene?"

"My bar," he retorted. "Therefore, it's inherently my fuckin' business."

Mei's glower deepened, and she muttered, "Touché."

"What's with the happy-go-lucky schtick?" he continued, crossing his arms across his barrel chest. "You and Bea decide to swap personalities for the day or somethin'?"

Mei blew a raspberry through her lips and threw her hands in the air. "Jesus, Eugene, it's called *being friendly*. You should try it sometime."

"Like you're such an expert," he quipped, but a little twitch in his mouth said he enjoyed this kind of banter.

Her sigh was beleaguered. "You know, I was trying to do my good deed of the year, and you totally ruined it."

"Good deed?" I asked because as much as I was enjoying the exchange, I was tired of being lost.

Mei winced and gave me a weak smile. "Uh, I may have recognized you from that night at the clubhouse when Boner brought you over? We didn't meet officially, but my Old Man is Axe-Man, or Axe as you used to know him, and Boner is an idiot, but I love him, so I've heard a lot about you."

"Mei..." Eugene said like a warning.

She rolled her eyes at him. "Fine! Boner *may* have mentioned that you had a cosmetology certification, and Axe-Man *may* have mentioned Lin was looking for someone at the salon." She shrugged.

"So...you were, like, waiting for me to show up?" I asked, confused because there was no way she could have known I would be there that morning.

"It was actually just a coincidence," she admitted. "Boner and I were still working out how I might run into you. He thought the grocery store, but I figured maybe the mall? And, uh, I hate shopping, so I didn't relish the idea of just hanging out in a mall all the time until you showed up. He should've asked Bea because she loves shopping and she's friendly as hell, but she's super pregnant, and Priest basically isn't letting her out of his sight. Besides, I'm the one with the connection to Lin's, so..."

She stopped talking because I was laughing.

I couldn't seem to stop.

God, Aaron Clare was fucking *wonderful*.

Mei and Eugene shared a look but let me have my slightly hysterical giggle. I wiped a tear from my eye, careful of my liner.

"He's crazy," I said finally. "I can't believe you agreed to do that."

Sincere kindness softened the edges of Mei's precisely drawn features, and when she spoke, her tone was deeper and filled with warmth. "I'd do anything for Boner, and I know he'd do anything for me. That's the way our crew works. It's a ride-or-die kinda loyalty."

My lips twisted instantly. "I know people like to say that, but c'mon, no one wants to die for anyone else. Hardly anyone is that selfless."

Mei stared at me for a long moment as emotions worked behind her eyes.

"I could tell you a lot of stories about The Fallen that prove different, but they aren't mine to tell. I'll only say this, Boner took a knife to the gut for me and the Old Ladies without hesitating. I was abducted and buried alive, but the club saved me. You know what the first thing Boner said to me when I saw him after that? 'I'm sorry I wasn't there diggin' with the others to keep you outta the ground.' And I know, if they'd let him, Boner would've been digging next to the others even as he bled out if it meant keeping me alive."

A chasm cracking open at my center made me shudder as if someone had ripped out the backbone of my life. I felt unbalanced by the hope that filled the bloody cavern. Longing tasted like acid on the back of my tongue.

Mei reached over to touch my clenched hand on the counter, her fingers light against the faint bruise marks I hadn't thought were dark enough to conceal on the inside of my wrist.

"If I've learned anything in my life, it's that heroes come in all shapes and sizes, but the best heroes are the ones who are a little tarnished themselves. It means they're literally willing to do anything to keep the people they care about safe. It means they can understand a little of the hell you've been through."

"You're saying Boner's like that," I murmured, my voice lost to the chaos of emotions wreaking havoc on my insides.

"I'm saying they are *all* like that," she corrected softly. "And it extends to the women, too. We take care of our own at all costs." She paused, wrapping her hand around my wrist so that her fingertips matched the bruise points, and I shivered at the gentleness of the touch against the cruelty of the one that left those marks.

I sucked in a shivery breath, trying to get myself under control. I wasn't usually so emotional, but being back with Rooster was a daily barrage against my mental health, and then being infrequently faced with the blinding kindness of Aaron and his family was almost too much to bear.

"You've just gotta let us," she whispered, looking from me to Eugene, who flinched imperceptibly at the implication, scowled fiercely, and then turned on his booted heel to check on a man at the other end of the bar.

"You don't know him," I told her quietly. "I had a crush on a boy when I was thirteen, and Rooster found out. The kid wasn't at school the next day because he'd been a victim of a hit-and-run. Ten broken bones. Rooster sat on the edge of my bed while I cried and told me the only important men in my life were him and his club."

Mei's expression tightened, and I winced as her grip did on my wrist.

"I can't imagine what he would do to Aaron for getting involved in my life," I admitted. "And I've lain awake thinking about it at night. I grew up in the club, Mei. I know what happens to traitors and enemies. I've heard them tortured, seen them maimed, watched them beg on their knees in front of Rooster only to have him put a bullet between their eyes. There's nothing romantic about dying at his hand. Not for love and loyalty and certainly not for *me*."

"In my experience, people have a much better idea of our own worth than we do ourselves. I struggled for a long time, thinking I didn't deserve love, and I was a much worse person when I shunned it. I'll probably never think I'm good enough for Henning Axelsen because he's the best man I've ever known. But it makes him happy to love me, and God knows it makes me happy to let him and love him right back." She shrugged. "Something to consider."

"You don't know me." The words were filled with the frustration that bubbled and churned where Rooster's lifelong abuse met Aaron and the Entrance chapter of The Fallen MC's kindness. My gut hissed and churned like the Bermuda Triangle, thoughts drowning in the riptides. "Not you and not Aaron."

No one! *my conscience screamed*. No one knows you, and no one ever will because *he* won't let them.

"No," Mei agreed, sliding from the stool to her combat boots. "But I've got trust issues a mile wide, and Eugene hates just about everyone he meets, and yeah, Boner might have told us about you, but you wouldn't have a job here, and I wouldn't be offering to take you to meet Lin if we didn't think you were worth knowing after only a few minutes of talking to you."

She turned and started walking to the door. Distantly, I noted that her almost ethereal beauty was contrasted by ripped black skinny jeans and a paint-splattered Streek Ink Tattoo tee she'd cut off at the sleeves and hem to reveal her toned arms and belly. She looked like some kind of kick-ass avenging angel.

And I wanted to go with her more than my next breath.

Toward Lin's Beauty Emporium and my dream job, toward a group of people who embodied the kind of loyalty I'd only ever dreamed about, toward Aaron and the safe, passionate security of his arms.

But I thought of Grouch after Rooster had let him go, broken nose and orbital socket, eye swollen closed, shoulder dislocated, the fingers of his left hand crushed by some kind of tool. He'd been broken, sobbing as Rooster tossed him his keys with a vague threat not to go to the cops and took off.

And he was just a civilian.

Not part of the club Rooster hated through to his marrow.

Mei realized I wasn't following her and turned, cocking her head for a moment before extending her hand to me. "Come on, Blue. You don't have to see Aaron, and you don't have to take the job if you don't want it. Just come get your nails done with me." She showed me the chipped black polish on her bitten-down nails and winced. "You know you don't want to be responsible for me staying like this."

A breathless laugh left me. "They are tragic."

"That's not the first time someone's said that about me, believe it or not," she joked, wiggling her fingers at me. "You're going to give me a complex if you don't take my fucking hand. I'm not usually the touchy-feely type, and I can't face the rejection."

I laughed again because I could see how she and Aaron would get along, her sharp sarcasm and his teasing charm. I thought I might pay all the money I'd buried in a lockbox in the backyard of the Raider's clubhouse to spend just half an hour with them.

So I sucked in a breath, reminded myself that I was bold and brave, and stood to take Mei's hand. It was warm in mine, small but strong.

And the smile she gave me, a true one that made a dimple pop in one cheek, was worth the effort.

Aren't we all? SINNERS

CHAPTER TEN

Blue

AARON

You angry?

Completely.

AARON

God, what I wouldn't give to taste that anger on your tongue.

Aaron, it only annoys me even more when you're sexy and charming while I'm trying to be mad at you.

AARON

Yeah, it's part'a my charm ;p

I should be angry, but how can I be? Lin and Mei are amazing. Eugene was grumpy but kinda sweet in his own way. I get to work doing something I love.

AARON

Mission accomplished. You can be angry with me any day if it means you're happy the rest'a the time.

Stop it!

AARON

??

Stop trying to make me fall in love with you. I told you, this isn't happening.

AARON

It's already started, Blue baby. Best you can do now is hold tight and enjoy the ride.

OF COURSE, Aaron's friends made it so that I could have my cake and eat it too.

Rooster expected me to work at Eugene's to gather intel about The Fallen and the underworld of the Sea to Sky so I would work there three nights a week, Thursday through Saturday. But from ten to six, Monday to Thursday, I'd be a cosmetologist at Lin's Beauty Emporium.

How fucking cool was that?

Lin had only recently branched into offering hair styling services, and I was her second hire there, so I had my own chair and station in the salon. When I had gaps in the schedule, I'd do nails and make-up for special events.

It might have seemed like such a little thing to anyone else, but when I walked in that first Monday morning and saw my station with an ice-coloured neon sign that read *Blue*, festooned in blue and silver balloons with a card sitting on the white countertop that read 'Blue Baby,' I burst into tears.

Lin was the only other person there that early, and after giving me a brief hug, she busied herself with opening the shop so I could have the semblance of privacy to read Aaron's card.

Blue,

Don't think Lin'll go easy on you. Already got half the club's Old Ladies booked in to see you this week 'cause they're all nosy as hell. They're harmless, for the most part.. just avoid Harleigh Rose if you can. She'll have you confessin' all your sins before her nails are dry. Wish I could be there to see you shine your pretty light on everyone you leave a little more beautiful today, but I got a vivid imagination, so I figure I'll be alright.

Happy for you, my girl.

ABC.

I BLINKED DOWN at the chicken scratch scrawl, thinking it was the prettiest thing I had ever seen.

"Hey, Lin? Do you have any magnets?" I called.

A few minutes later, the card was in the corner of the rounded mirror at my station. I took a selfie sitting in the chair, surrounded by the balloons Aaron had bought, smiling into my reflection and sent it to him.

Blue: A document of the happiest moment in my life.

It was later, at a more forgiving hour of the morning, when I was just finishing with my first client, an older woman who worked at the local library, when Aaron responded.

Aaron: We gotta work on that. You deserve a whole life'a happy.

The other girl who did hair was a few years older than me, but she was an outgoing, happy-go-lucky woman named Mal with blonde-tipped dreadlocks and flawless dark skin. She had me singing along to Taylor Swift by the time I was done with my morning clients and had to head to the nail station for my next appointment.

That was how he saw me when he came ambling through the doors, eyes closed, a bottle of gel polish held like a mini microphone in one hand as I sang the lyrics to "Gorgeous."

When I opened my lids at the sound of the chair scraping against the floor on the other side of my station, Aaron was sitting in it, elbows braced on the table, tattooed, ring-laden hands fisted under his chin.

My breath arrested in my lungs, struck by his sheer beauty.

God, I'd almost forgotten how terribly gorgeous he was in the few days since I'd last seen him.

Those dark eyes gleamed like water on a moonlit night as he grinned at me.

"Hey, happy girl," he said softly.

It took me a full second to recover my wits. When I did, I looked around the salon as if any of the White Raiders would be lying in wait.

"Aaron," I hissed. "What are you doing here?"

"I lied. My imagination wasn't good enough. Had to see you in your element," he declared. "Glad I did 'cause I've never seen happiness look so fuckin' good on anyone else."

Some of my panic dissolved in his sweetness. "It's not safe to be seen together. Rooster keeps an eye on me. Does random drive-bys."

Aaron raised his dark brows, opening his palms for me. "He drives by, all he'll see is a guy in desperate need'a a little self-care."

I gaped at him. "Are you seriously suggesting I do your nails?"

"Paws and claws," he agreed soberly, but his eyes shone with mirth so bright I had to blink away the sun spots.

A giggle escaped before I could slap my hand over my mouth. When I was under control, I said, "Well, as much as I would *love* to do that for you, I have a client. Claire Lafayette."

Aaron's grin was wide and triumphant. "Claire for Aaron Clare and

Lafayette's the surname of Zeus's and Priest's women, Loulou and Bea."

"So you're my noon appointment," I clarified, a little dazed.

Aaron slapped his big, scarred and tattooed hands on my pale blue mat and wiggled his fingers. "Hop to it, Blue. These suckers've never been seen to, so it'll probably take you a while to get them up to snuff."

Emotion surged up my throat so strongly, I almost gagged. It was joy so sharp it made my teeth ache. Unbidden tears stung the back of my eyes and pooled in the ducts.

"Hey, hey," Aaron crooned, leaning forward to tuck a lock of my hair behind my ear and cup my cheek. "What happened to the happy?"

"I am happy," I whispered through the crush of tears in my throat. "I think it's just a shock to my system."

His full mouth flatlined, and I watched his gaze dip to the exposed line of my throat that my hair had been covering. I'd covered the vivid bruises from Rooster's choking grip with about a pound of concealer, but Aaron's eyes were too keen. I swallowed thickly as his hand trailed from my cheek along the soft edge of my jaw to my throat, palming my neck the way Rooster had done, touching the bruises like Mei had on my wrists. His touch was feather light, thumb dragging softly over my tripping pulse. I watched as emotion stormed through his expression and then as he visibly swallowed it down and shifted back, dropping his hand.

When he smiled, it was almost normal—bright and arrogant in that way that made women combust. But I could see the tightness beside his eyes and knew he was making an effort to be cool so he wouldn't ruin my happiness.

Fuck, how was I ever going to resist a man like him?

An outlaw biker who'd come to get his damn nails done just to see me.

I sucked in a tremulous breath and smiled back at him as I took his hands and laid them over the bolster. "You do know I'm going to have to paint them something real pretty...I'm thinking blue."

Aaron laughed, that gorgeous sound deep from the belly, and I wanted to throw myself into his arms and beg him to laugh with me every day for the rest of my life.

"Blue suits just fine," he agreed.

I took a moment to stroke over his big hands, tracing The Fallen MC skull and flaming wings symbol on the dorsal side and the four thick silver rings on each hand. I lingered over the signet ring etched with spidery calligraphy, trying to read the letters upside down.

"Ximena Sofia Escalante," he answered my unspoken question. "It was my mother's ring and, before that, her mother's. The eldest daughter was named Ximena in my family until my sister was born."

"Why the break in tradition?" I asked as I started to prep my station to give him a manicure.

He hesitated for a moment, that energetic vibrancy dimming in a way that made me stop what I was doing to search his morose expression.

"My parents died a few weeks after she was born in a car crash. When we went into foster care, they decided Ximena was too hard for people to say, so they used her middle name, Elsa."

"I'm so sorry," I said, taking his hands to give them a squeeze. "Were you always Aaron?"

"Aarón," he said in a rolling Spanish accent, amplifying his name to even more beautiful heights. "But it was easier to go by Aaron. There isn't a huge Latino community in the province. Honestly, I got lucky with the club. I didn't learn Spanish until I patched in and got the chance to speak it with Nova and his Old Lady, Lila, and Ares, Zeus and Loulou's son. Lou's tryin' to learn, but she can't roll her r's for shit."

I laughed, rolling mine on my tongue.

Aaron shot me a heated, lazy grin. "Why did I know you'd be perfect at that? Makes me think what else you could get up to with that tongue."

I bit my lip to hide my smile. "Behave, we are at my place of work."

"Woulda taken you out properly, you gave me the chance," he reminded me.

"I'm married," I countered. Even the words felt like a knife I'd stuck through my own chest.

I pulled out the nail drill and flicked it on, only to watch Aaron's eyes blow wide.

"What the fuck is that?" he asked suspiciously. "Didn't come here to get tortured, Blue. Coulda asked Priest for a session if I wanted to get fucked up."

The laughter that burst from me was so loud, some of the other patrons turned to see what amused me. I caught Lin's eye, but she only shook her head with an indulgent smile.

"It's a nail drill, silly." I took his hand to show him how gently I could press the tool to his nail to clean up his cuticles. "We do dry manicures here, which means no soaking in water or chemicals. It's more precise."

I laughed again at the face he made but continued to work on his ragged nail beds. There was motor grease under his nails and dirt ground into his skin.

"I don't even know where you work," I admitted softly because it was so strange to know he was almost a perfect stranger to me while everything in me yearned for him on an atomic level.

I felt I had known him all my life or, if not known, that I had been waiting for this man to arrive.

Not to save me, exactly, but to give me the hope I needed to endure my circumstances and find my way out of them.

"I'm a mechanic at Hephaestus Auto," he offered easily. "The club owns the garage, and we put most'a the prospects to work there 'til we figure out what other skills they might have. Ransom's provin' to be real good with bodywork, and Carson's got a mind for engineerin', so we're puttin' him on the newer models that need diagnostic scannin' and shit. Pigeon hates it, so Nova and Axe-Man are thinkin'a takin' him on at Street Ink Tattoo to see if he's any good at that."

"What if he's not?" I asked, curious about how the inner workings of The Fallen played out.

The Calgary chapter and now the White Raiders were different beasts entirely. What Rooster said went, so even if the brothers didn't like their work or their chores for the club, they did them without fail.

Aaron shrugged. "Then he can do whatever the fuck he likes. We got some other companies and shit, too. King works at Hephaestus to fill in sometimes, but he and Curtains and Axe-Man mostly run the club financials and businesses. Buck's got Edge Truckin'. There's a shit ton Pige can do and if he doesn't like any'a it, then he can get a job outside'a the club. Plenty'a brothers do."

He peered at me for a second, probably taking in my look of disbelief. "It's not slave labour, Blue. We only get the prospects doin' work for the club 'cause they usually come to us with no money and no fuckin' idea what they wanna be doin' with their life other than ridin'."

"What do you want to do?" I asked, hiding behind a sheaf of blue hair as I worked on his thumb. "With your life."

He was quiet, but the silence held weight as if he was giving my question serious consideration. When he finally spoke, it was more muted than usual, somber in a way that etched the words into my bones.

"Used to want for nothin' really. Felt like a miracle I had a family after losin' my parents and then Elsa. A family that saw me and wanted me for exactly who I was. I got more brothers than most folks and so many women to love and be loved by, their kids to spoil rotten, it just seemed...I donno, selfish maybe? To dream'a more."

He paused because I had, the nail drill discarded on the table, my fingers hovering over the nail polishes as I stared transfixed at the man before me.

"Then I met you, and it wasn't like anythin' I had before became less. It was that I realized how much more it could be with the right woman to share it all with."

"Aaron," I breathed. "I hate to sound like a broken record, but you don't know me very well, and honestly, there are dozens of other women out there who would fall at your feet with ten times less baggage than me."

He shrugged. "Don't want any'a them. I wake up every mornin' with the colour blue behind my closed lids and a punch to the gut when I open them to find you're not sleepin' beside me."

My heart felt pulverized by his words and the hope they invoked. Who knew hope could be so brutal? Who knew it had fists and claws and teeth?

"I talk in my sleep and hog the covers," I retorted because I couldn't give him any of the mess in my chest. I didn't know how to articulate it.

He grinned. "I run warm and sleep heavy, so that suits me just fine."

Just for that, I picked a pretty pale blue from the options and brandished the wet brush like a weapon, a maniacal grin on my face as I bent to start with his pinky.

"Just a shade lighter than your hair. Love it."

"Aren't your brothers going to make fun of you?" I asked because in the Raiders, if a man showed up with painted nails, even done by his daughter, he'd probably be beaten as well as ridiculed. They subscribed to entirely outdated views on masculinity and machismo.

"Nah, they've done stupider shit to get noticed by their women." He leaned in conspiratorially. "You know, King was Cressida's student when they met. Left her poems pinned to apples every day on the side'a her desk 'fore she agreed to go out with him for real."

"Oh my gosh, that's so cute!"

"So what's Blue's version of an apple poem?" he asked, curling his hand around mine to still me, bringing me closer so his mouth was an inch from mine and his devastatingly handsome face was all I could see. "'Cause baby, I'm gonna find what you want and need and give it to ya until you agree to be mine."

"You'd be taking on an entire club to get me," I pointed out, a little breathless because his breath was *sweet* like cinnamon candy, and I wanted so badly to see if it tasted the same.

"Hate to break it to you, Blue, but we were takin' them on already. They're comin' for what's ours, and even if you don't acknowledge it, that includes you."

"One night together doesn't make me your possession."

"'S not about me possessin' you," he argued. "Don't you get that yet? It's you who's got your name carved into my bones now, Blue. It's you who's got possession over me. I'm just askin' ya to give me some relief, and let me try to convince you I'm worth inkin' onto yours."

But I feel you there already, and it scares me, *I thought but didn't say.*

If I ever thought to dream of the perfect man, it'd be you. Blue nails and all.

He searched my eyes like an archaeologist with a careful, deliberate intent, stirring up things I wanted to keep buried.

"For now, I'm just a man gettin' a manicure from the best girl in Entrance," he said, slowly leaning back in his seat, a manly sprawl of spread denim-clad thighs and slouched, broad shoulders that made my mouth water. "For now, I'm just askin' to get to know you a little more. So play a game with me."

I peered at him through my lashes, unable to resist the wicked little grin on his mouth. "I like games."

That grin widened. "Excellent. So would you rather hafta live in the nude for six months or not be able to bathe for one year?" When I laughed, he added, "I gotta tell ya, I got a preference for you pickin' to live in the nude."

I DID his fingers and his toes, but he demanded a cobalt blue for those "the same shade as your hair." By the time I finished, he had the other women in the pedicure stations beside him gasping for breath as they laughed over his story about the night Curtains and he tried to install a new laundry machine and ended up setting fire to their house.

"I still feel the trauma every time I do laundry. It's my excuse for bein' lazy, at least," he finished, eyes crinkled, pink mouth split wide by the kind of smile that dazzled like a sunrise at dawn.

You could love him if you let yourself, *a little voice whispered in my head.* You wouldn't even have to try.

He was just a lovable man. Confident enough to get a mani/pedi and regale other clients about his trials and tribulations. Sexy enough to make my gut pool with heavy warmth. Even his feet, long and lean with tanned skin and high arches, were absurdly attractive, and I'd never before entertained the idea of a foot fetish.

He was a supernova or a daytime eclipse, something so outlandishly magical it was impossible to look away.

So I stopped trying.

When I went to dump the water out, I heard one of the women approach him and ask him for coffee. The bottom dropped out of my stomach, and all the happy hope that inflated me rushed out on a whoosh of punched breath.

I waited, arms straining as I held the heavy tub over the sink, unwilling to spill it because I wanted to be able to hear his response.

"Sweet'a you, but I'm taken."

My heart commenced thudding inside my chest.

"Girlfriend?" the woman asked dejectedly.

"It's complicated, but I'm waitin' for her to un-complicate it by lettin' me take her out on a date."

What would a date with Aaron look like?

I wanted to know so badly that it was as if every molecule in my body was magnetized to his. But it was also impossible to ignore the fact that Rooster would kill him, and maybe even me, if I went back on my oath not to run away again.

In fact, knowing my father, he wouldn't stop at Aaron and me. He'd kill Grouch and Zeus and the entire club, the final spark to ignite the bonfire of hatred he'd compiled against perceived wrongdoings by The Fallen MC over all these years.

My happiness simply was not worth that price.

Aaron must have seen the conviction on my face when I came back to his station because there was a frown between his dark brows that didn't suit him well at all. I led him to the front of the shop silently, and when he tried to pull out his wallet at the reception stand, I waved him off.

"My treat," I stated firmly. "As thanks for everything you did to help me that night."

That frown tightened into a glower. "Don't insult me by implyin' I need payment for services fuckin' rendered, Blue."

The sigh that unwound from me was as long as an unspooling ball of yarn. "I didn't mean it as an insult. Honestly. I just...I wanted to do something nice for you, and I don't have anything else to offer."

He stepped closer, boxing me into the small space behind the reception desk, one hand against the wall and the other gentle at my hip. I was so much shorter than him that the owl tattoo inked on his neck was as high as I could see until he tipped his head down and gave me those coal-dark and burning eyes.

"You're the only thing'a worth I want, and that's got nothin' to do with owin' me anythin'," he announced.

"Aren't you getting tired of playing this game with me?" I asked wearily because I was.

Tired and suddenly so lonely I just wanted to hug myself in the back room for a few minutes.

"See, that's the problem here, Blue. You think this is a game, and it fuckin' well isn't. This is *life*, mine and yours, and I'm tryna tie them together in a way I know in my bones is gonna last if you let it."

The little bell over the door chimed as someone came in so I pushed him away and tried to get my breathing under control. Only for Aaron to grab my hand and pull me toward the exit, calling to Lin over his shoulder, "Blue's takin' a five-minute break."

"Aaron! It's my first day. I can't just––" My words tumbled to a stop when the door closed behind us, and he dragged me to his gleaming Harley parked at the end of the row beside a massive truck. He pushed me gently into the gap between the two and then pressed himself against me, a hand to the truck and another tangling in the back of my hair.

"Now, I got you for a second, I need you to listen to me, yeah?" he said, low and serious, eyes pinned on mine so I couldn't look away, couldn't even blink. "I'm not some frat boy or Otto fuckin' Fuck Up you gotta worry about protectin' or protectin' yourself from. I'm a brother'a The Fallen fuckin' MC, the baddest club in the fuckin' nation, and I can not only safeguard myself from my enemies, but I sure as fuck can keep you safe from yours. You only hafta ask me, and I'd burn down the fuckin' world for you."

"Why?" I asked, the word like a knife held to his throat, a demand and a threat all at once. "Why would you do that for me, though?"

His entire countenance softened, melting against the heat of my anger until his body was flush with mine, and I imagined I could almost

159

feel his heartbeat through the layers of his leather cut, shirt, flesh and bone.

He tilted my head back with the hand woven through my hair and lipped at my Medusa piercing before pulling back slightly so I could read the sincerity in his eyes.

"The real question is, who, havin' met you, would offer you anythin' different?" he paused when tears pushed at the corners of my eyes, his other hand cupping my cheek. "I don't hafta know your middle name or where you went to high school or what kinda shows you like to watch to know the quality'a your soul. I saw it shinin' from your too-blue eyes the minute I entered that gas station, and I've been lookin' at it ever since."

"I'm not that great," I promised, but at some point, I'd clutched his wrists with my hands like I couldn't bear for him to move. "Honestly, ask anyone I've ever known save Grouch, and maybe Axe and Cedar."

"I'm not that great either," he said with a little shrug. "We can be not that great together."

I laughed, slightly hysterically, but then slumped deeper into his body and let the last of my tension leak out through my mouth.

"I'm tired," I whispered, a terrible confession. "I'm tired of living like this, and it only just started. It's...I thought I got away, you know? And now it's so much harder to withstand."

"Yeah, baby, I know," he murmured, pressing a kiss to my forehead. "And I'm gonna help you stand tall and strong to endure it 'til we can get you outta there safe, yeah?"

Another gusty exhale stirred the thick lock of hair falling over his forehead. How could I resist a man who seemed as strong as Atlas offering to carry some of my burden on his shoulders?

"Yeah," I whispered so softly it was mostly air. "Okay."

"Okay," he agreed, the shape of his smile pressed to my cheek. "That's my girl."

"I want to be," I confessed, grasping his wrists even tighter. "But I'm legally already someone else's."

"Well," he said, completely undeterred. "I'm sure we can find a way around that. But for now, I'm gonna use the next two minutes'a your break to make out with my woman. You got any objection to that?"

I grinned against his mouth and then closed my lips over his in answer.

And when I returned to work two minutes later, I felt like I was walking on air even with the anchor of Rooster, Hazard and the White Raiders still tied around my ankle.

CHAPTER ELEVEN

Boner

BLUE

> Hey, Trouble. I dreamed of you last night.

> Oh yeah? Maybe it was the same dream I had.

BLUE

> We were riding on your bike along the beach, right on the sand, and I had my hands in the air. I felt so free that the next minute, I became a bird and took off into the sky.

> Yeah, no. In my dream, you were ridin' my face. Woke up hard as iron, and my fist ain't anywhere as pretty as your sweet mouth or pussy.

BLUE

> You haven't even had my mouth on you yet.

> Yeah well, a man can dream. Literally.

BLUE

I'm just about to start my shift at Eugene's, please don't turn me on!

Can't stop thinkin' about puttin' my mouth on you again. You got so nice and wet for me, baby, that I could just slide right on in to that tight little cunt.

BLUE

I'm ignoring you now.

Don't ignore me and leave me here with this boner! You're responsible, you gotta give me somethin' to tide me over.

BLUE

image

I STARED down at the selfie Blue sent me in the mirror'a the ladies' bathroom at Eugene's Bar and wished like hell I was there with her and not waitin' at the side'a the highway for Pigeon to a take a leak on our way to our monthly check-in with our dealers in Vancouver.

But that was what you got when you were in charge'a the prospects.

Carson pushed outta the gas station with a bag'a Twizzlers, three'a them stuffed in his mouth.

"You get anythin' for me?" I asked, brow raised.

He hesitated mid-step--it was always good to know I could be intimidatin' when I set my mind to it--and then held out the bag'a red candy.

I snatched the entire thing from him and stuffed it into the back pocket'a my jeans before takin' a rope for myself and chompin' off the end. "Thanks, man."

Carson scowled but didn't refute my claim. He wasn't exactly the most easygoin' kid, but he went against the grain'a his nature to be cool with the brothers and his chores for the club. When he'd left football behind 'cause'a its association with his fuckwad father, he'd been set adrift, and if it wasn't for Benny, King and Cressida leadin' him to the club, I wondered how dark he woulda gone down the rabbit hole'a his own mind.

It also drove him crazy that we hadn't given him a nickname yet, even though the guys and I had all told him it had to come naturally. There was usually a story involved, some hilarious or fittin' meanin' that needed to spring to mind for it to stick.

It wasn't somethin' you wanted to rush.

Still, he was always the first prospect to volunteer for anythin', which was why he was on this run with me. Pigeon was there 'cause it was his turn to ride out with me, and King had tagged along to keep me company lookin' after the kids.

"You got that face on," King noted as I chewed through the sweet rope. "You gettin' through to Blue?"

Carson snorted. "Dude, you're really askin' when you can see the man's got painted nails?"

I wiggled them at King. "She does a good fuckin' job, thank you very much."

King chuckled. "Yeah, 'cause you know so much about beauty."

I ran a hand through the long top half 'a my hair and batted my lashes at him. "True. Most'a my good looks are all natural, but I know more about it than you."

"'Cause you got a crush on a beautician," he quipped.

"Cosmetologist," I corrected with a haughty sniff. "Don't even know the fuckin' lingo."

King rolled his eyes. "Datin' one and he thinks he knows everythin'."

"Dude, you wrote poetry for Cressida for like...weeks. Don't think you're one to talk," I argued as Pigeon finally came outta the station toward us.

"You think I still don't write my woman poetry, you're mad," he countered. "You get a woman like Cress, you don't take her for granted for a fuckin' *day*."

Yeah, I thought, lookin' back down at the selfie'a Blue, lush breasts pushed together in a white tank, full sleeve of blue inked tattoos on her left arm and the piercings in her nose and upper lip. She looked like somethin' outta a fantasy novel or the pin-up posters I'd hoarded at foster homes as a kid.

Somethin' way too fuckin' good for the likes'a me, but what did I care?

I'd work to earn her and fight to keep her.

"Hey, man, you think Lion would know anythin' about getting an uncontested divorce?" I asked as Pigeon swung a leg over his bike and settled.

"What do you know about uncontested divorce?" Pige asked on a snort.

"What Google told me, dipshit," I shot back, shovin' him to show I wasn't actually angry.

"Yeah, or you could call White," King suggested, mentioning the club's lawyer. "He'd have a good answer for ya."

I shot off a quick text to White and Lion askin' them both about it, then put my phone away to ride out with the boys. It was a grey June mornin', the type'a weather that made locals call it 'Junuary'. The blue tinted glass'a Vancouver's skyline came into view, spires reflectin' the dark clouds, and it started to rain the second we swerved into the downtown Eastside and our first stop'a the day.

Jelly Hock lived in a crumblin' buildin' with a Condemned sign on it even though there were no plans to knock it down and never would be. Jelly owned it and lent the various rooms out to his low-level thugs who peddled our product exclusively in the neighbourhood. He'd grown up poor and didn't like to spend any'a the money he made on upgradin' his life. Instead, he had a weird habit'a buryin' it in Burnaby and Langley, in random locations he said he kept coordinates of only in his head.

But the man did like to eat, and when we entered the apartment, I expected to find him sittin' at his kitchen table with a plethora'a of take-out containers and a mouth slick with sticky sauce residue.

Instead, I found the door to the apartment blown open, and Jelly Hock slumped over the table, pale cheek pressed to a rank dish'a days-old crab rangoon.

"Fuck," I cursed, pushing the door wide open so the men behind me could see the situation. "Pigeon, stay on the door."

"We go in, we could be cornered," King argued as I stepped into the mess of an apartment.

"There's a fire escape out the kitchen window, but if someone laid this as a trap, you'd think the meat would be fresher." I moved to Jelly, grabbed a pair'a disposable plastic gloves from my pocket, and snapped them on one hand before checkin' his pulse. His skin was hard and cold, a wavy texture I could feel even through the latex. "He's been dead a minute."

"Fuck," Carson echoed, and not 'cause'a the dead body. He was at the fridge, readin' the colourful alphabet letters arranged into a sentence.

White Raiders are coming.

"Poetic," King scoffed, takin' a photo with his phone before muddlin' the letters up with his leather-covered elbow. "How the fuck did they know Jelly was one'a ours?"

"It wouldn't be that hard to find out." I closed Jelly's eyes outta respect and moved away from the stank'a the crab and days-old body. "What's strange to me is that no one fuckin' noticed him in here before us."

"Uh, Boner? King?" Pigeon called from the hall.

A moment later, the sound of sirens, growin' louder fast.

"Fuck," we cursed together before gettin' the fuck in motion.

King and Carson went for the door, but I knew Jelly, and he hid valuable intel in the mini-fridge in his bedroom behind a fake panel, so I headed there.

"Boner!" King yelled.

"Go on, I'll meet you by the bikes," I replied, already racin' into the bedroom and droppin' to my knees in front'a the fridge. I flinched at the odour of rotten food inside when I swung it open, holdin' my breath as I worked my fingers in the panel to pry its icy walls away. Food and beer bottles rolled out onto the floor at my knees, but I ignored it to collect the elastic band-wrapped roll'a papers and another'a cash in a small cubbyhole.

The sirens were piercin' now, comin' down the street a block or two out if I had to guess.

I shoved the papers into the back pocket'a my jeans opposite the fuckin' candy ropes and sprinted through the apartment to the kitchen. The window was swollen in the frame from age and water damaged, firmly closed despite my gruntin' efforts.

The sirens stopped.

"Fuck," I cursed again, usin' the barrel'a my gun to knock out the glass so I could carefully bend myself through the openin'.

The fire escape groaned and hissed under my weight, rusted and missin' a few slats at my feet. So it wasn't any surprise when the fuckin' ladder wouldn't descend more than two feet.

Inside, voices called loudly over the stomp of feet.

I dropped through the small square, grabbin' the handle'a the ladder in both hands to use my momentum to pull it farther down. It dropped another foot and stuck with a screech.

Below me was a pile'a garbage waitin' for pick up includin' a dumpster'a cardboard and plastic to the right'a my feet.

"Fuck, this is gonna hurt," I muttered.

The crackle of radio feedback sounded in the apartment above me, and someone hollered to another cop about a dead body.

I dropped.

Hopin' I wouldn't be joinin' Jelly in the afterlife.

It was only two stories, but hittin' plastics and cardboard was not a soft landin', and the breath whooshed outta me like I'd been sucker punched. I lay there for a moment to catalogue my aches--nothin' life threatenin' and no broken bones save a potentially bruised rib or two-- and then scrambled to the edge of the metal bin to climb over.

"Hey!" a cop above me yelled, leanin' over the fire escape. "Stop right there."

I'd never been good with people tellin' me what to do. Jumpin' down from the dumpster, I set off at a sprint down the back alley before turnin' right, headin' to where we'd left our bikes two blocks down.

Behind me, sirens started up again.

Goddamn, it had been a minute since my last police chase.

I shucked my cut, tossin' it behind a garbage can with a silent apology, and flipped the hood up on my grey sweater as I picked up speed.

My bike was the only one left, but that was the way it shoulda been.

It wasn't every man for himself in the club, but it sure as hell was get the fuck away from the cops as quick as you can.

They didn't exactly love The Fallen.

I swung my leg over the bike, startin' the engine with a loud purr just as a siren whooped behind me. Thankful my helmet obscured my face, I gunned the throttle and took off through the streets of Vancouver.

I'd grown up in the city and still knew it well enough, thanks to all our business there, to give the cops a merry little runaround. They couldn't follow down some of the narrow lanes in the residential area I veered into, and then when they caught sight'a me again, I was two blocks ahead, cuttin' to the left to head toward the seawall. They'd expect me to head right to get outta town, maybe disappear into the traffic leadin' out to Burnaby.

Which was why I took the seawall, cuttin' down off the street to take the pedestrian walkway on my bike, grateful it was a Thursday and the weather was shit so I didn't have to contend with too many tourists as I flew around the curves and then cut back up to the road to head into Stanley Park.

By the time I was in North Van, there was no sign'a the cops on my tail.

Still, I didn't pull over 'til I reached our next destination, a pretty house backin' onto Grouse Mountain where one'a our biggest distributors lived.

Shelly Byers's Mercedes SUV was in the driveway when I walked up, havin' stashed my bike a few blocks away for good measure, but no one answered the door when I rang.

That was not like Shelly.

She was the kinda PTA mum who colour-coordinated her kids' clothes and had a schedule for each member'a the family on the kitchen fridge. You told Shelly a time, and Shelly'd fuckin' be there lookin' like she stepped right outta some Brooks Brothers' catalogue.

So where the fuck was she?

I texted King my location as I walked around the side'a the house, grateful Shelly lived in a posh neighbourhood with huge, treed lots separatin' each house from view'a the others. There was no movement in the windows and the doors were locked. But I could see a spill'a toys in the livin' room that was totally outta character for Shelly.

"Fuck."

Someone had got to her.

At the very least, they'd tried.

"You good, brother?" King asked, joggin' up behind me with Carson at his back. "That was fucked back there."

"Don't worry about me. Shelly's not here," I said and watched King's face close down.

"Shit, they're really comin' at us," he muttered. "You check the house?"

"She's not here. We can break in to check, but she's got a good alarm system, and we'd have to get Curtains involved. I'd rather not hang around long enough to see if those fuckers set another trap for us. But give me a second here," I asked, turnin' my back on them to pace 'cause movin' always helped me think.

I was good with people, which was an important skill when you were a member'a an outlaw organization filled with the kinda personalities that usually made people uncomfortable or terrified. So 'fore I'd been in charge'a the prospects, I'd been one'a the main brothers on the ground connectin' with our network. Nova, King and Buck were all good options too, but they were busy with other work for the club, and talkin' to people was no hardship for me.

I'd always been able to talk my way outta scraps, and Curtains always fuckin' hated that I had a memory like a steel trap.

Both things worked to my advantage in a situation like this.

'Cause I remembered once, over coffee at Shelly's marble-topped kitchen island, she'd mentioned how happy she was with her cut lately. It meant she could buy that cabin her husband always wanted up in Whistler.

Ding fuckin' ding, I bet we had a winner.

My phone was in my hand taggin' the speed dial for Curtains's number 'fore I explained shit to King and Carson.

"Sup, bro?"

"You helped Shelly set up that off-shore corporation last year," I said, cuttin' straight to it. "You able to access records'a purchases she made under the company?"

"Sure, could do it in my sleep. Why?"

"Just do it, brother. Look for any land or houses purchased in the past year near Whistler."

I hung up without another word, knowin' Curtains was already on it, and the results would be texted to me in the next few minutes.

"You think she's hidin'," King confirmed, noddin' slowly. "Okay, let's head up there now, and we should have the info we need by the time we get there."

"You don't think they killed her too?" Carson asked as we broke into a jog headin' back to our bikes.

I snorted. "Shelly's smarter than Jelly. She's the kinda woman's got a backup for her backup plan."

"This is not lookin' fuckin' good," King murmured as Carson fell back a step to avoid some trees.

"No, brother, it's not," I agreed, but some part'a me—the part that made outlaw a good fittin' mantle over my shoulders—gnashed its teeth like an overaggressive dog on its leash. I was almost *happy* Rooster's lot was comin' for us 'cause I wanted any fuckin' excuse I could get to go at him.

And if that had a whole lot to do with avengin' the marks I'd seen collarin' Blue's throat a few days ago, well, so much the fuckin' better.

THE CABIN WAS A PRETTY little pinewood number at the edge of a development near Lost Lake outside'a Whistler Village. Unlike her home in North Van, it was wreathed with neighbours, so I went in alone first with King, Carson and Pigeon followin' one at a time, slinkin' through the shadows to surround the house in case'a any issues.

I went right to the front door.

The sound'a children's laughter could be heard through the pane'a glass.

Shelly's face, when she caught sight'a me through it, was brittle enough to crack in half.

"What the fuck are you doing here?" she hissed as soon as the door was open, slippin' out to close it behind her.

She was barefoot in a little cardigan set that made her look like a Stepford wife, but there was watercolour paint on her cheek from one'a her kids, and she tended to curse worse than some'a my brothers.

I'd always liked the contrast in her.

"Hey, Shell," I said affably, leanin' a shoulder against the wood post. "You don't call, you don't write, so I figured I'd come see what the hell drove you outta town without a word to your dear old friend, Boner."

"Jesus." She shook her head, eyein' the neighbourin' homes 'fore reluctantly takin' my hand to drag me inside to the first room on the left.

Apparently, havin' me inside was better than bein' seen chattin' it up with a tatted biker even though I'd ditched my cut.

"What the fuck happened, Shellster?" I asked, softenin' my tone 'cause I noticed her hands shakin' as she closed the double doors'a the office for privacy.

She was pale when she turned to walk around the desk and took a seat, her usually immaculate nails chewed to the quick. When she finally locked eyes with me, they were bloodshot and ringed in dark circles.

"They came to my goddamn house, Boner," she said through bared teeth. "Charlie and the kids were home playing in the back. He said some guys were watching them, ready to take action if I didn't 'hear him out.'"

Anger turned my insides into serpents, hissin' and coilin' in my gut.

Shelly was a drug dealer and a damn good one, distributin' through a high-end network'a execs, stay-at-home mums, and bored university students, but she was still a mum and a good one at that. Fuck, she'd started this gig with us to pay for aides for her daughter with Down

Syndrome.

"Who?" I gritted out.

"Said his name was Rooster. Called himself a 'friend' of the club." She rolled her eyes and opened the drawer to pull out a pack'a cigarettes. After puttin' one in her mouth, she offered me the pack, but I shook my head. "He wanted to renegotiate the deal I had with you. As in, drop The Fallen and take up with the White Raiders. I told the fucker I hadn't even heard of his precious White Raiders, and he did not like that."

She lit the cigarette, the cuff of her sweater fallin' back to reveal a vivid bruise on her wrist.

Fuck.

"Shell." I leaned forward and extended my hand, palm up, so I could examine it.

After a tremblin' hesitation, she laid it in my hand and exhaled a long cloud'a smoke. "I'm fine. Thank God, Wes Potter drove by in his squad car because he forgot something at home. He saw these huge-ass fuckers talking to me in the yard and asked if I was okay. Obviously, I said no. Wes waited with me for them to leave and even checked the house. Charlie and I gathered our shit and drove up here as soon as it got dark."

"When was this?"

"Last night. I knew they'd be back, and this morning I got a text from Vaughn. You know him? He works with Mags Marie over in Port Coquitlam? Apparently, they fucking got to Mags and killed her when she refused to work for them. Vaughn agreed to take over when they threatened him too." She sucked in another deep drag from the cigarette. "What the fuck is going on, Boner? I did not sign up for this level of bullshit. My kids were home!"

"Hey, I hear you," I said, low and smooth, gently pattin' her arm above the bruise before lettin' her go. "Seems they're targetin' our dealers like this. I found Jelly dead in his apartment."

She scoffed. "Jelly was an idiot with tons of enemies. It could have been anyone who killed him."

I arched a brow. "Yeah, if there wasn't a pattern now that I hear they came for you and they got to Mags Marie. I'm real sorry about this. You know we'd never want you or your family harmed."

Somethin' in the line'a her shoulders relaxed a bit. "I know, Boner. I wouldn't be working with you if I didn't think you were a group of rebels with good hearts, but this is too much. I have to think of my family."

"And I have to think'a mine," I countered. "You can't just stop workin' with us, Shell. You run North Van, for fuck's sake. It'd cause serious issues for more than just our chapter if we closed up shop."

"Well then, what're you going to do about these bastards?" she spat. "I want them dead, Boner."

"You and me both," I promised. "Let me think on it, yeah? We just got this info, so I need to talk to my Prez and the brothers about our course'a action. But we will not leave you hangin', you get me? In fact, if you want, I'll leave Pigeon here with you. Call him your cousin or whatever the hell and take him with you wherever you go 'til we get this fixed, yeah?"

She stared at me querulously for a moment before tappin' out her cigarette and pullin' a can'a Febreeze from the same drawer she'd stored her smokes in.

"Fine, leave the kid. He's a little awkward, but Midge loves his tattoos. I'll keep shit going, but my family stays here with Pigeon. I'll make trips back to the city as need be."

"Agreed." I leaned a hand onto the desktop and chuffed her lightly under the chin. "Thanks, Shell. I promise, personally, I'll see this doesn't happen again."

"The only reason I'm not getting on a plane to Mexico is because I know that, Boner," she told me quietly, touchin' me briefly on the cheek. "Now get the fuck out of my house."

Aren't we all?

SINNERS

CHAPTER TWELVE

Blue

I WOKE up Friday morning lying in the bathtub with a brutal crick in my neck and my left leg so numb it wouldn't support my weight when I tried to stand.

I'd closed myself in the bathroom because it was the only room in the house with a lock.

And last night, the Raiders had a party.

I'd almost forgotten what their parties were like, relegating the memories to the deepest recess of my brain. They were rowdy to the point of chaos, breaking chairs and bottles, throwing each other through windows or into walls when inevitable scuffles broke out over stupid wounded pride or drunken declarations. There were no Old Ladies allowed in Rooster's club, so the only women were biker sluts, women who were usually hooked on drugs or danger who needed the Raiders for their hit of either substance. When I walked in after my first shift at Eugene's, Meatloaf was fucking someone right beside the door. He'd sneered at me when I walked in, balls deep inside a woman who was screaming loud enough to wake the dead.

It didn't get any better the deeper into the house I went.

Rooster was being fellated as he casually drank whiskey with his Sergeant At Arms, Macho, and when he caught my eye across the crowded living room, he beckoned me to his side with a snap of his fingers.

I was exhausted.

Thursday was my double duty day at Lin's and Eugene's, and both jobs were physically and socially taxing. All I wanted was to fall into bed, text Aaron for a minute, and escape into dreams.

But I knew better than to say no to Rooster.

So I picked my way through the warm bodies writhing together to the rock music spilling tinny and crackling through an old speaker and stopped at his side.

"Grab us some more beer, girl," he said, meeting my eye as he pet the blonde head of the woman on her knees in front of him. "Make yourself useful like Crystal here."

I fought against the shiver of revulsion that moved through me and turned to do his bidding. Before, when I was young, I hadn't grown into myself yet so none of the brothers had even looked at me too long.

But I was decked out in glam make-up, tiny denim shorts, and a yellow top that emphasized my curves for my shift at Eugene's, and one of the Raiders let his appreciation be known by tugging me into his lap before I could get by.

His face was between my breasts, motorboating me loudly, beer-wet lips against my flesh before I could push him away. When I tried, he gathered my hands in his ham fists and pulled down hard to keep me still.

He pulled away laughing, ruddy-faced and clearly high out of his mind from the dilation of his pupils.

"Let go," I seethed, baring my teeth at him.

"Or what?" He chuckled, rubbing his bearded cheek against me.

"Or Hazard'll have your eyes plucked from your skull," I warned, hoping that Hazard's legendary temper hadn't cooled in the eight years of our separation.

The biker, I thought his name was Piston, winced a little and then almost threw me off his lap. I crashed into the coffee table behind me, whacking my hip so hard I had to swallow a cry. Piston and his buddy next to him laughed at me, but I didn't stick around to make an issue of it.

The kitchen was a relief after that, only Aunt Rita sitting at the table in her housecoat with a biker slut who was crying softly, holding a frozen bag of corn to one cheek. Sympathy moved through me for a moment looking at her smeared make-up and bad extensions.

I wondered what kind of path she'd wandered down to end up in this place voluntarily.

But I couldn't afford to help her, not when I couldn't even help myself.

So I just paused after grabbing a six-pack of cold ones and offered, "You can sleep in my room if you need space. The last one on the second floor on the right."

She'd blinked at me, checking me out in one sharp look before sneering. "I don't need your help, bitch."

I shared a look with Aunt Rita, who only shrugged, long ago inured to all kinds of biker behaviour as Rooster's spinster sister, and left the room.

I dropped the beers while Rooster was busy coming down that girl's throat and then diligently handed over my first paycheck and the scant information I felt comfortable telling him about gossip at Eugene's. Mostly that The Fallen realized they were under attack from someone, but they had no clue who. That got a wild, smug laugh from my father before he dismissed me to take a celebratory shot with his brothers.

I disappeared up the stairs, grabbed my pillow, and locked myself in the bathroom. I thought about taking my secret phone with me, but it was too risky in case someone broke down the door (it had happened before) or I couldn't get back to my room before everyone woke up in the morning.

Instead, I used the phone Rooster had given me and called the only number I had memorized.

"Faithy?" a sleepy voice answered, growing alert with every word. "Faithy, is that you?"

Tears pooled at the back of my eyes, but I didn't stop them from running down my cheeks as I whispered to the only man who'd ever treated me like a daughter, "Hey, Grouch."

"Honey." The one word throbbed with heartache. "God, I hate that you are back with them."

"Yeah, me too."

"I wish...I wish you'd let me help you. I can give you some money. You can catch a bus or a train out of here."

"I told you," I said, so tired each bone in my body felt like an anchor. I imagined filling the tub with water and sinking beneath the current. At that moment, it seemed like the only way to find peace. "Rooster would kill you. Look at what he did to you already because of me."

"I don't want you worrying about what happened to me. I only wish I could do more. I could take Ruth and Jensen, and we could go with you," he offered.

A sob fell from my mouth before I could catch it. I knew how much Grouch loved it here. He'd immigrated to Canada with Ruth to Toronto and crossed the country until settling here because it reminded them of the mountains back home.

"Even if I could let you do that, he'd find a way," I said through the clutch of tears at my throat. "He's like...the devil, Grouch. And I sold my soul to him at birth. I don't think I can ever get away."

"You can and you will," he declared imperiously. "We'll find a way."

I focused on breathing so I wouldn't fall to absolute pieces.

"What about that boy who gave me the parcel to deliver to you?" he asked into the silence, a little hopeful, a little afraid. "He seemed...capable. He told me he was the one who helped you the night of the break-in."

"Yeah," I said, my breath lost to the memory of Aaron swaggering into the gas station and the recognition that he was trouble. It was ironic really because I was the one bringing trouble to him. "He's..."

"You like him."

"You saw him, right?" I tried to joke. "He's my type to a T."

"No," Grouch said slowly. "He's got kind eyes. Otto never had none of that, and from what you've told me, neither did Hazard."

"Yeah," I agreed softly, thinking of those ink-dark eyes and long lashes and the way they crinkled at the sides when he smiled. "I think he's the kindest man I've ever met apart from you."

"The kinda man who's good to know. Don't turn him away, Faithy. You think I didn't recognize his cut, you're blind. Those men've been keeping Entrance safe from outside riffraff for a long time."

I laughed a little wetly. "Only you would say that about a group of outlaw bikers, Grouch."

"I never judge a book by its cover," he reminded me. "If I had, I would have robbed myself the opportunity of loving a girl as sweet as you just because she stole some things from my store."

His sweetness seeped into the broken skin of the wounds I'd acquired in Rooster's home and burned like acid.

"Love you, Grouch," I whispered, exhaustion sweeping through me.

"Love you, girly. Don't lose faith," he joked as he always did.

"I already have," I murmured, half-asleep. "Faith's gone, but I have hope for Blue."

HAPPILY, everyone was passed out when I left the farm. It was still too early to start my shift at Eugene's, but there was somewhere else I had to be.

Lion Heart Investigations was above a bakery in downtown Entrance called Honey Bear Café so the stairwell smelled like warm butter and coffee. The name was written in gold on waxy glass set into the door at the top of the stairs, and when I knocked, an enormous, long-haired, bearded man opened the door as if he'd just been on his way out.

"Hey," he grunted, granting me the tiniest smile before he stepped back to let me in.

He had the look of an ex-con, a look I recognized from half the men I'd grown up with. It was the look of someone haunted by ghosts of their own making. He was handsome in a way that felt threatening, the big muscles, the tattoos, and the scowl lines carved into his tanned face, but when he gave me his eyes, I found a sweetness lurking there.

"Leavin'," he hollered over his shoulder into the depths of the office before nodding at me and starting down the stairs.

"See ya, Sander," someone called back from behind a slightly opened door at the back of the room.

I walked toward it, noting the lack of a receptionist, and knocked lightly on the doorframe before peeking inside.

"Uh, hello?"

The P.I. I'd looked up online sat before me at a big wooden desk with scarred cowboy boots resting beside the keyboard and a tablet in his lap. When he turned his gaze to me, I was shocked by the vividness of his green eyes against his tanned skin and golden hair. He was beautiful like cowboys in old Hollywood films were beautiful, weather worn in an attractive way that spoke of too much time outdoors.

I wondered if being beautiful was an entry requirement for Entrance.

When I'd last seen him, it had been in the low lights of The Fallen MC clubhouse late enough at night, after hours of adrenaline, that I hadn't given him a proper look.

"Hey," Lionel Danner said, dropping his boots to the ground to stand up to greet me. His hand was rough around my own, but his grip was warm and gentle. "Faith Cavendish. I didn't expect to see you in my office."

He gestured to the studded leather chair across from him, so I sat and offered a weak smile. "Why doesn't it surprise me that you know who I am?"

A little shrug. "It's my job." He rubbed a hand over his stubbled chin as he considered me. "And Boner was pretty frantic to find you after you disappeared on him."

Instead of guilt, warmth infused me.

"Oh," I said, looking at my freshly done nail art to hide my blush. I'd hand-painted a little owl on each index finger because they reminded me of Aaron.

Lion's chuckle was friendly. "Never seen the guy like that, so I was happy to help."

"Like what?" I indulged myself in asking.

"Serious about someone. You might not know him well yet, but Boner's our jokester, so when he says something serious, we all perk up and listen."

I nodded because I could see that. "We all hide behind something."

His eyes flashed with interest, but he leaned back in his chair as if we were just having a casual chat. "Very true. And what can I help you hide or find today, Ms. Cavendish?"

"Actually." I swallowed the fear blocking my throat and squared my shoulders. "I was hoping I could help you."

"Oh?" His eyebrows jumped up. "How might you do that?"

God, why was this so hard?

I knew it was the right thing to do. The only thing to do if I wanted to get myself out of this mess of a life I was living. So why was I reluctant?

Rooster and Hazard were bad men who had done awful things to me. This was my chance to take my power *back*.

But years of abuse and power imbalance stood between me and Lion Danner like an unscalable ice wall. I'd spent so long *not* talking about it when I was young and then even in my years away from them that it was like I didn't have the vocabulary to talk about my abuse.

Lion sat forward, his handsome face earnest and open. "Is this about your father?"

I nodded, trying to swallow down the beginnings of a panic attack.

"Okay," he soothed. "You know, I've never been in a situation like yours. But my wife was in an abusive relationship before we got together. He tried to rape her with a knife, and she ended up taking his life to save herself. She wouldn't mind me sharing that with you, I think, because she'd get you needed to hear this. You aren't attacking him by protecting yourself. You aren't doing anything wrong. In fact, you're doing the only thing that's right for you."

I sucked in a sharp breath to mortar my flesh to my bones so I wouldn't fall apart in front of a virtual stranger.

"You know," he continued. "Harleigh Rose and some other women in the club went through hell and back before they got their happy. Maybe I could give you some numbers in case you needed to talk to someone."

"Aaron told me to avoid Harleigh Rose," I admitted before I could curb my response.

Thankfully, Lion only tipped his head back to laugh. "Yeah, I can see that. People think I named my company after myself, but honest to

God, I named it for her. She's my lion-hearted girl. Braver than anyone else I know 'cause she took her own life back for herself. She can be a little intimidating, but she's the best kinda woman to have in your corner. And I think she'd like you."

His gentle manipulation was obvious, but truthfully, it helped to hear their story.

I wanted happy so much I burned.

And somehow, Aaron had got all tangled up with my definition.

Maybe, if I was brave and bold, I could have both.

So I opened my mouth and said, "I want to help you take down the White Raiders. I don't care if you use the information I get and give it to the cops or to the club, but I want to be free of them."

"Okay," he said simply, as if this wasn't the biggest wish I'd ever had laid bare in front of him, like my bleeding heart still warm from my cracked-open chest. "We can do that."

"Yeah?" I asked, almost wincing at the hope in my tone.

"Not gonna lie to you, Faith. It's a dangerous prospect. Your father and his crew are gunning hard for The Fallen, and they find you are working against them, maybe even with The Fallen, it could end badly." He opened his palms wide. "I'm just laying out the facts so you know there's a slim chance of a bad ending, but I'll do anything in my power to make sure that doesn't happen."

"I'm living there anyway to keep people I care about safe. So I figure I can make the sacrifice worth it in two ways if I try to help you put them away while I'm at it." My hands twisted in my lap, damp with nerves and adrenaline. "I know it's dangerous. But if the only move I have to make is sacrificing my queen to end this, I'll do it."

Lion leaned across the table slightly, grass-green gaze intense. "And I'm saying you aren't the only piece on the board anymore. You've got me, and I gotta sense you've got The Fallen if you want them too. I suggest with the adversary we're facing? You tag them in. They can more than take care of themselves and you."

"I don't want them to know I'm doing this," I clarified because I didn't think Aaron would take it well, and I *needed* to take action for me. "I think they've got their hands full already, and I want to remain an anonymous source."

"That's probably best," he agreed. "There's been some developments and I'm not so sure there isn't someone on the inside working with the Raiders."

"I can try to find out who," I suggested. "They don't tell me much, but they also don't care much where I go or what I do in the house."

He considered it with an unhappy frown. "Fine, but be careful. I'll give you a burner so we can stay in touch."

"I have one," I offered, blushing even though he didn't know I had it so I could have a lifeline to Aaron. "I can give you the number. Only one other person has it."

He ducked his head to grab a pen, but I could see his slight smile. "Good. So try to keep an ear to the ground and let me know what you find. If anything goes down that you think spells danger for you, you call me, yeah? Not after it happens, before. And I don't give a fuck if it's a false alarm. Call me anyway so I'm on standby to help you."

"I'll be fine," I told him, the words automatic on my tongue. "Before I go, what do you know about getting an uncontested divorce?"

His head snapped up, eyes bright and when he saw my expression, a slow smile pulled his lips wide. "Not much, but I know a guy who can help."

"I don't have a lot of money, but I could sell something," I offered even though it broke my heart to think of selling the ring Aaron had found for me.

It was hidden in the mattress beside my secret phone because I wasn't sure Rooster wouldn't take it for himself.

"No, you let me worry about that, okay?" He held up his hands when I opened my mouth to protest. "And if you think you're getting special treatment because Aaron's head over boots for you, you're wrong. You're getting special treatment because you're a woman in trouble, and that's just how we do things here. You understand?"

I felt jittery, like a child hopped up on sugar, only the substance that had me tweaking out was kindness. So much of it, so unexpectedly after a lifetime without that, was overloading my system.

"Yeah," I whispered. "But I will pay you back."

"Honest to God, Faith, the best payback you'll give me is getting safe and clear of those criminals."

The smile felt twisted on my face. "So you discriminate against certain criminals but not others? Your bio said you used to be a cop."

Lion rubbed absently at a place on his chest, eyes distant. "Monsters wear all kinds of labels—cops, bikers, politicians. I've found it's how a person acts and not what they associate with that determines their goodness. Met some of the best men I've ever known in The Fallen and that doesn't discount meeting some of the worst through them either."

"It's complicated," I agreed.

His grin was wry, but I matched it with one of my own, feeling the bloom of camaraderie unfurl between us.

"The best things often are," he confirmed.

And I knew both of us were thinking about Aaron.

CHAPTER THIRTEEN

Boner

I'D SPENT YEARS WATCHIN' soulmates find each other, and I'd never once thought'a findin' that for myself.

It just seemed too good for the likes'a my luck and my life.

Findin' the club had been my once-in-a-lifetime miracle, so was it really fair to give a man more than that?

I hadn't thought so.

But now, leanin' against the first booth inside Eugene's Bar watchin' Blue serve her customers, I couldn't help but think she was made for me. Maybe it had nothin' to do with fairness, or maybe it did. Perhaps we'd both lived through our own trials and fuckin' horrible tribulations as some kinda payment for the wealth'a happiness that was comin' to us.

Would I change anythin' if it meant I got the chance to meet Blue that night at Evergreen Gas? The chance to have someone for my own again after years of loneliness?

The ache'a missin' Elsa would never cease, but she was safe, at least.

Hidden from the triad, livin' life on her terms. I had to find comfort in that, even if it meant we couldn't have a normal siblin' relationship. Even if it hurt like pressure on an old bruise to see King and Harleigh Rose fuckin' around and laughin', Dane and Lila spendin' quiet moments together out in nature slowly reconnectin' after years apart.

Curtains wasn't blood, but he was my brother, my best friend, a different kinda soulmate.

And if Elsa hadn't been taken by Seven Song, I'd never'a met Curtains or the club.

So even though it fucked with my head, I stood there watchin' this girl I wanted down to my bones and found some kinda peace for all the chaos'a my life, believin' it had led me to these people and this moment.

This girl with the ocean eyes and cornflower-blue hair and curves like some pagan fertility goddess. This girl whose spirit had weathered the worst kinda storms and emerged somehow still sweet with an edge of sass and independence that made my dick hard and my breath thin inside my lungs.

As if sensin' my gaze, she turned from deliverin' drinks to a table'a women and looked directly at me. The smile that claimed her full mouth was brighter than any'a the ones she'd been dolin' out around the bar.

And it was all for me.

I waited for her to saunter over to me on her high heels, hips swayin' enough to hypnotize, just so I could relish the sight'a her comin' toward me. When she stopped a foot away, head tipped back to maintain our gaze, I had to blink away the sun spots at the dazzle'a that sweet-lipped expression.

"Hey, Trouble," she teased, pokin' me in the chest over The Fallen patch on my cut.

"Hey, pretty Blue," I returned, achin' to pull her in for a kiss and resistin' only 'cause it was a busy weekend night at the bar and more than just The Fallen found refuge at Eugene's.

"I wasn't expecting you tonight."

"Couldn't stay away," I admitted with a little shrug. "'S been two full days since I saw you, and that's too fuckin' long."

Her entire face softened with awe, and fuck, it felt good to be on the receivin' end'a somethin' like that.

"Has anyone ever told you that you're really very lovely?" she asked, steppin' just a little closer as if she couldn't help herself.

"Nah, but I don't give a fuck what anyone else thinks'a me."

"You really don't, do you?"

"Care about my Prez, my club and their families, but outside that, hell no. You gotta earn my care."

She tipped her head coquettishly. "And what did I do to earn yours?"

I took a risk and glided my hand nearest to the booth around her hip, needin' to feel the soft heat'a her skin. "You were more brave and beautiful than anyone I'd ever seen."

She swallowed thickly, somehow shocked. "I...I always try to be brave. It's cool you saw that in me. Sometimes, I'm worried it's a lost cause."

"You're here, aren't you? Survivin' and thrivin' as much as you can even livin' caged." I bent closer. "I'll find the key to get you out, baby. Just like I got you outta that cage at Evergreen, yeah? I'm workin' on it."

And I was.

After the shit show in Vancouver yesterday, I'd spent the entire day at the clubhouse with Z and the brothers, figurin' out a game plan.

We knew where most of the fuckers lived or spent their time. Out at that farmhouse near Furry Creek. The advantage to them choosin' such a rural location meant we could take them out without havin' to worry about drawin' too much attention. Lion had shown up midday with a strange look on his face and offered some'a his own intel on the White Raiders, claimin' they had a party every Thursday night where all twenty-three men in the club should be present.

So in two weeks when all'a our brothers were back from runs, we were plannin' to hit them with the full weight'a The Fallen and crush them for good.

"You could still leave now," I reminded her.

"No, I told you, they wouldn't rest until I was found, especially if they knew I'd run to *you*. And I can't risk Grouch."

Understandin' clicked into place. "That's why you went back to them."

She bit her upper lip but nodded. "They took him, and when I made the exchange, I swore a blood oath that I wouldn't run again."

"Fine," I said, spittin' it like a curse. "You won't run. We'll make them do the runnin' if they're lucky enough to get away alive."

"Blue," one of the other servers called, indicatin' some'a her tables. "Stop flirting with Boner and get to work."

"Cindy," I hollered back. "Don't be jealous just 'cause Blue's the prettiest girl here tonight. I know you're used to ownin' that title."

Cindy rolled her eyes and waggled her finger at me. She was forty-five and gorgeous, but after a brutal divorce, she'd been feelin' like shit for the past few months, so I'd made a point to flirt with her and shoot the shit after her shift to keep her company.

"He's dangerous," she told Blue as she passed by to the other side'a the bar where a country rock band was settin' up on stage. "Silver-tongued devil."

Blue laughed that pretty, chimin' laugh and beamed up at me as she said, "Good thing I'm not easily charmed."

"Ah, well, I brought somethin' I'm hopin' will change that," I offered, pullin' the ungainly brown-wrapped package out from under my arm.

"What is it?" she asked, a little suspicious but mostly excited, rockin' forward on her toes as she touched her fingers to the paper.

I grinned. "Bought you flowers."

"Uh, I hate to break it to you, but you should *not* wrap flowers in brown paper. They should be in water in like...a vase."

I laughed, pushin' her forward by the hip. "Take your break now, and I'll show you what kinda flowers remind me'a you."

"My break's not for another hour," she argued, diggin' in her heels as I ushered her toward the bar and the door leadin' to the back rooms.

"Eugene, Blue's takin' her break," I shouted to him where he was slingin' beers behind the bar.

He only shot me a warnin' look. "Don't have sex in my office."

"Wouldn't dream'a it," I promised 'fore we disappeared through the door into the hallway.

"Aaron! You can't speak to my boss like that."

I shrugged, haltin' at the break room when I heard the sound'a women's voices inside and turnin' instead to open the door to the storage room. It smelled like beer and damp wood inside, an oddly pleasant combination especially underscored by the sweetness'a Blue's perfume.

"Why are we in here?" she asked.

"Privacy," I said a moment 'fore I crowded her into the wall and claimed that pink mouth the way I'd been hankerin' to since the first moment I saw her that night.

She tasted like bubble gum, the cool metal'a her Medusa piercin' a sexy contrast to the warmth of her slick tongue. Her surprised reluctance melted in a moment, her tray clatterin' to the ground at our feet so she could sink both hands in my hair and pull me even deeper into the kiss.

It took all my willpower to break our mouths apart and even then, I dragged my lips down her throat to her collarbone, nippin' at the skin there in a way that made her nipples bead behind the thin cotton'a her shirt.

A groan worked its way outta my throat, but I was too excited to see her unwrap her present to give in to lust first.

"Open your gift," I told her, still placin' open-mouthed kisses along her throat.

I could feel the vibration'a her laughter beneath her skin. "I will if you stop kissing me, but I don't really want you to stop."

"Greedy girl," I teased, palmin' one'a her heavy breasts to feel the hard peak'a her nipple and tweak it between two fingers. "Be good and open your present, Blue, and I'll be sure to give you another after you do."

Her eyes were blown straight to black beneath that long fringe'a lashes when I stepped back to hand her the three-foot package I'd leaned against the door. My heart fuckin' ached to see the way she stared down at it, a kid on Christmas who'd never been given any gifts 'til now.

Suddenly, I was fuckin' *nervous,* and I was never nervous.

The gift felt silly, really, not real art, not real expression like a poem or a paintin', but it was all I had to give. All I was really good at besides fixin' up a bike or car, or talkin' my way into people's lives or makin' someone laugh.

And I wanted her to have this 'cause what gift could I get a girl who couldn't show she was startin' to become mine?

The rush'a blood in my ears was almost loud enough to drown out her sweet little gasp as she tore open the paper and revealed the bouquet'a flowers I'd made for her.

Bunches'a blue and pink flowers tied with a bow all in neon coloured tubin' against a clear acrylic base.

"Aaron?" she breathed, lookin' from the sign up at me.

Wordlessly, I took it from her and plugged it into an outlet near the door, restin' it atop one'a the many kegs'a beer in the store room. With a flick'a the light switch, the room plummeted into darkness lit only by the pinks and blues'a the neon sign.

I walked back over to Blue, where she stood frozen against the wall, starin' at the sign with her hand in front'a her parted mouth, eyes made neon by the lights I'd bent into shape for her. I pushed a lock'a electric blue hair from her cheek so I could palm it, tiltin' her head up for a small kiss.

"Wanted to buy you flowers, but I knew you couldn't take them home with you, so I figured this would have to do," I explained.

"They're so beautiful," she whispered thickly, damp eyes reflectin' the shape'a the flowers in the dark as they stared up at me almost helplessly. Her fingers reached up to cling to the shirt beneath my cut. "No one's ever made me something before. Let alone something so lovely."

Somethin' unlocked inside my chest like I'd been given access to a previously closed chamber of my heart. At that moment, I would've reached inside my own chest to gift that to her if it meant keepin' that soft look'a reverent joy on her face.

"I'm glad you like them," I said a little awkwardly 'cause there was this strange heat in my cheeks and angst in my bones that seemed like... bashfulness, and I wasn't used to it.

"I love them," she corrected, gettin' on her tiptoes so she could haul me down for a kiss. "Prettiest flowers I've ever seen. Where did you get them?"

The back'a my neck itched with heat, so I scrubbed at it as I pulled away. "Uh, I made 'em."

She blinked. "You actually *made* that? Like with your hands?"

The chuckle dissolved the last'a my uncharacteristic shyness. "Yeah, Blue. It's a hobby'a mine, I guess you could say. Makin' neon art. Eugene was actually the one to teach me. Half the shit on the walls in the bar is mine."

"Wow." She looked over at the sign and back at me. "Oh my gosh, you must have made the sign at my station at Lin's, too? You're amazing, Aaron. You'll have to tell me how you do it someday."

"Yeah?" God, I felt like a kid, giddy bubbles in my gut, warmth bloomin' in my chest.

"Yeah," she said firmly. "But not now, I only get fifteen minutes for my break, and I can think of better things to do."

"Oh, yeah?" My voice dropped three octaves, gravelly from bein' pulled up from my gut.

Her wicked grin flashed neon bright 'fore she dropped to her knees and went for my belt. My breath shuddered outta me when her nimble fingers made quick work'a the clasp and zipper, openin' my jeans to slip a hand into my boxers and pull out my rapidly hardenin' cock.

She hummed with pleasure at the sight'a me in her grip, lickin' her lips unconsciously as she stared at me.

"I love that you're pierced," she groaned before liftin' my cock to lick over the ladder'a metal rungs on the underside'a my shaft.

I shivered at the pleasure, shoulders rattlin'.

"I don't know if I can even fit my mouth around you," Blue admitted, settlin' more comfortably onto her knees and raisin' her other hand to wrap it alongside the first on my length. "But I'm going to love trying."

"Shit," I hissed as she opened that pink mouth around my tip and sucked me inside.

She couldn't fit much'a me inside, and the frown'a frustration on her face shouldn't'a been so hot, but my girl wasn't a quitter. She pulled off, lookin' up at me while she spat on my cock once, twice, and then slicked me up with a twist of both fists 'til I was totally slick with spit and precum. Rock hard now, she could barely fit me in her small hands, and the sight'a that was hot enough to make my spine tingle with electric heat.

"Fuck," I ground out as she bent her mouth to my head again, suckin' hard as she twisted her grip on my dick, each hand in a different direction.

My head thunked against the wall, hands flyin' to her head to bury in that thick, silken cobalt-coloured hair to hang on for dear fuckin' life as she threatened to suck my life force through my cock.

It was wet and messy, spit smeared over her chin, pantin' around my tip while she squeezed precum onto her tongue before sinkin' back down just a little too far to test her gag reflex 'fore pullin' up and wringin' me with her dexterous hands.

Every inch'a my flesh was on fire, my very fuckin' bones rattlin' with the pleasure she was sendin' like shock waves through my core. In the dark, only the light'a my neon flowers to guide us, it felt like we were alone in the world, absconded in a den'a pleasure and safe to indulge in the furious need we'd been harbourin' for weeks now.

It'd been too long, and my patience was beyond frayed.

So I wasn't surprised when her wet fingers brushed low over my piercings, my balls, and pressed into that sensitive span'a skin behind them that my control ripped to shreds with an almost audible tear.

I swallowed half the roar that rose in my throat and bent double, pullin' her up by the armpits so she was suddenly in my arms. I was already walkin' to the back'a the small room, her full, sweet ass in my hands, her wet, gaspin' mouth against mine as I lowered her onto the shallow metal rim'a a beer keg. She clasped the edges to balance as I reached between us to push up her denim miniskirt and pull down her panties in two quick moves. Her pussy was already slick, pink and prettier than any art I could ever make for her.

When I told her that, she hauled me in close with one hand fisted in my shirt while the other grasped my cock, bringin' it tight to her hot cunt.

"You're not ready for me, baby," I warned her between suckin', luscious kisses. "Be patient."

"Fuck patience." She bit at my lower lip with sharp teeth. "I've waited weeks to feel you stretch me open on this big cock, and I'm not waiting any longer."

A red mist of pleasure blurred my reality and the edges'a my usual control. The heat and slick'a her pussy against the head'a my cock seared through me, tuggin' me by the balls to bury myself inside her even though I knew she was too tight to take me like that.

But when I reached down to slide a finger inside her, she hissed and snapped her teeth at me. It was feral, animalistic, her eyes black as she leaned back to bare her little teeth.

"Fuck me, Boner," she demanded.

And the shreds'a my control vanished in the echo'a my club name in her mouth.

I pressed inside slow but unyieldin', conquerin' her inch by intractable inch. She shivered and shook in my arms as I held her by the round curves of her ass, pullin' her down on my shaft as I thrust deeper and deeper.

"Boner, Boner, Boner," she slurred, lost to the sensation'a bein' overfull as I worked myself to the hilt inside her. "God, yes. You were meant to fill me up like this."

"Fuck yeah, baby," I grunted as I ground into her, the piercings at the base'a my shaft lightin' up with pleasure so bright it left white spots in my vision and made Blue *keen* in my ear. "You're on birth control, yeah?"

She unlocked her teeth from the side'a my throat to gasp, "Ah! Yeah."

"Good," I growled, pullin' her slowly off my cock 'til only the bulbous head remained inside her, the pink clasp'a her pussy so pretty around my blood-dark shaft. When I snapped my hips forward, her head fell back between her shoulders bonelessly. "'Cause I'm gonna fuck you hard and fill you up with cum knowin' you'll spend the rest'a your shift with my seed leakin' outta your swollen pussy."

She convulsed in my arms, limbs tightenin' to vises around my torso, teeth scrapin' over my pec through my shirt. "Jesus, Bones, yes! Please. I wanna feel like I'm yours."

"You are mine," I grunted, movin' a hand from her ass to her hair, wrappin' it up tight in my fist so I could cant her head back, and her lust-dazed eyes were pinned on mine. "Now in the dark, tomorrow in the light. Painted in neons or sunlight or starlight, you're mine, Blue. You get me?"

I wished I could fuck her hard enough to brand my possession into every inch'a her, inside and out.

"Are you sure?" she asked on a breathy hiccup, clingin' so tight, her pussy a hot clutch around me that threatened to steal my sanity, that for one moment, I almost didn't hear the heartbreakin' uncertainty.

I gave her every last inch'a my cock, grindin' her down on me 'til she was impaled, and then loosened my hold on her hair to wrap my hand gently around her throat. The bruises Rooster had left were gone, but I knew she understood my gesture by the flutter'a her lids and the little whimper that leaked from her throat.

Holdin' her like that, inside her and around her and balancin' her completely in my arms, I tried to convey just how fuckin' safe she was with me. How I'd protect her and cherish her with my body. Instinctually, I curved around her further, like a shield against the world.

"Never been so sure'a anythin' in my whole fuckin' life," I whispered like a confession 'cause it felt holy holdin' her here in the dark with only my neon light to guide us. "You give me a chance, I'll show you just how fuckin' wonderful you are, Blue, and I think I'd be happy to spend my whole life doin' it."

"Don't make me fall in love with you," she begged, but she was only holdin' me closer. "I won't be able to handle it if I lose you."

"Won't promise not to love you and definitely won't promise not to try my fuckin' damnedest to make you love me, but I fuckin' swear it, Blue," I promised, solemnly. "You won't lose me if you don't wanna."

"I don't wanna," she echoed after a moment. "I want to be yours more than anything. And I want you to be mine."

"I already am," I said, startin' to fuck into her again, slow and steady, a meetin'a the ocean lappin' at the shoreline. "Feel like I was born with your name written on my bones, and I was just waitin' to find ya."

"Bones," she gasped, and the transformation'a my nickname felt right in her mouth.

So I kissed it off her tongue and increased my tempo, just long, smooth strokes in and outta her greedy pussy, a grind at the base so she could feel the effect on her clit and the ridges'a my piercings inside'a her. And every time she gasped my name, I swallowed it down my throat like a drug. It sent me higher and higher 'til finally, the hiss'a my name streamed through her lips, and she imploded around my cock, shockin' pulses that milked me so hard I had no choice but to come too. The deeply coiled pleasure at my spine sprang loose, and I jerked as I spilled inside her, comin' so hard all I could see behind my squeezed shut lids was neon blue.

My neon Blue.

I pumped her full'a cum like I'd promised, wringin' the last'a her orgasm from her in little jerks and shudders. And when we were finished, I collected her up into my arms, still connected, and hugged her close. She buried her head in my neck, pantin' softly against my rapid pulse, and dug her nails into my back.

We stood like that a long time, and that quiet intimacy, almost more than the bone-brandin' sex, meant everythin' to me.

'Cause it was peace.

And my girl hadn't had a lotta that in her life.

So it felt fuckin' brilliant to be the one to shelter her.

"I'm heavy," she protested after a while.

"Nah, you feel just right."

"I have to go back to work, then," she said on an unhappy sigh.

I made an unhappy sound in my throat, but she was right so I carefully pulled her off me and settled her on her feet, bracin' her arms as her knees wobbled. She laughed at my cocky grin. When I bent to pull her panties up, I pressed my lips to her mound in a little kiss and then pulled her skirt down.

"There, presentable again even though my cum's gonna be leakin' outta ya all night," I proclaimed.

I wished fiercely I could bottle her laughter.

"I like it," she admitted, bitin' into her lip.

"Me too." I reached beneath her skirt to pat her pussy, already moistenin' her underwear. "Gonna be hard again when I climb into bed thinkin'a ya. Be a good girl and send me a photo'a your puffy, cum-wet pussy 'fore you clean yourself up, yeah?"

A little shiver made her teeth click together. "Yeah, I can do that."

"You okay?" I checked, bendin' at the knee to bring me closer to eye level. "You seem shaky."

A huff'a air through parted lips. "I feel shaky, honestly. Probably because you're changing my whole world."

"For the better," I agreed.

"Yeah," she said softly, movin' her hand to palm my neck the way I'd done to her, fingers brushin' the wings'a the owl tattooed there. "Why the owl?"

I could feel the grin hangin' crooked on my face. "Figured I could use a little wisdom in my life." When she only narrowed her eyes at me, I gave in with a shrug. "It's a symbol'a self-actualization. I wanted to be courageous and insightful enough to create a good life for myself despite my circumstances. First tatt I ever got."

"It suits you," she complimented.

"Why the bluebird?" I asked 'cause I'd been wonderin', too.

It took place'a prominence on her left deltoid, surrounded by leaves and flowers.

"Bluebird," she said with a small, wistful smile. "My mum called me that when I was little before she left. It's why I first dyed my hair and got this tattoo. They're symbols of hope and good news arriving soon."

I smoothed her hair away from her face to kiss her forehead, her pierced nose, her sweet mouth. Empathy for her made pain pulse through me like a wound carved outta my centre.

"It's okay," she whispered, soothin' me even though she was the one needin' it. "I have a feeling it's finally arrived."

And when she tugged my ears down to kiss my mouth, I knew there was nothin' in this world I wouldn't do to make that hope for joy a reality.

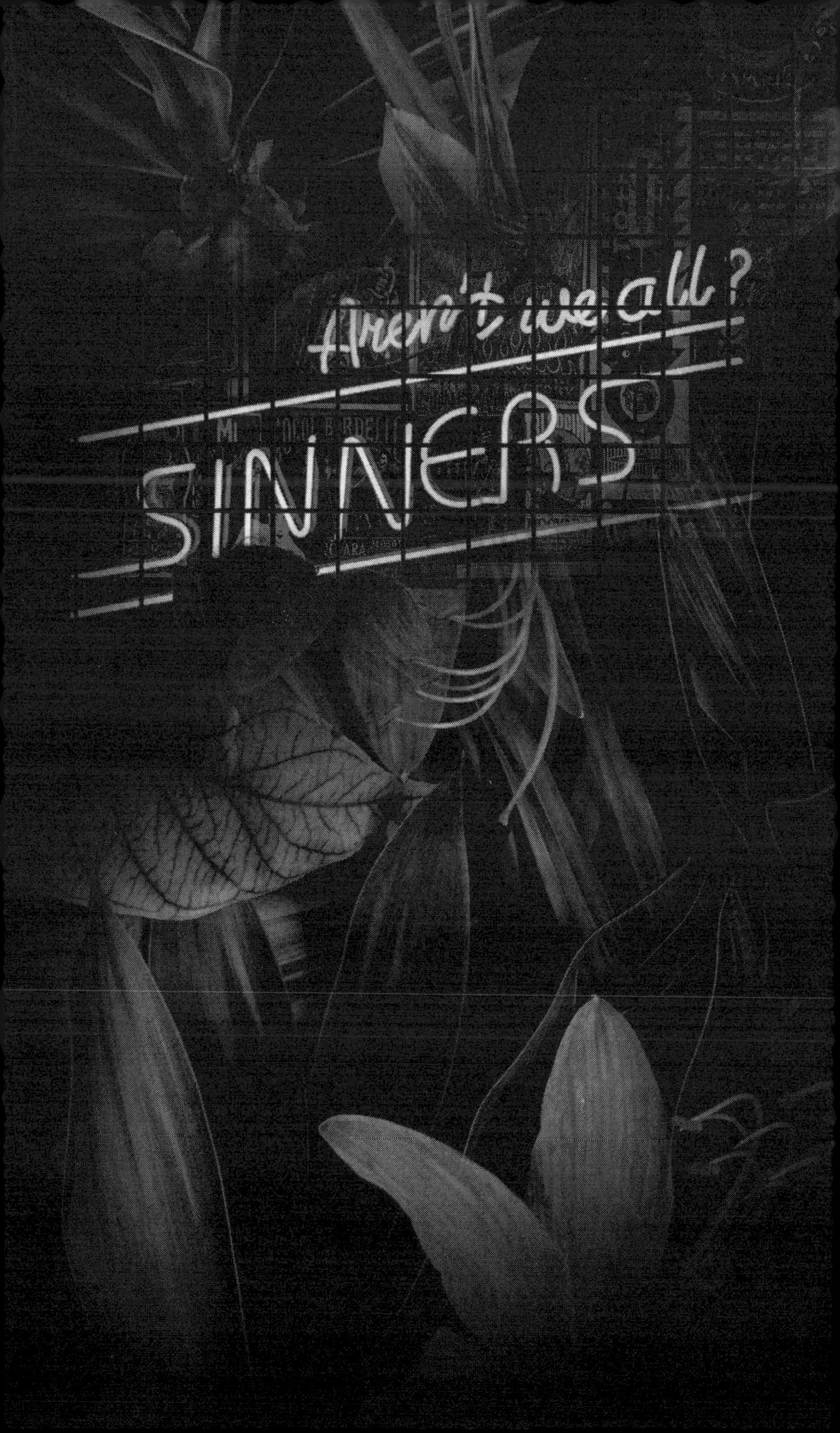
Aren't we all?
SINNERS

CHAPTER FOURTEEN

Blue

I T WAS DISORIENTATING to live two lives simultaneously that were so wildly different. One heaven and the other hell. My time with the Raiders at the Furry Creek farm and my time with Aaron and at work with Lin and Eugene, The Fallen men and Old Ladies coming in for appointments and beers respectively as if they wanted to get to know me just as much as Aaron did.

Well, maybe not just as much.

When we weren't together, which wasn't nearly as much as either of us would've liked, we were texting.

Bones: I miss your mouth.

Bones: And your pussy.

Bones: I want to put my tongue inside'a you.

Blue: My mouth or my pussy?

Bones: Don't make me choose.

Bones: No, wait, pussy.

Blue: Are you always this horny?

Bones: You can blame yourself for that. It's gotten so bad I pop a boner when I just see the colour blue.

Two weeks passed in perfect, TERRIFYING BALANCE.

I loved going to work. Helping other women feel beautiful might have seemed trivial to some, but it filled my heart with joy. Confidence was so hard won in a society that told us we had to be perfect in all ways and all things, especially as women. So seeing the look of awed gratitude and self-love on the faces of my clients was incredibly rewarding. To my surprise, I even loved serving at Eugene's, and not just because it kept me too busy to spend much time at the Raiders' farmhouse. The clientele was an eclectic bunch from bikers to Entrance locals to those passing by on the way to or from the north looking for a cold beer to combat the hot June air. I met someone new and fascinating almost every day and squirrelled away the cash tips in my back room locker to keep Rooster from claiming them as well as most of my paycheck.

Rooster was busier than usual, too, working on securing funding from that unknown 'sponsor' who wanted to see The Fallen ended. But there was chatter about issues back in Alberta. Apparently, Hazard had forcibly taken over a small independent club in Lethbridge that resulted in serious casualties on both sides.

I was happy to hear it because it meant my husband, in name only, would not return for another few weeks.

Which gave Lion, the lawyer he introduced me to, Mr. White, and me enough time to file the paperwork.

Apparently, I could be legally unwed in as little as three weeks.

I hadn't told Aaron yet. Mostly because I was terrified something would happen and the uncontested divorce either wouldn't work or wouldn't even matter in the end. But also because I was a closet romantic and the idea of handing him my divorce papers as a gift was too good a dream to give up on.

In the meantime, I was having a secret love affair with the best man I had ever known.

If you had told me a few months ago I'd be falling in love with an outlaw biker, I would have laughed you out of the room, but it happened so naturally. From the very first moment I'd seen him swaggering into the gas station looking like a bad boy wet dream, he'd been leaving little pieces of himself inside me and stealing sections of my soul for himself.

And that was before he'd put on the full-court press of the past two weeks.

He spent time at Eugene's every single shift I worked, even if it was only for an hour just to flirt with me when I passed by on my rounds and steal a make-out session in the break room. He came into Lin's for a haircut so I could get my fingers in that gorgeous head of dark hair, trimming the sides close and leaving the top long enough to flop over his forehead without product or push back from his face like a modern-day James Dean. That day, it was me dragging him into the parking lot for a quick tussle in the back seat of my Mazda.

The best part, though, were the signs.

He left them all over town at places he knew I'd go.

The night after we fucked in the store room, there was one hung up against the same wall we'd made out against, red lights curved into the shape of a voluptuous woman, the kind of thing you might see at a strip club.

But I knew it was modelled after me by the plush form and the short, wavy hair.

There was "I licked it so it's mine" hanging up over the server's station in Eugene's one day, "You are exactly where you are meant to be" at Lin's another, and "Miss me yet?" glowing pink inside the door of Revved & Ready clothing store when I went on Lila's recommendation to pick up some new clothes for work.

My favourite appeared in Honey Bear Café & Bakery where Mei had asked me to meet her for coffee so I could meet her best friend and Axe-Man's daughter, Cleo. They were sitting beneath it, one word repeated three times from dark to light shades of blue. *Baby, baby, baby.*

By the look of smug pride on Mei's face when I gaped at her, I knew she and Boner had orchestrated it together.

"He made me one," Cleo had confessed in that soft, almost muted voice of hers. "Because I have...issues sleeping in the dark."

"What's it say?" I asked, without probing about what trauma had left her with awkwardly chopped hair and a gaunt face with haunted, sunken eyes.

A flicker of a smile around a sullen mouth. "Fuck the monsters."

I'd laughed gently, falling more in love with him for taking care of this girl who clearly needed all the gentle attention she could get.

It gave me the courage to ask, "Have you ever thought about doing something with all that pretty hair, Cleo? I'd love to get my hands on it."

She'd blinked at me, subconsciously leaning closer to Mei, who put an arm around her shoulders. I watched patiently as she chewed her lower lip and then confessed, "I told Mei once I thought about maybe dyeing it pink."

"Like Chibiusa," Mei added with a little grin for her friend before explaining to me. "From Sailor Moon."

I didn't know the reference, but I nodded because Cleo's flawless pale skin and sage green eyes would look stunning with pale pink hair.

"When you're ready, I'm your girl, okay?" I offered. "And speaking from experience, having fun-coloured hair automatically makes every day a little happier."

"Yeah?" she'd asked, her gaze peeling back my layers with nimble fingers. "If you say so."

And she said it like she believed me.

She didn't make an appointment or anything, but I couldn't say I was shocked when she showed up at Lin's and asked if I could trim her unruly bob into something a little sleeker.

And I couldn't say we both didn't tear up when we looked at her stylish, tousled bob in the mirror, and she'd asked me through a tight throat if I had time to do her make-up too.

Without hesitation, I'd pushed back my next client and painted Cleo's beautiful, tragic face in soft colours that made her eyes pop and the bruises beneath disappear. When Kodiak, one of Aaron's brothers whom I didn't know well because he barely spoke, came into Lin's to pick her up, he'd hesitated for a full second with his foot raised mid-step before he recovered.

When I told Aaron about it later that night at Eugene's, he just shook his head, curled an arm around my waist, and murmured, "Not everyone's as reckless as me, baby Blue. I saw you and knew in my bones I had to have you no matter what 'cause I knew I'd be good for you if you just let me in. The Bear doesn't think he's good for anyone and definitely not for Cleo after everythin' she's been through."

"What's she been through?" I whispered, almost afraid to ask.

It was late enough that the bar was almost empty, and I was the last server in the place. Eugene had entrusted me with my first closing shift with the kind of ceremony I'd come to expect from him.

"You're closing tonight," he'd said, sliding a set of keys along the bar top so they hit my hand where I was making paper napkin rollups with cutlery. "Don't fuck it up."

And of course, Aaron was waiting it out with me, nursing an IPA as he sketched out a new design for a client at the garage who wanted a *pickle* riding a motorcycle on the side of his gas tank. Curtains, King and Cressida had kept him company for a long time, but King and Cress had a baby at home, and Curtains seemed a little awkward around me, so he'd left when they had. I knew it bothered Aaron that his best friend was the only member of The Fallen family who seemed to have an issue with me, but I figured I should leave them to hash it out.

Honestly, even though I wanted the red-headed hacker to like me, he was the least of my problems.

"I'll tell ya when you kick the stragglers out," Aaron said, pulling me back to the present.

He wore that somber face, brows pinched, stubble-shadowed jaw tight with strain.

I knew it wouldn't be a good story.

But when I finally closed and locked the front doors behind Bruce, one of our local, friendly drunks, and went to sit on Aaron's lap at the table, I realized nothing could've prepared me for the truth about Cleo's history with The Prophet serial killer.

When he finished speaking, I sat mutely in his lap, eyes fixed unseeing on a neon sign over his shoulder that depicted a cupid with devil horns and a forked tail.

"She went through hell," I murmured, finally, heartbroken for the sweet, brittle girl I hardly knew.

"Yeah." Something in Aaron's voice, a graveness I'd never heard before, drew my gaze to his. Those dark eyes seemed to be filled with the ink I needed to write out the feelings battling inside my chest.

"Not one of you is without scars, are you?" I asked.

"No," he agreed. "Curtains's mum was killed on Christmas mornin' when he was eighteen. A serial killer murdered Bat's wife, brutalized Cleo, and stalked Bea. Loulou's fought and beat cancer twice, and she's only twenty-three. Zeus's been to jail twice, both times with two young kids at home, once for savin' an innocent kid and the other 'cause he was set up by a corrupt cop. Cress's been nailed to a chair and lived through believin' her husband was dead for months just like the rest'a us. Lila's dad killed her mum in front'a her when she was fuckin' six years old. Wrath's woman was killed by her father, and Harleigh Rose stabbed Lion in the fuckin' chest to save his own life. There's no shortage'a sad stories amongst The Fallen."

"I guess it bonds you." I thought about my brother Red, a total stranger to me now and even back then. Rooster's differing forms of neglect and abuse had merely formed a wedge between us. If I saw him now, I wondered if I'd even recognize him.

"You could say that. All'a us have felt broken at some point in our lives, maybe even wondered if it's worth it to go on. We've been disillusioned and lost, and the club gives people a purpose to tether them and a long lead to give them the slack they need to recover on their own terms. No one here has to be any one way or one kinda person. The lines are blurred 'cause we all learned the hard way that life's painted in shades'a grey instead'a black and white."

I hummed my agreement as I processed his biker wisdom, stroking the owl on the strong column of his throat like a touchstone. So I was still a little lost in my thoughts when he jostled me in his lap to straddle him, his big hands palming either side of my face.

"I think it's how we all know deep in our bones when we fall for the right person," he murmured, eyes dark and intent on mine, expression almost harsh with sincerity. "They add colour back to our greyscale lives. Just like you added the colour blue to mine."

"Bones," I whispered because transforming his nickname felt as right as the taste of it on the back of my tongue. As right as the feeling he alchemized in my skin, blood and bones. "I don't understand how I got so lucky to have you in my life. I know being together in secret isn't enough, but it's better than anything I ever had before."

"It's enough," he swore like an oath signed in his own blood. "It's more than enough to spend any minute with you. We'll get to it one day, the ever-after shit without the obstacles between us, but 'til then, Blue, I'm more than fuckin' happy with what I got right now."

There was a gasp of hot air between our mouths, and then he kissed me, and that felt like a promise too. Like a solemn pledge to love me and take me however I came for as long as I wanted to give myself to him. I ate it off his tongue and fed it back to him with all the near-violent lust and yearning in my heart. My nails scratched the short hair at the back of his neck, then reached up to tangle in the long, silken strands so I could pin him to my voracious mouth. He matched my hunger with a fierce growl that rumbled between my teeth as he stood suddenly, my weight perched in his arms, to stalk over to the pool table.

He lay me down slowly, the muscles in his torso and arms flexing around me like iron. It did something to me, knowing that all that strength was being used for tenderness and not violence. Under other circumstances, I might have cried, knowing that this outlaw, this man who had no doubt killed and beaten and potentially maimed, would *never* lift a hand to me. Even more than that, he would use that Olympian strength and street-smart strategy to protect me against anything that came.

I tore my lips from his, suddenly overcome by the need to show him just how alive and fearless he made me feel.

"Sit down," I murmured against his lips as he tried to kiss me again.

"Kinda have other plans goin' right now, Blue." His mouth moved to my ear, teeth nipping at my lobe, then down to the sensitive skin of my neck where he placed luscious, open-mouthed kisses.

I shivered, trying to hold on to my slippery willpower. "Trust me, you'll like this. Just sit down for me."

In the past, my orders had no weight in the bedroom with my husband. It was an authoritarian space with Hazard as the master and I the lowly servant.

But here, in the middle of a biker bar, Aaron proved that my voice would always matter to him.

Slowly, coiling that hard, lean body back from mine with infinite care, he stepped away from the pool table until his knees hit the chair behind him. Without tearing his heated gaze from me, he pulled it out and sat down.

Even in the dimmed lights, I could see the thick wedge of his erection tenting his jeans.

Power soared through me, lightening my bones until I felt like I could fly. A bird freed at least momentarily from its cage, all I wanted to do was preen my feathers and show off exactly who I was to the only man who had ever deserved it.

I tugged my phone out of my back pocket and secured it to the Bluetooth speakers in the bar. A moment later, "Caged Bird" by Myles Cameron spilled through the room. It was a song I listened to every day on my way to work because it reminded me so much of me, of us, and I'd been meaning to share it with him.

It was just sexy enough, the beat rich and erotic, to use it now to strip off the last of my shields.

Aaron watched with lowered brows, tongue touching the edge of his mouth as I sat on my knees, sliding on the felt until they were as wide as I could comfortably spread them. My hands found my breasts through my yellow floral sundress, plumping them in the structured cups so that they spilled dangerously over the fabric. The stained glass light above the pool table cast me in golden light, every inch illuminated so there was nothing to hide. Not the soft thickness of my spread thighs as I slowly teased the hem of my dress up over the pale skin or the swell of my hips and the slope of my trembling belly. There wasn't a hard surface on me, all exaggerated curves and the slight dip of my waist between them.

But all the ugly voices that had taken residence in my head in the tone of my father, his brothers, my soon-to-be ex-husband were all crushed under the sheer intensity of Boner's lust-filled, reverent gaze on every inch of my body.

"So fuckin' gorgeous," he said like words were pulled from him, an exorcism of deeply buried belief. "I could never get tired'a lookin' at all'a the beauty that's you."

His praise stoked the fire in my gut even higher and fanned the flames of my confidence until I felt like a goddess on that black felt.

I lifted the dress over my head and threw it at him.

He caught it in one hand, brought it to his face to inhale the scent of me, and then dropped it on the table without taking his gaze from me for a second.

Clad only in my simple blue bra and panties, I tipped forward onto my hands to show him the heavy sway of my breasts as I rocked to the throbbing beat, circling my hips and tossing my hair.

"Fuuuuck," he cursed softly, squeezing his cock through the denim. "You're killin' me."

Good, I thought gleefully, sliding my leg through my hands and then flipping over to face away from him, ass bared for his regard. I twerked my curves, jiggling my ass in a way I knew looked sexy because it even turned me on when I caught sight of it in the mirror over the bar.

I looked shameless and sensual, a temptress winding a spell around a man who was helpless to resist it.

Tossing my hair over my shoulder, I saw Aaron sprawled in the wooden chair, thighs splayed, hand still clenched hard over his erection.

"Touch yourself for me," I told him in a voice I barely recognized, deep with lust and power. "Pull that thick cock out and show me how much I turn you on."

Aaron slouched deeper in the chair as he slowly undid the big silver buckle of his belt and then dragged the zipper of his jeans down tooth by tooth. I was almost panting as I moved sinuously to the music, gaze hooked by his steady, intentional movements.

"You see what you do to me?" he rasped as one hand dipped into his boxers and pulled out that huge dick, thick and heavily veined, the head already plump and plum purple with blood.

I wanted to fall to my knees and lave it with my tongue.

But this was *my* show, and Aaron was the one who would end up on his knees for me.

I sat back on my heels, my ass plumped by the pose. Facing away from him still, I undid the hook of my bra and let it slide down one arm, then the other before dangling it off my fingers and letting it drop to the floor. I knee-stepped to the side so I was in profile to him and arched my back, breasts proudly displayed, an s-shaped presentation of every one of my curves.

I could hear his shuddered exhale over the current of the next song and grinned smugly at the results of my lewd display. I'd never done anything like this. I had never before felt empowered by my own sexuality, and in truth, it was both of us turning me on now. Every incredibly gorgeous inch of him and every inch of me, beautiful because I *liked* myself and so, wonderfully, did he.

Shaking my hair back in a blue swirl, I faced him again, extending my legs one at a time as I shimmied out of my panties so I was naked under the spotlight of the pool table light. I tossed the damp garment at him and watched with cat-like contentment as he snatched the cotton from the air and wrapped it around his erection.

"Fuckin' stunnin'," Aaron growled, his fist tight around that straining shaft, the tip wet with precum as it slid through my panties. "Touch yourself for me, baby. Show me how wet you are."

I shivered as my fingers delved from between my breasts, down my stomach to the slick heat between my thighs. A quick dip inside my aching entrance and then I lifted my fingers to the light to show him how wet I was. His mouth fell open on a ragged gasp as I slid them slowly into my open mouth and sucked.

"Jesus fuck," he said, his entire body tensing in the chair. "I'll die if I don't get my hands on you."

"Then come here," I beckoned, leaning back on my elbows as if I did this kind of thing every day.

While inside my chest, my heart thudded like a war drum and my blood ran so hot I thought it would set fire to my skin.

When he stalked across the space and reached for me, I placed my high-heeled left foot against his chest to stop him temporarily.

"I don't think I'm quite ready to take you," I drawled, but a little smile played at my mouth because this was *fun* in a way sex never had been before.

A wicked grin played around Aaron's full mouth in that short dark beard. I laughed in shock as he growled, tugging me by the hips up into the air slightly so he could bend and fix his mouth to my pussy like a starving man.

I fell to my back on the table, scrambling for purchase against the felt as he feasted on me. The wet, slick sounds of his mouth working over my clit, fucking into my core, sucking at my lips and biting at my inner thighs were sexier than the heavy bass of the song pulsing through the speakers. When I couldn't find anything to sink my fingers into, I clutched at his shoulders and hair, writhing even as I pulled him closer.

The orgasm that came too quickly almost scared me, barreling toward me like a runaway train. When it hit with one sucking kiss over my clit, I fractured limb by limb, every part of me imploding around the bright hot sensation at my core.

"Bones," I cried out, shaking apart in his firm hold.

"Yeah, baby," he encouraged, licking lightly at my clit to pull even more pleasure from me without turning it to agony. "Gimme that sweet cum."

Before I'd even finished, he was fucking into me with two fingers, twisting and rubbing until that place inside me lit up like one of his neon signs. Pleasure throbbed through me in shocking, vibrant waves reducing my thoughts to rubble.

"Bones, Bones, ohmygod, *fuck*!" I chanted as he took me higher and higher in a slow, steady build this time.

"Gonna make you come 'til you beg me to stop," he warned me almost viciously. "Can't get enough'a the way you taste."

I shivered as he shifted the fingers inside me to press a thumb over my asshole, circling and pressing just enough to bring the nerve endings buzzing to life. It felt as if I was going to come straight out of my skin, sensation stripping me of everything but the feel of Aaron inside me, anchoring me to the world by those clever fingers and smooth tongue. Desperate for something more to keep me from evaporating into nothing, I grabbed his hand from my hip and tugged it to my mouth, clamping my teeth around the pulse beating hard against the thin skin of his wrist.

Aaron swore savagely against my wet folds before flicking my swollen clit and pressing that seeking thumb just inside my tight ass.

My body tensed like a strung bow, arching off the pool table, thighs clutching his head, hand fisted in his hair and the other around his arm so I could bite, bite, bite down on his flesh, the taste of him coalescing with the final blow to my system that shattered me into pieces. I pulsed aground his fingers, legs shaking, voice trembling around a scream that was muffled against his flesh as I came and came and came until I was floating in a white mist of gentle contentment.

Only the feeling of Aaron's heavy cock slapping against my pussy shocked me back to life. I came to with a gasp, eyes wide at the electric sensation as he gently beat my cunt with his steely hard length. His eyes were full black as he knelt over me at the edge of the pool table. He'd discarded his jeans, boxers, shirt and cut, so every inch of his naked form glowed golden above me, coiled and ready to spring into action.

A sudden thought had me saying, "Put your cut back on."

He shuddered but shook it from the tangle of his shirt before tugging it on. The open leather framed his muscle-quilted torso, the silver chains above the tight pecs and the stack ladder of muscles in his abdominals. It drew my gaze down farther to the short copse of black hair at the base of that spectacular cock, thick and heavy as he slapped it in rhythm to the music against my swollen sex.

"Fuck me, Boner," I begged, arching back, letting my legs fall open even wider.

He splayed a hand on my chest, pinning me to the felt in a way that felt possessive and so right the touch burned straight through to brand my bones.

Something about him at that moment was almost scary. All the good humour and fun-loving charm were stripped from his expression, revealing the strong bones and the eye-squinting brightness of his desire to own me like this.

"You're mine," he told me in a rough, biting tone as he lifted my hips onto his thighs and angled his cock to my entrance. "Do you feel it?"

A slight rock of his hips slotted him just inside, but he didn't rush, swaying back and forth a little deeper every time until I was hypnotized by the oceanic rhythm and the erotic tensing of all that golden-tanned muscle framed by the cut that made him the outlaw, the *man*, he was.

"Yes," I hissed as he pressed impossibly deeper and deeper. "I feel you in my fucking bones."

"Yeah," he grunted, taking my hand to press it to his chest so I could feel the wild hum of his heartbeat. "Bone deep, Blue."

"Bone deep," I agreed on a shocked breath as he tugged me up into his arms so I was impaled on the wide length of him and straddling his knees.

He held me still with one hand on my hip and the other coiled around my hair so he could fuck up into me, slow and slight so every thrust ground the hair at his base against my sensitive clit. When my eyes closed as another orgasm started to curl around my hips, he tugged sharply on my hair.

"Eyes on me while I take this pretty pussy," he ordered.

Oh yes, I loved this side of him. Dark and dangerous and stripped of that veneer of civility.

"Watch me as I take you apart," he said as he snapped his hips brutally up into mine so pain edged the pleasure cutting through the ribbons on my sanity until I was only hanging by a thread.

"Keep those fuckin' gorgeous blues on me while I come deep inside you. Love leavin' my cum in this gorgeous cunt, knowin' you're mine more than anyone else's."

"Yes," I cried as my neck lost tension and my head fell back between my shoulders, my hair tickling my sweaty shoulders. "I love feeling you when you're gone. Sometimes, before I shower when I get back from work, I use it to touch myself. Fucking your seed back inside me."

"Fuck yeah," he growled, dipping his head to nip at my neck. "Such a good girl for me. One day soon, after I come inside you, I'll eat you out and fuck you again. Love the taste'a me merged with you."

My head snapped forward, teeth boring into Aaron's pec as my orgasm electrified my senses, vision whiting out, then fading to black like a power outage. Limbs shaking in the bracket of his strong arms until suddenly they were limp. Pussy spasming, milking him, desperate for that promised cum, and the moment I felt him grunt against my throat and kick inside me, heat flooding my sensitive folds, I called out in triumph.

And even though he held tight in the aftermath, his knees no doubt hurting from the unforgiving felt, our skin too sticky for comfort, I felt freer than I'd ever been. Like Aaron had broken open my glass cage and let me taste a life I might have if I believed in him. One where I'd never have to worry about the monsters under my bed again.

"Bone deep, Blue," he said into my hair, stroking a big, rough hand down my spine. "Forever."

"Bone deep," I echoed because it was the truth.

No matter what happened, this man was a part of me now, as elemental as my blood and marrow.

But I couldn't give him back his forever because I was still too scared, one foot still deep in the mire of my past, to trust in his belief that a girl like me living the life I did could ever have the "ever-after shit."

CHAPTER FIFTEEN

Boner

THINGS WERE ABOUT AS good as they could get, which should've been enough to warn me of the incomin' storm. Life never stayed peaceful for long in my world. It was the price'a the kinda joy we sought and rules we made. Someone was always gunnin' for what was ours and we'd spend our lives tryna defend it. But it was easy to be complacent when I spent my days workin' my dream job at Hephaestus Auto with my brothers, visitin' Blue at Lin's to take her take-out curly fries and milkshakes for lunch from Stella's Diner 'cause my girl was addicted, shootin' the shit with brothers or locals at Eugene's at night just to be in her orbit, steal a word or a kiss or two.

It was funny how simple heaven could be. The right girl, the right friends, laughter, and harmony. It was all I needed to feel like a fuckin' king, like the world wanted me to gorge myself on the kinda happy I never imagined couldn't last.

Even knowin' my girl went home to the wrong house at night.

The only way I could stand it was knowin' she was so busy workin' two jobs and Rooster was so busy tryin' to take over *ours* that she rarely saw him or the club members for any length'a time long enough to do her harm. And I checked for bruises every time I could.

What I couldn't check for were the cuts beneath the skin.

But I tried to temper those with all the love I had wellin' up in my heart.

And by puttin' my own plans in motion.

Just that afternoon, I'd driven Grouch Pederson and his wife and kid to Tsawwassen to catch the ferry to Victoria. They'd be spendin' time with the local chapter there under a man named Bolt who swore he'd make it safe for them 'til we could get the Raiders taken care'a.

Grouch'd been hesitant with me at first, but after a couple'a hours in the SUV I'd borrowed from Cressida where I made his kid laugh and charmed his wife with stories about Blue, he'd warmed up.

Enough to wave his family on to the terminal when I dropped them off so he could offer me his hand.

"Won't threaten you if you hurt her," he said mildly. "Because I don't have any doubt you could kill me in a few very creative ways. But I will say, she's a great girl despite everything she's been through, and she deserves the best."

I'd tipped my head. "Respectfully, Grouch, she's a great girl *'cause'*a everythin' she's been through. Endurin' Rooster and Hazard and Otto made her brave and independent and full'a love for the small things in life. It made her the woman I love."

He blinked, a little shocked. "Well, that's not a bad way to look at it. I'm just saying, please, don't be one in the long line of men who've disappointed her."

"Since the moment I met her, I've been workin' to get her free'a the past. Does that seem like the kinda man who'd ever fail to be there for her?" I asked sincerely.

His lips twisted. "No, I guess not."

I'd nodded, knockin' my fist against the door 'fore I opened it and climbed in. The window was down so I could look at him as I started the engine and said, "Take care'a yourself. She'll want you to walk her down the aisle one day."

I'd left him gapin' a little, my laughter trailin' out the window behind me.

Now, sittin' at Eugene's watchin' Blue shine her beamin' light on every table she spoke to, I felt a contentment I'd never known. The only thing that coulda made it better was tyin' us tighter with laws, with customs and ceremonies, with shared ink and shared memories, any'a the ways I could make her more my own and make myself more hers.

I wanted to own her blood and bones and be owned that way in return.

But she was fuckin' *married,* and the thought'a it burned.

The forbidden aspect'a our affair had long since grown stale. I wanted to take her home at the end'a the night. Out to dinner at La Gustosa. To parties at the clubhouse with my brothers and their families.

I wanted fuckin' everythin' with Blue.

"Never seen you smile like that," Curtains said from my left, nudgin' me with his shoulder so I turned to face him. "Not even when you get the occasional win against me in *Call of Duty.*"

I scoffed. "Occasional, my ass."

"Leave your ass outta it," he quipped with a grimace. "I see it way too fuckin' much as it is livin' with you."

"Hey, you've got your section'a the buildin'. You don't need to see me half-naked if you don't wanna."

"Not when you come into *my* kitchen every mornin' to steal *my* food," he argued, freckles fadin' against his flushed cheeks as he got riled up.

I shrugged a shoulder as if I didn't find it hilarious when he got worked up. "You always have the good cereal."

"You could buy your own," he suggested acidly, but I knew there was no real threat there.

Curtains and I bought an abandoned buildin' on the edge'a Main Street a few years back and renovated it to turn it into somethin' that would work for us. He lived on the right side, and I lived on the left, but we had a shared third story that was basically a giant man cave with games, a bar, a pool table, and anythin' we had a hankerin' to add to our collection'a fun and games.

We lived together 'cause we were best friends and also family. We lived together 'cause we'd both been without family for so long, we honestly couldn't stand to live on our own.

No one got me like Finnegan "Curtains" Ramsey.

But I had the feelin' Blue could, one day.

"That sugary shit will rot your teeth out," I scolded him.

"You buy that bran crap and only eat it like once a week, just get the good stuff, and you won't have to eat all'a mine!"

"Are you two seriously arguin' over cereal?" Axe-Man asked as he pulled out a chair and sat in it, pullin' Mei into his lap as soon as he did. He looked at his woman with a weary sigh. "How the fuck do you put up with these two?"

Her smile was sharp in her pretty face. "I always love people who are willing to bleed for me."

They shared one'a those looks then, one filled with understandin' and love, that I'd always looked away from uncomfortably before. Now, I felt an echo'a warmth in my chest thinkin'a Blue and the looks we shared.

"She values a good sense of humour," Loulou added as she draped an arm around my shoulders from over the top'a the booth behind me.

"Boner and Curtains are one of the secrets to the club's success."

"Oh yeah?" Zeus asked, appearin' behind her like an overlarge bracket, movin' her blonde hair off her neck to press a kiss there. "Thought the secret was *me*."

Loulou shivered but pretended to be unaffected. "No, they can cut any amount of tension with the knife of their hilariousness. I'm pretty sure you'd all have been in way more fights if they hadn't been there to de-escalate things."

"Maybe they should be in charge then, huh?" Z growled against her neck.

She squirmed, twistin' in his hold to look down her nose at him. "Maybe they should be. You *are* getting old."

Z's blade-grey eyes narrowed, and a second later, Loulou was yelpin' as he flung her over his shoulder and stood beside the booth with her legs pinned to his chest.

"Gotta sort this one out, brothers," he said calmly, swattin' her ass firmly when she wriggled too much. "Have fun without us."

"Zeus!" Loulou protested. "I was having fun."

"You'll have more fun in a minute," he promised as he strode out the doors'a Eugene's, our catcalls and whistles followin' him out.

Blue appeared beside me with a low whistle of her own and a tray full'a fresh beers for the group. "Well, that was kinda hot."

"Yeah?" I lassoed a hand around her hips to tug her into my side, a little loose from a few beers and the fuckin' unreal sex I'd had with my woman in her car 'fore her shift. "I could carry you off caveman style right now."

"Don't you dare," she said, but she was laughin', and I didn't think I'd ever seen her so at ease. She was settlin' into the routine'a her life, bloomin' under the light'a our relationship like a flower too long without sunshine. It was fuckin' beautiful to witness. "Eugene already made a comment about tainting his product in the storeroom."

Laughter rushed from my belly. "I think we both know every bit'a evidence he could've found wound up inside ya."

"Bones!" she hissed, slappin' at my arm, which only made me laugh harder.

Dane and Bat laughed across from me.

"Bones, eh?" Curtains drawled, lookin' at Blue with those sharp eyes rovin' over her the way he did over code, readin' somethin' others couldn't. "You know, it's Boner, yeah?"

I wedged an elbow into his side in retaliation.

"Yeah, but I think Bones suits him better," she said softly, not even lookin' at my best friend, just smilin' at me.

Curtains snorted softly, finishin' the rest'a his beer before placin' the glass a little too firmly on the table.

"What's your problem?" I demanded.

"Don't got one."

"The fuck you do," I argued. "You do not act like this."

"I better get back to it," Blue murmured, excusin' herself 'fore I could keep her at my side.

Still, it gave me the opportunity to turn the full weight'a my scowl on my brother. "What the fuck, Curtains?"

He just pulled a full pint Blue had laid down on the table into the bracket'a his arms and glared into the amber surface.

I looked up at Dane and Bat for a second, but they were sharin' one'a their damn looks no one else had the key for, so I ignored them.

"Dude," I said, tryin' to control myself. "You get I'm into this girl, right?"

Curtains rolled his eyes. "I'm not blind or deaf, and you won't stop talkin' about her, so, uh, *yeah*."

"Is that a problem for you?" I asked, incredulously.

I didn't date seriously, but I had a rotation'a women through my life over the years, and Curtains was never anythin' but his usual dumbass, awesome self with them.

So I didn't get this.

And the tension made my teeth ache.

"This is it for me," I told him, an edge'a desperation like a blade cuttin' into each word. "You get that? Blue's mine."

"She's fuckin' married, man, to a member'a the White Raiders," Curtains reminded me, knuckles white around the glass. "She's the kid daughter'a Rooster Cavendish. The man who put Axe-Man away for three years and who's actively gunnin' to take down the club. She is *not* yours; she's theirs."

"She's as much theirs as an animal in a fuckin' cage, and you know it," I seethed, seein' red and not just 'cause Curtains was a ginger.

For the first time ever, I wanted to hit my best friend in the fuckin' throat.

"I'm just sayin', you're jeopardizin' the club by doin' this secret affair shit with her. Especially when it's not that fuckin' secret, seein' as you're flirtin' with her in public and plantin' those neon signs for her everywhere she goes."

I blinked at him like I'd never seen him before. "What the hell, Curtains?"

He rolled his lips between his teeth, then cursed under his breath. "Never mind. I'm outta here."

I sat numbly as he climbed over the back'a the booth instead'a askin' me to get out so he could storm outta the bar.

When I looked up at Dane and Bat, they were both watchin' me with varyin' expressions'a sympathy.

"What am I missin' here?" I asked 'cause King was at home with Cressida and their kid, and Z had left with Loulou.

That left them, Wrath and Kodiak playin' pool in the corner, and Axe-Man and Mei who'd pulled out a sketchbook they were both drawin' in as they spoke softly to each other.

Bat and Dane were my best option.

It was the latter who winced and offered, "He could be jealous."

I gaped at them. "Jealous? What the hell's he gotta be jealous about?"

"Um," Mei interjected. "Maybe the fact that the woman he's loved is lost to him, probably forever, and now he has to watch his best friend falling in love?"

"Or he's worried you're gonna leave him or spend less time with him now that you've claimed an Old Lady," Bat said over the rim'a his beer bottle before takin' a pull. "I'm no expert on romantic relationships, but I get friendship, and this is classic."

"Even though she was thrilled for us, Cleo had a hard time adjusting when Henning and I actually got our heads out of our asses and started seeing each other," Mei admitted, and Axe-Man smoothed a soothin' hand over her thigh. "We're a family, all three of us, but obviously, it changes the dynamic."

I blinked down at the scarred wood tabletop as I digested their words.

'Cause they made a fuckuva lotta sense when they laid it out like that.

Curtains and I had trauma-bonded over savin' Elsa only to lose her again, and even though I'd dated and Curtains fucked around to keep the edge off, there'd never been anyone we brought into our family'a two.

'Til I met Blue.

Curtains had this wholehearted belief that he'd never settle down with anyone but Elsa. No matter how hard I tried to convince him she wasn't comin' back.

So there he was, thinkin' he'd probably live his life alone, but at least he had me, who didn't give a shit about love and marriage and all that crap.

Then I did.

And I wanted it with a woman who was by no means a sure thing.

Which meant he was probably fuckin' scared for me, that if things didn't work out, I'd end up like him. Married to a ghost, an idea I used to know.

Not to mention, I *had* been spendin' less time with my buddy so I could sneak what time I could get with Blue. It wasn't like we'd stopped hangin' out. I still ended up on the third story'a our house every day shootin' the shit with him, but we weren't exactly inseparable anymore.

"Fuck." I dug the heels'a my hands into my eyes. "I should go talk to him."

"Probably," Dane and Mei said simultaneously.

Bat and Axe-Man only sipped their beers, happy to stay outta my shit show.

"Alright." I stood to get goin' and say goodbye to Blue when the familiar growl'a motorcycles spiked outside and then settled into silence.

I hesitated, 'cause it was late and most'a the brothers were at home with their women or doin' fuck all at the clubhouse. Uneasiness prickled the back'a my neck.

And a moment later, my premonition was proved right when a group'a bikers wearin' cuts embossed with a skeleton ridin' a motorbike swaggered into the bar in a cloud'a cigarette smoke and loud cussin'.

The White Raiders had arrived.

There were only four'a them to the six of us, seven if you counted Mei who was a black belt badass in her own right, but the bar was filled with civilians, too, and there was no way we'd get away with a public fight without the cops comin'.

For one glimmerin' moment, I thought about sittin' down and resumin' casual conversation with the brothers 'til it wasn't so conspicuous'a me to leave.

But then one'a the Raiders spotted Blue, frozen like Bambi in the scope'a a hunter's rifle, and I knew there was no peaceful way outta here.

"Hey, bitch," one'a them called out to her. "Hard to believe you're still the same frail, ugly little thing Hazard used to own."

"Still owns," another muttered, clampin' a hand on his shoulder. "He won't like it if you try somethin', Geyser."

"Try?" Geyser snorted, strollin' to Blue with his hand cuppin' his junk through the denim. "I don't gotta try for shit. Look at her all grown up and lookin' like a true biker slut, now. She'll beg for it. Won't you, Faith?"

I was outta the booth and stompin' toward them without any thought to the consequences when Blue firmed her slightly tremblin' mouth and punched her chin into the air.

"I will not. And Bandit's right, Hazard will eat your balls for breakfast if you lay a finger on me. So you want a brew? Sit down and I'll bring it to you. Otherwise, get lost. I'm sure the clubhouse has the kind of entertainment you're looking for."

Pride surged through my chest, washing away some'a the red haze'a anger obscurin' my vision.

Fuck, she was magnificent.

Eugene appeared behind her, mammoth and scowlin' darkly.

Geyser, idiot though he was, stopped in his tracks and glared right back 'fore gesturin' to his buddies to the right'a the room near the live band, grabbin' a table at the back.

The tension in the room lowered instantly, but I still went to the bar, proppin' my elbow on the counter as if I was askin' Eugene for a beer and not checkin' on my girl.

"You okay, Blue?" I murmured, keepin' my eyes forward.

"That was nothing," she said as if that was reassurin' and not totally fucked.

"Please, don't go back there," I whispered, feelin' like blades were slippin' between every rib, each breath a struggle. "Can't stand you bein' in danger like that."

"I won't put the people I care about at risk," she said, ironclad, implacable.

"Grouch and his family caught the ferry to Victoria this afternoon," I told her. "They're stayin' with a buddy'a mine who'll keep them safe if Rooster decides to go lookin'. You don't have any excuses left."

The soft look she'd worn when I mentioned Grouch faded to a scoff at my last sentence. "No more *excuses*? I'm sorry, but you seem to have forgotten what I told you the other day." She punched her chest over her heart. "I love you bone deep, Aaron Clare, and if you think I'm going to let my own father or shithead excuse for an absentee husband come after you and your family, you're an idiot."

She turned on her heel and stalked off to take beers over to the Raiders who'd seated themselves on the other side'a the room.

I blinked after her, wonderin' how I'd fucked that up so bad. When I wandered back to the table, Mei only shook her head at me slightly.

"You're stayin'?" Axe-Man asked 'cause he knew I wouldn't leave Blue when the Raiders were here.

I nodded, pulling over one'a the fresh brews even though I knew I was done drinkin' for the night.

It was later.

The summer sun had set leavin' the breeze cool through the opened windows and the patrons'a Eugene's were loud with mirth. It was a great atmosphere with the country rock band puttin' on a great show and my friends all around me. Mei had gone home to work on her latest graphic novel, and Kodiak had trailed out at some point after frownin' furiously at his phone, but Bat, Dane, Wrath, Axe-Man and I were still shootin' the shit.

Blue hadn't stopped by once.

Which was good, I knew, 'cause the Raiders had caught sight'a our crew an hour into their drinkin' and sneered at us the rest'a the night. It was easy to tell they were itchin' to start shit, but Eugene'd brought out his shotgun for a cleanin' up at the bar, which seemed to deter them.

In the end, it wasn't even Blue who started the fight.

Tempest Riley, Bat's nanny and a one-time club slut, had come into the bar on a warm breeze, the air stirrin' her long, dark red hair and liftin' the hem'a her short, white dress so it revealed the bottom curve'a her bare ass. Heckler called her 'Bunny' 'cause'a her not-too-distant resemblance to Jessica Rabbit, and the Raiders took notice.

Catcalls and a few barks like a dog broke through the bar. One'a the bikers fell to his knees pantin', and another called out, "Hey, Red, you need a seat, my lap is free."

Tempest ignored them, goin' straight to the bar instead'a comin' to sit with us.

I looked across the table to see Bat's and Dane's eyes both fixed on her back.

"You guys fightin'?" I asked.

Bat's eyes slid slowly away from Tempest, and he took a deliberate draw from his pint. "She's the nanny. She doesn't hafta talk to us on her time off."

Dane's pale blue eyes stayed locked on her, though, and I wondered if it was gonna be awkward, him datin' Bat's nanny if it ever came to that. Tempest avoided club shit, but we'd all heard what a fuckin' godsend she'd been with his twins, Shaw and Steele, especially after their mum died.

"Get your hands off me."

The cold voice cut through the din'a the bar and drew my attention again.

One'a the Raiders, the guy named Bandit, was in her space at the bar, his hand half-up her skirt high on her thigh.

Bat and Dane were up only seconds 'fore the rest'a us.

Tempest wasn't an Old Lady, but she was still a de facto member'a our family and *no one* fucked with one'a ours.

Let alone scum like the Raiders.

Dane made it to them first, haulin' Tempest off her stool to drag her behind him.

Meanwhile, Bat, war veteran with two tours in Afghanistan under his belt and Sergeant At Arms for The Fallen MC, reeled back and landed a brutal punch to Bandit's jaw.

I could hear the crack'a bone ten feet back.

The Raider, not more than twenty really, fell to the ground with a broken yelp, jaw noticeably broken.

"Fuckin' brphen," he wailed inarticulately.

"Fuck," Wrath and I cursed in tandem as the rest'a the Raiders surged from their table into the action.

I grabbed the one that veered closest to me by the shirtfront and slammed my own fist into his soft gut, the big silver rings on my hand actin' like brass knuckles to deepen the hit.

Still, dude was big, so he didn't go down.

He swung a wild fist at my head that I ducked, but not quick enough, the edge'a his knuckles clippin' my ear so it burned with impact.

Around me, chaos as the rest'a the men erupted in a good old-fashioned bar brawl.

I caught'a glimpse'a Tempest smashin' her pint glass across a man's cheek, the skin splittin' instantly, his head reelin' back.

Huh, I hadn't known she had it in her.

Wrath slammed a barstool into another Raider, grinnin' wildly as he crumpled to the ground.

The guy I was fightin' decided to dispense with pleasantries and launched himself at my middle, tacklin' me to the floor. I grappled with him, usin' the floor as leverage to flip him onto his back and follow it up with a punch to the face that lay him back down when he lurched up.

BOOM.

The reverb from the shotgun echoed through the bar and dust from the destroyed wood panelin' rained down on the floor.

"Enough," Eugene bellowed, cockin' the shotgun again. "You want the cops here, Blue's got 'em on speed dial. Otherwise, lower your fuckin' fists and move away."

The Raiders stirred first, skulkin' a few feet back with jeers still locked over their mouths.

Eugene leveled the gun at the man called Geyser who stepped forward when I winked at him. "You wanna try me, motherfucker?"

Geyser scowled but lifted his hands. "Fine, you assholes are just lucky Daddy saved you."

"Daddy?" Eugene asked with a blink before plantin' a hand on the bar and hoppin' over it to press the shotgun directly to Geyser's chest. "Who're you callin' Daddy, boy?"

Geyser's bravado withered in the face'a Eugene's bulk, but there was bitterness and rage in his eyes as they swept over us 'fore he turned on his heel and stormed outta the bar.

The rest'a the Raiders followed, one'a them helpin' the broken-jawed Bandit through the doors.

"You want help cleanin' up?" I asked Eugene, surveyin' the two broken stools, crushed glass and overturned table.

"No, just get the fuck outta here," he ordered wearily. "It's too late for more trouble, and you lot are always at the center."

"Fair enough," I agreed.

"Leave through the back just in case those fuckers are waitin'," he suggested as Blue came out from behind the bar with a broom and dustpan.

I snagged her arm gently and tugged her into my front.

"Hey," I said softly, bendin' at the knee to look into her eyes better. "Is my girl okay?"

Her sigh was weary. "Yeah, Bones, I'm okay. Violence is kinda the modus operandi of my life. You're not hurt?"

"Nah, those assholes? Like they could get a hand on me," I boasted just to win that small little smile curvin' her mouth. "On the other hand, yes, I'm gravely injured. I think a kiss would make me feel better."

She grinned, shakin' her head as she lifted my red knuckles and kissed them gently.

"Not exactly where I'm hurtin', seein' you in those shorts," I corrected with a leer at the short denim leavin' acres'a pale skin bare for me to ogle.

"You're ridiculous," she said on a huffin' chuckle. "How can you make me laugh even when I'm annoyed with you?"

"It's an art form," I admitted with faux sincerity. "I gotta head out, but you stay safe, yeah? Eugene'll walk you to your car."

She rolled those blueberry eyes. "It's like ten steps from the entrance."

"Eugene'll walk you to your car," I repeated, all trace'a amusement gone. "Need you safe. You don't wanna leave the Raiders' house, fuck, I hate it, but I respect your decision. Doesn't mean I want you takin' unnecessary risks."

"It won't be for long," she promised, every inch'a her softenin' as she leaned into me. "I-I found something this morning that I think should help."

"Whaddya mean 'found somethin'?" I demanded. "Blue, do not put yourself in danger snoopin' around! We got this handled."

"I'll do what I can," she decreed like a queen 'fore her court.

Her independence and sass shouldn't've been such a turn-on when I was tryin' to keep her safe, but it was.

"What'd you find?"

"I told Lion about it," she said, then winced at my glower. "I may have been feeding him intel when I found it."

"Blue," I growled, torn between rage and pride for my brave girl. "Fuckin' stop that. I refuse to be phoned from the hospital or the cops sayin' you've been hurt."

Or killed.

She pursed her lips, then sighed. "Okay, okay. I'll cool it on the detective front, but only because I think Lion has it covered. Apparently, Otto's agreed to testify against Rooster in the jewelry theft case for a reduced sentence. The law moves slow, but it should mean they'll get him eventually, right?"

The law could fuck itself.

We'd learned the hard way that cops fell down on the job or were too corrupt to do it in the fuckin' first place. The only way I'd rest happy was if I saw Rooster put in the ground my-fuckin'-self.

"Relax," she said softer, steppin' close to place a hand on my hip. "I'll be careful, I promise. Everything is going to be fine in the end."

"You believe that?" I had to ask 'cause there was always a hesitancy in her, a thin barrier that was still erected between her heart and mine.

Like she didn't believe everythin' would be okay.

Like I was a dream she was livin' only for a short time.

I refused to let that be the case.

"Yeah," she whispered, tippin' her head back so that blue hair cascaded in a waterfall shimmer and her vivid cobalt eyes caught the bar lights and burned neon. "You make me believe."

I stamped a firm kiss on her lips 'cause the Raiders were gone, and I didn't give a fuck. I needed her to know how much I fuckin' cared about her. How much she'd rocked my goddamn world.

When I pulled back, she was blushin' prettily.

"Keep your phone near tonight," I whispered. "I'm thinkin' I'll need a little stress relief."

I waggled my brows at her and let her laughter rain down on me.

"Let's go, Romeo," Wrath said, clampin' a hand over my shoulder to pull me back toward the hallway.

I tipped my chin up at my woman before lettin' Wrath spin me forward. I slung an arm around the taller man and sighed.

"I'm in love," I told him. "Head, heart and dick. The trifecta."

He was startled into snortin' and rubbin' a fist into my hair, somethin' he'd learned from Z that annoyed the shit outta me.

I was shovin' him with a sharp laugh when we emerged through the exit door out back and rammed into the back'a Bat and Axe-Man.

"What the fu--" I started, and then the shot went off.

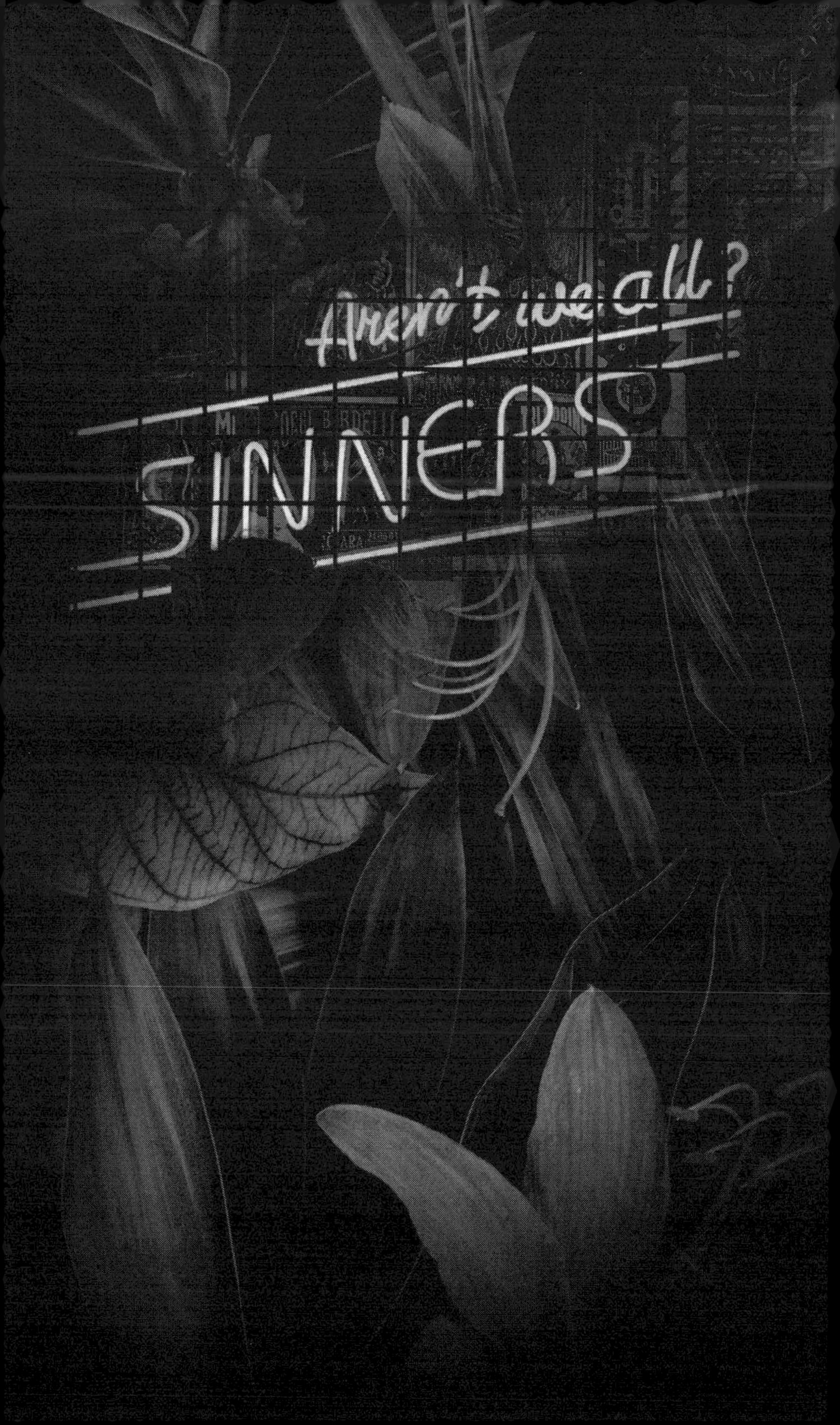
Aren't we all?
SINNERS

CHAPTER SIXTEEN

Blue

I WAS CARTING two garbage bags filled with the broken detritus from the bar brawl down the back hall when I heard a ruckus above the usual bar cacophony of loud music, louder voices, the clatter of boots and heels on the floor, and dishes in the small kitchen.

A noise like something slamming into the wall behind the bar.

I hesitated, straining to listen but unable to hear much beyond the country rock band's throbbing bass and drums.

After a moment, I continued toward the back door, easing it open to peer through the crack into the poorly lit back lot.

Chaos reigned.

The White Raiders had not gone home with their tail between their legs.

And the original four had been joined by four more.

Eight Raiders to five Fallen brothers and Tempest.

Only it was obvious the Raiders had got the jump on The Fallen because Axe-Man had a knife in one shoulder even as he fought someone and Bat...

Bat was on the ground slumped halfway behind the dumpster for protection because he had a bullet in one thigh.

Tempest stood in front of him like a guard dog, a huge silver gun in her hands steady and trained on the action as if she planned to shoot anyone who stood still for long enough to get a good shot.

Aaron was on the ground under Oscar who was two hundred and sixty pounds of muscle and lard. I winced as his meaty fist landed in Aaron's face, his nose blooming with blood at the contact.

Without thinking, eyes trained on my man as he was hit again and again, I shoved the door open so hard it banged against the opposite wall loud enough to pop off like a gunshot.

"Hey now, what's going on here?" I yelled loud enough to pause the fight.

Loud enough, hopefully for Eugene to hear inside the bar.

Geyser used the moment of stillness to fling himself away from Axe-Man and land next to his gun, where it'd been kicked into the dirt. He trained it on the closest target.

Aaron.

Geyser turned his head to sneer at me. "Get the fuck back inside, Faith."

No.

No, no, no.

Every self-preservation instinct I had fell away to focus on someone other than myself.

All the bravery and boldness I'd been shoring up inside myself surged forth.

There was no way I would let him hurt Aaron.

None.

Consequences could get *fucked*.

I turned my head slightly to catch Tempest's eye, relieved she was looking at me even though her gun was still raised and ready.

Please, I tried to convey with my eyes.

And then, I used every single ounce of my strength to throw the bags of glass and broken wood right at Geyser's head.

Tempest followed my cue and shot Geyser just as he staggered under the weight of the bags.

Right in the arm holding the gun at Aaron.

It fell to the ground with a dull thud, and The Fallen surged into action.

It would have been amazing to watch, the way Axe-Man pulled a man's arm straight, turned his back on him with it still in his grip and broke it in two over his shoulder. How Dane stepped up to the man straddling Aaron and snapped his neck with a single, easy twist of two hands on his head. While the man slumped to the side of him, Aaron reached for the bloody, discarded gun and shot Tyre in the knee before he could attack Wrath from behind like he'd clearly been aiming to do. Wrath was preoccupied by pounding in Gauntlet's face.

It would have been amazing to watch if Macho hadn't made a grab for me.

"Fuckin' bitch," he growled as he carted me into his arms, ignoring the way I struggled. "Let's see what your old man thinks about you interferin' in club shit, huh?"

He started jogging with me over his shoulder toward the gleam of bikes in the dark just as Eugene's shotgun boomed through the air again, and he shouted for everyone to stop where they fuckin' were.

Macho didn't listen.

He swung a leg over the bike and settled me over his lap facing him. "You make me crash, I'll kill you and bury your body. Tell Rooster you ran away again."

Behind me, boots pounded against the earth as the Raiders, those who could, ran from Eugene and The Fallen.

"I didn't do anything," I protested. "You just startled me while I was taking out the garbage––"

"Shut the fuck up, bitch," he growled before biting my ear so savagely I cried out, and a moment later, the warmth of blood slid down my neck. "You can explain yourself to fuckin' Rooster."

My heart dropped into my belly, churning in acid.

Because I knew what Rooster would do if he thought I'd turned on him, especially for The Fallen.

He'd kill me.

MACHO DRAGGED me off the back of his bike by the hair. I fell to my knees in the dirt and tried to find my feet as he pulled me forward across the lot and up the shallow stairs of the porch. Instead of opening the screen door, he threw me through the warped mesh, so I fell straight through the door and landed on the jagged screen, the edges cutting into my forearms.

"Found her," he hollered, pounding his chest as he released some kind of war cry. "Found her for you."

I didn't mention that Rooster knew where I was––that he'd *sent* me to work there. It wouldn't do any good. But I hoped he would put an end to the violence, turning the air to static, because I knew I'd be at its pinnacle.

Instead, the boots that thudded heavily––unevenly––over the floor were not the black motorcycle boots embossed with roosters on either side like my father's.

They were cracked-leather, brown cowboy boots attached to black jeans that covered one wiry leg and one amputated at the knee, a prosthetic replacing the calf and foot he'd lost to a roadside bomb overseas.

Hazard was back.

I looked up with my heart lodged in my throat, throbbing so hard I gagged as my eyes locked with his pale grey ones.

"If it isn't my wife," he drawled in that prairie accent. "On her knees where she belongs once again."

Time had been unfairly good to Hazard. He had always been thin but strong, a corded rope of steel leaning forward at the hips like he was walking into a perpetual wind, but age had put some more meat on his bones, filling out the wide shoulders and long arms. His hair was mostly grey, underlaid with black so it looked almost metallic and complemented the cold grey of his eyes. Even though there were harsh lines beside his eyes and mouth, he was still handsome enough to pull women whenever he wanted.

Including the one pressed to his side, his arm wrapped around her waist with his fingertips stuck down the front of her jean shorts.

The face of evil never had an ugly face to match, and it was one of life's greatest injustices.

"She fuckin' threw a bag'a garbage at Geyser," one of the men behind me tattled with serious glee.

"Protectin' The Fallen bastards," another, Meatloaf, added.

They were rabid dogs slavering at the mouth for blood.

"I wasn't," I said quickly, pulling myself to my knees and then trying to stand before Macho's foot planted between my shoulders and sent me sprawling. "My boss sent me outside to take out the garbage. When I saw people fighting, I panicked. I don't know what half the club even looks like!"

"Bullshit," Macho spat, planting his foot in my back so I couldn't get up.

"Tyre got shot in the fuckin' leg, Geyser in the arm, and one'a them killed Oscar."

"Someone go to the bar, get Oscar's body if they didn't take it with 'em," Hazard ordered. "Where's Tyre?"

"Denny took him to the hospital."

"Where's Rooster?" someone asked. "He'll want to punish her."

"Rooster had to make a trip to Alberta, but he left me in charge," Hazard said, stepping closer so his boot nudged my nose. "And this is my wife, in case any'a you forgot that and thought to touch her."

There was a vibrating pause where every man tried to stay as still as possible to avoid Hazard's wrath and scrutiny.

"Were you a bad girl, Faith?" he asked me in that sinuous voice that coiled around me like a hissing cobra, choking my neck.

My mind fell back eight years when I was sixteen again, begging him not to hurt me, obsessing over being meek and quiet enough to avoid his ire.

It hadn't worked well, but it was my only tactic.

I had spent the last near decade trying to grow through the cracks in the foundation Hazard and Rooster had poured over my soul, and suddenly, it was all for nothing.

Because here I was on the ground beneath a boot, being ridiculed and abused as if it was my destiny.

And the thought of Aaron, his dark eyes bright with humour like a star-filled night sky, his quick smile and unfailing kindness, felt like a great cosmic joke. Cruelty so painful it cracked my bones into pieces beneath my skin.

"I don't care what she did at the bar," Hazard declared into the silence as the toe of his boot lifted off the ground and resettled over my hand. "Everything else pales in comparison to the true betrayal. You left me,

Faith. Without a word. Do you think I can let that slide?"

"Hazard," Cedar said. Hope sparked briefly like the flame from a broken lighter. "Rooster won't be happy if you damage his daughter too badly."

Hazard's laughter was jagged and rusty. "Rooster's not here, and she'll heal. She always does."

"Still--"

"Shut up," he snapped as he dropped slowly into a crouch. It had to hurt his knee, he'd always avoided the position when I was with him, but he clearly wanted to make a point.

And it was made the second the cold edge of a knife skimmed my cheek and pushed my hair away from my face. Fear sluiced through me like frigid water, freezing every inch of me until even my heart seemed to cease beating.

He leaned closer, the hot breath of his voice against my cold cheek.

"I heard you're a workin' girl now. You know I don't like my woman doin' anythin' but servin' my needs, so you'll be stoppin' that right...*now*."

The crack and crunch of bone registered a curious moment before the pain flared lava-hot beneath my skin. A scream ripped from my lungs as pain brutalized my hand, shooting up my arm into my chest and throat.

Hazard's boot was crushing my hand, breaking the bones in at least three fingers, though the hurt encompassed so much more than that.

Neon colours burst behind my eyes, splashes of bright pain painting the inside of my brain. It did something to short-circuit my brain, transmuting that broken, frail teenage girl into the woman I'd strived hard to become in her absence.

As I writhed, pinned to the floor like a bug, agony collapsing my chest in that long, brutalized scream, I resolved that this was it.

This was the last *fucking* time they hurt me.

The last time they took something precious from me.

Because without my hand, even my left one, I couldn't do hair or nails or even make-up. I couldn't do any of the things that brought me joy, any of the talents I'd worked so hard to learn, any of the things that made me *me*.

"Fuck you," I shouted through the pain.

"Fuck me?" he hissed, grinding down so hard I thought I might black out from the pain.

"You're a fucking monster!" I screamed, loosening the door on the years of hatred buried inside my heart.

I thought of the sign Aaron made Cleo.

Fuck the monsters.

"Fuck you, fuck you," I screamed as his hand wrapped in my hair, and he dragged me to my feet before bringing his elbow down hard on the side of my temple.

I was out before I could fall to the ground.

And when I came to, in the bathtub of all places, I wished I was still unconscious.

Because Hazard was cutting into my face with his knife.

When he noticed my eyes and the scream building behind the tape over my mouth, he grinned.

"No one will want you when you're this ugly," he said, almost conversationally, as he dragged the knife in a line of fire from my ear to the corner of my taped mouth. "No one but me, Faithy. You got real pretty over the years, so I figured I should bring all that ugly inside you back to the surface."

I passed out before he could do the other side.

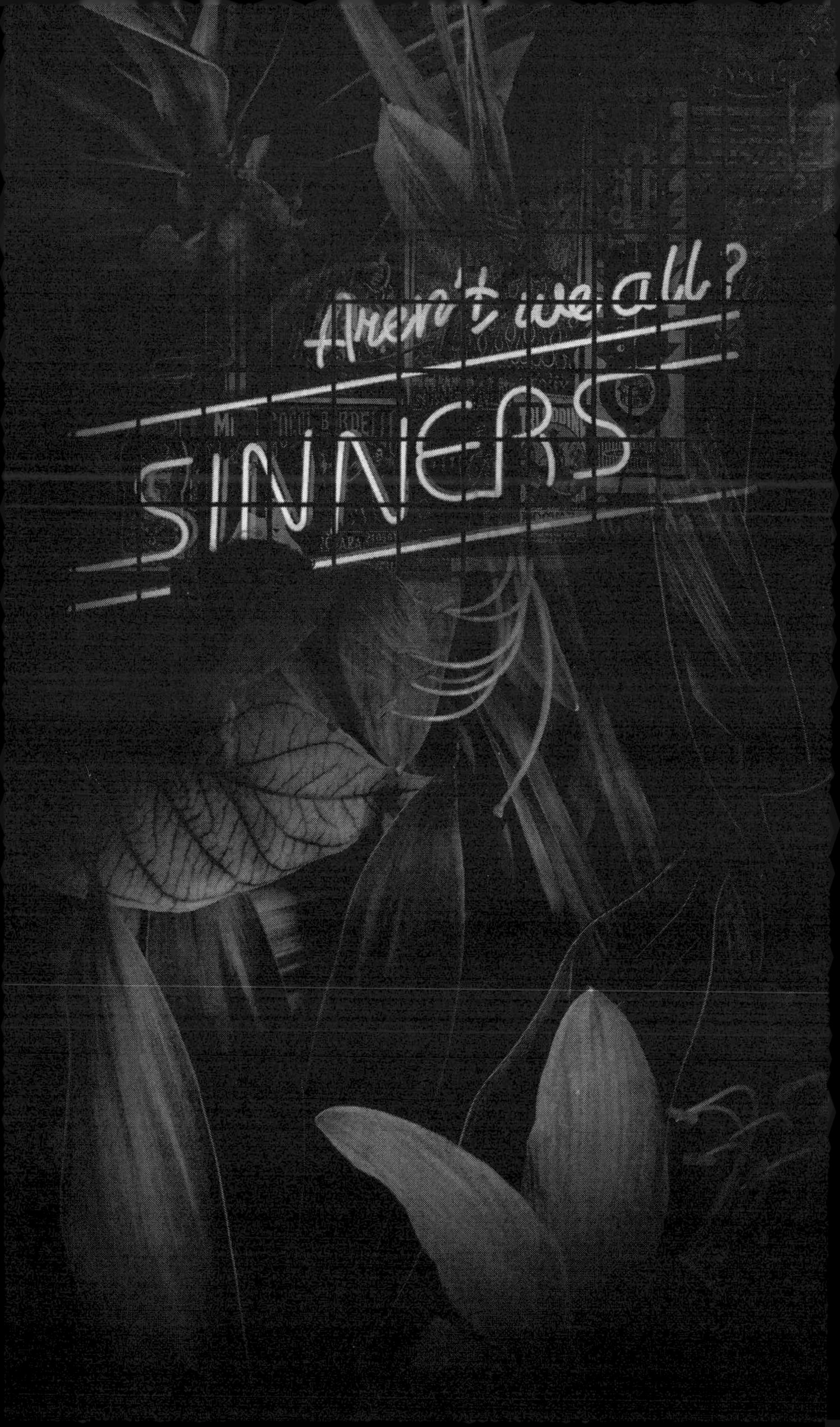
Aren't we all?
SINNERS

CHAPTER SEVENTEEN

Blue

WHEN I CAME TO AGAIN, I was still in the bathtub, but my mouth was free of tape, and only Aunt Rita was in the room with me. She sat on the closed toilet lid right beside the tub, gauze and medical scissors in her hands, fingertips wet with blood.

"I'm so sorry, Faith," she whispered softly, her age-creased face crumpled and damp like a used napkin with tears and snot.

She'd been crying for me, then.

My entire head hurt, face to neck, and my left hand was on fire where it lay limp across my chest, but the rest of my body had been spared. It seemed Hazard only wanted to make his point by scaring me.

"How bad is it?" I croaked.

It hurt badly enough to think it had to be grotesque, one side of my face suddenly made into a bloody mockery of the Joker's smile.

Aunt Rita's fingers trembled as they fluttered ineloquently. "Oh, it'll heal."

Shame burned through me, brighter than the actual pain.

"Help me up?" I asked quietly, trying to adjust so I could stand, but my good hand slipped on the blood from my wound that stained the side of the porcelain.

I must have struggled when he cut into me.

Aunt Rita stood to offer me her hand. She was old but as strong as an ox, pulling me easily to my feet. My head swam, vision popping with bursts of colour and darkness. I closed my eyes to settle myself for a moment and then carefully, hand still in my aunt's, stepped over the rim so I could stand in front of the little stained mirror above the sink.

I didn't open my lids until my right hand was curled over the edge of the sink because I knew when I looked at my reflection, I wouldn't like what I saw. Sucking in a deep breath, I told myself that no matter what I looked like, Aaron would still want me because his feelings for me were bone-deep and not superficial.

It didn't help as much as I wanted it to.

Because the truth was, I'd fought hard to find myself beautiful, to emphasize my assets and forgive my flaws. I'd learned everything about cosmetology so I could make others feel as pretty as I'd learned to make myself believe I was.

The idea of being scarred across the face was the exact right way to pierce the heart of the confidence I'd built in Rooster and Hazard's absence.

My 'husband' had been back for less than a day, and he had already reduced me to rubble.

"Even before you left," Aunt Rita spoke softly into my ear as she gripped my shoulders comfortingly. "Even at your unhappiest, you only had to smile at someone to become the loveliest girl in the room."

A sob bubbled up my throat and stuck there.

"I am a selfish old lady stuck in this life and its ways, but I always hoped you would find happiness somewhere else. Happiness that brought that smile out every day instead of once or twice a year." She paused while I sucked in a shivery breath. "I think you've found that now, outside of these walls?"

I nodded even though it made my head pound to do so.

"Well, then, whoever is on the other end of your happiness will still love the shape of that smile, even if it's a little scarred."

I tried to breathe through my nose to stop the tears, knowing from experience that the saline water would sting the wounds, but it was a lost cause. When I opened my eyes, the first thing I noticed was the blue of my eyes.

It was vain, but I always tried to match my hair to the same shade, a rich cobalt blue. They popped even more vibrantly against the bloodshot white and the livid red wound stretching from the edge of my left ear to the corner of my mouth. Hazard's hand was steady enough to make it seem like an exact straight line except for the end which flicked up beside the end of my lips. Aunt Rita had used butterfly bandages to close the wound, but some blood had sluggishly leaked from the edges, merging with my tears to drip pinkly from my chin into the basin.

"Fuck," I cursed, squeezing my eyes shut again.

There were no clear thoughts in my head, only emotion that filled me to the brim until I felt like I couldn't talk or think or even breathe.

Vaguely, I was aware of a knock on the door and Aunt Rita shuffling over to crack it open to speak to someone.

"How is she?" Cedar's voice whispered.

My chest clutched, but I didn't turn. It had been years since I last saw him, and the time felt like a chasm between us. We had been something like friends back then, but I had no idea what kind of man he was now.

Actually, I was inclined to think he wasn't a *good* one given the company he still kept.

"I'll keep her in here tonight with the door locked so he can't get to her again," Aunt Rita was saying. "He did a number on her sweet face."

"Goddammit," Cedar cursed, his fist thumping against something. "I'm sorry, Faith. I should've stepped in."

It went unsaid that unless he'd put a bullet in Hazard's brain, he would have done as he pleased anyway, and Cedar would just have suffered for trying. Once, back then, he'd stepped in to stop Hazard from hitting me, and he was cut from the club funds for six months, not to mention the bruised face he'd turned up with the next time I saw him.

"He's leaving," he continued. "We've got a meet with the man who's takin' us on."

"Who?" I asked, eyes snapping open so I could turn and drill them into Cedar. "Who is it?"

His mouth worked, pursing then flatlining before he uttered quietly, "A man named Javier Ventura."

I had no recognition of that name, but I filed it away for later.

"Thank you," I said because I had the feeling he knew exactly where I would take that information.

He'd always been too smart for this lot.

He dipped his head. "Take care'a yourself, Faith. We'll be gone for hours, and we're takin' a few men, but it'll still be a pretty full house. Don't do anything stupid."

His tone was all wrong, though. Not a warning, but a suggestion.

I shuttered my gaze and turned away with a small nod.

"If you cut across the left fields, you hit the road eventually," he said even softer before disappearing behind the door.

Aunt Rita gripped my good hand. "Are you going?"

"I have to," I admitted because it was the only light at the end of the tunnel illuminating a way through this darkness. "A...friend got Grouch and his family away today. I-I wish I could take you, but––"

She snorted, waving to her haggard face. "I made my choice a long time ago, ducky. I only wish I could help. I have some money saved——"

"No," I insisted. "I kept my cash tips from Rooster so I have some, too. And I think, where I'm going, they'll take care of me until I can get on my feet."

In fact, I knew they would.

The Fallen took in strays like an animal shelter, cobbling together the kind of found family that shouldn't have worked on paper but did beautifully in real life. Military veterans, orphans, black sheep, lost souls, the odd psychopath—all of them broken and made whole by their connections to each other.

A totally different organism than the blood family I had and the ways of this club and the one before that.

"Wait until they've left and everyone's settled down," she whispered. "And let me clean that cut again."

I laughed, a shocked little bark because hope had momentarily blocked out my memory and the pain from the wound. And suddenly, it was a little more bearable because I knew that I'd already taught myself to find happiness when life was hard, and a little scar wouldn't change that.

"I'll miss you," I told Aunt Rita while she cleaned my face with stinging antiseptic because I would, so much it momentarily robbed me of breath.

She was a constant in my life with Rooster, the only one to ever kiss my forehead or tuck me in sometimes as a child and the only person to offer me solace when I'd returned as an adult. It felt wrong to leave her behind, but then, she'd never left herself.

"I'll miss you, but every time I think of you, I'll imagine you with this smile," she said, touching the edge of the tremulous expression on my mouth. "Now, I'll go gather some of your things so you're ready. Try to wrap your hand with the rest of the gauze so you don't damage it worse."

"There's a phone and mum's ring in the lining of the mattress," I said. "That's all I really need."

"I'll grab what I can," she promised before squeezing my hand again, dropping it and leaving the room.

I locked it behind her, sucked in a breath, and fell to the edge of the tub because my knees were suddenly weak. I'd been so overwhelmed that I hadn't thought to worry if Aaron and his friends had made it out of that fight relatively unscathed.

And if he had, I didn't even know where he *lived* because I'd never dared to visit it.

So I'd head for the clubhouse, but it was a good forty minutes by car to Entrance and my Mazda was back at the bar. If I was lucky, I could hitchhike, but it wasn't exactly safe on the side of the Sea to Sky Highway's winding, mountainous roads at night especially when the Raiders could notice me gone and come after me.

I could call Aaron to come meet me if he was well enough to do so, but I had to get a head start while I could get away. Besides, something told me if he knew what Hazard had done, Aaron would drive up to the house without fear and light it up, guns blazing.

I wasn't opposed in theory, but there was no way he could take out a house of twenty armed men by himself.

I waited for what had to be half an hour, but Aunt Rita didn't return.

Finally, unease turning my gut sour, I opened the door and headed into the hall. It was eerily quiet in the big, ramshackle house when usually voices were raised in laughter or conversation over the sound of music and the television downstairs. It was such an old house that it creaked and groaned as people stepped through it, but only the pop of warped wood under my feet could be heard.

When I rounded the corner to my room, Macho was there, leaning against my door with a cruel smile.

"Little Auntie had to make herself useful downstairs," he said with a mocking pout. "She seemed to think you needed shit from your room. Of course, you don't need three changes'a clothes to get ready for bed, do ya, Faith?"

Slowly, scalp prickling with dread, I shook my head.

"That's what I thought. Now, you're gonna spend the rest'a the night in your room, and I'm gonna drink my beer right outside the door. Fancy'a bit'a quiet anyway after those fuckers nearly killed us," he said with a saccharine-sweet smile that looked just as wrong on his ugly, mean face as a scowl did on Aaron's.

He lashed forward to yank me by the arm so I stumbled into his foul-smelling body, but at least he didn't grope me or anything.

This he explained by saying, "Fuckin' ugly mark the VP gave ya."

Fury burned through me, but I kept quiet as he pushed me into the room because I knew I could access my phone to text Aaron.

That was until Macho grinned widely at me, showing a blackened eyetooth. "Don't be lookin' for this." He raised my burner phone in one hand to give it a little shake. "I think Hazard'll be real interested to see what you have on your secret phone when he gets back."

Fuck, my world was falling apart around my ears all in the span of a single night.

"Please, Macho, it's nothing," I tried, stepping forward with a sweet smile because I'd been able to sway some of the men to go easy or keep things quiet before.

He laughed loudly. "Yeah, maybe that cute shit would work before he cut you up, but I got no desire to use an ugly bitch like you. And thanks for this." My mother's sapphire ring winked in the light where it was pushed down over the fat tip of his pink finger. "This'll bring me a nice little payload."

I lunged for it before I could help myself, but Macho only slammed the door shut on me, and the sound of a key turning in the ancient lock told me he'd found the key to the bedroom.

"Fuck," I breathed out on a sob, hitting my good hand against the door as Macho laughed to himself on the other side. "Fuck, fuck."

I let myself wallow for a few minutes before I hauled in a deep breath that burned my lungs and then let it out in a gushing stream.

"Okay," I told myself softly, turning away to pull a scarf from my closet to fashion a makeshift sling for my arm. "You can figure this out."

If Hazard came home and saw the text messages on that phone, he would quite literally kill me. If Rooster was here, it might have been different. Even though he was cruel, I didn't think my own father wanted me dead, but Hazard was another story entirely. So much more had happened to him overseas than just losing his leg; he'd returned home with a lost sense of pride and anger that flared like a supernova, taking out everything in its path.

After eight years of separation, the knowledge of my secret, rival-biker boyfriend would send him so far over the edge, I knew there wouldn't be much left of me to find if he got his hands on me.

So I *had* to get out of here.

Like hell I was dying in this pathetic place when I had love and happiness on the other side of the highway.

The window opposite the bed faced the barn, where I could see a few men shooting beer bottles in the dark, laughing uproariously when they didn't connect and taking gulping draughts of beer when they did. It was obviously some kind of drinking game that would leave them senseless, but there was no way I could leave that way when they had guns in their hands.

The window beside the bed was painted shut, but it overlooked the back of the lot and just below it was the covered porch where I could hopefully land when I dropped from the sill.

I just had to get the window open.

Thank God for my backup nail drill.

I dropped to the ground by the bed to fish out my backup cosmetology kit, fingers shaking with adrenaline as I wrenched it open and found my spare nail drill. Relieved tears flooded my vision for a second, but I wasn't even sure if it would work to grind away the paint.

The tool buzzed as I kneeled on the bed and brought it to the windowsill, so I kept an ear trained to the door when I brought it down on the paint and it started to peel away from the old, soft wood.

No one stirred outside the door.

So I continued, fingers cramping as I moved the drill around the seam of the window, once and then twice to work the paint and grit free. I sent up a grateful prayer that it was my left hand with the broken fingers and not my dominant right hand.

"Please, God or whomever, let this work," I begged as I curled my right hand fingers under the hinge and pulled with all my might, standing up on the bed to leverage everything I could.

Nothing, for one painful moment, and then a sharp crack and groan as it pulled away from the sill and slid up inside the frame.

I paused, breathing hard, listening for Macho.

Only the sound of music drifted in under the door.

With a huff to blow my hair out of my sweaty face, I heaved once more until there was enough of a crack to press myself through. It broke my heart to leave my mother's ring after Aaron found it again, but nothing was worth more than my life. So without hesitation, I kissed my nail drill and left everything behind, slipping awkwardly out the window to perch my ass on the sill.

It was still a decent drop to the veranda roof, and I knew the landing would make some noise, so I waited anxiously until the sound of shots and shattering bottles rang out again to push myself off the window.

And drop.

My landing was graceless, knees banging into the flat roof, hand skidding as I tried to catch myself, burning the skin off my palm. Even in the sling, my left hand throbbed at the jarring impact.

I froze, straining to hear if anyone would come to investigate.

There was a creak of the screen door opening and two sets of boots moving outside onto the porch below me.

"You hear that?"

"You know this place is a dump, probably just settling. It's humid as fuck so the wood's probably swollen."

"Like you know anything about construction."

"More than you."

"Get fucked!"

Their voices drifted back inside, but I waited for a few long moments before scooting to the edge of the roof and peering over. It was another fair drop straight to packed earth, but there was no other option.

I waited for another round of the shooting game when suddenly there was a whooshing noise and the sound of shattering glass from the *other* side of the house and a heavy thump from within followed by shouting.

The waiting game was no longer an option.

I dropped to the ground with a tiny squeak of fear and landed hard on my right side, but the blast of pain was dull and didn't stop me from getting quickly to my feet.

Another gunshot, so much louder than the ones by the barn, thundering through the air, it seemed to echo across the fields.

More cries.

I turned and ran toward the left field like Cedar had suggested. Cardio and fitness were not my friends, but I pushed as hard as my tired body and aching head would allow, my vision trained on the dark stalks of corn.

Relief made me light-headed as I hit the field and shoved through the crops, pushing them with my right hand, even though more battered my whole body as I plunged through the dense growth. I just had to get through this field and out the other side and I'd be so much closer to safety.

Then, out of the dark, something reached for me and in my haste to evade its grasp, I tripped over a slippery corn stalk and fell sideways.

Right into my pursuer.

We fell to the ground with a muffled thud, and I opened my mouth to scream even though it pulled open the wound at the side of my face. A hand covered my gaping maw, thwarting the sound, but I knew even when I tried to scream that no one would come for me.

This had been my one and only attempt to save my life.

And now I was caught on the ground in the pitch dark, probably minutes away from death.

"Where do you think you're runnin' to, little bitch?"

Piston's voice, recognizable by the nasal drawl even though it was so dark in the field I couldn't make out his features.

Terror punched me in the chest because this was the worst person to find me, save Hazard.

Piston had been leering at me for weeks, and if it wasn't for the threat of Hazard and the watchful eyes of Rooster, he would have taken me already. I could still remember that beer-wet texture of his mouth against my breasts as he'd forced his face between them one night.

And now he had the chance.

His laughter, putrid from sour beer, wafted over my face in triumph. He only had to pin my one hand above my head because my left was caught in the sling so he could use the other to reach for the button of my jean shorts. They were undone too quickly, even though I kicked and bucked beneath his heavy weight, screaming and shouting now that he'd released my mouth.

But there was no one to hear, maybe, or no one to care.

He reached for his own belt, pulling himself out of his jeans. I gagged, about to squeeze my eyes shut, when I saw the telltale movement of stalks swaying behind Piston's head.

Motion in the cornfield coming toward us.

I kept my eyes fixed on it as I shouted for help again and again.

"Shut up," Piston grunted as he released my hand to pull at my shorts.

I shoved the heel of my hand into his nose as hard as I could so his head snapped back. A moment later, something broke through the little clearing our struggle had made in the crops, a flashlight trained on Piston's form looming over mine.

And then *bang*!

A gunshot split the night, and blood erupted across the little clearing a moment before I lost myself in darkness.

CHAPTER EIGHTEEN

Boner

I**T TOOK** me just two minutes in the chaos of the brawl behind Eugene's Bar to realize that one'a the Raiders had taken Blue.

Just two minutes.

One hundred and twenty seconds too late to save her.

By the time I recognized her absence, the growl'a Harleys was already recedin' from the parkin' lot, tearin' onto the Sea to Sky.

"Fuck!" I'd shouted to the sky 'fore startin' to storm to my own bike.

"Boner, wait," Axe-Man said, grippin' my wrist tight so I was forced to stop and turn back to him. Brother was six foot four and built like a tank with long blonde hair like some kinda Viking, but there was no berserker rage in his eyes as they locked on mine, only calm control. And that was with a fuckin' push dagger embedded in his shoulder. "You think she's gonna go down for gettin' involved in this."

It wasn't really a question 'cause Axe-Man knew enough about the way Rooster ran a club to understand Blue intervenin' in the fight would bring hell down on her fuckin' head.

"You know she will. I gotta get to her."

"Do it smart," he urged, tuggin' me closer to palm the back'a my neck and shake me a little. "Call Zeus, get the rest'a the brothers to the clubhouse, get organized, and we'll ride out together. Take them down now instead'a later."

"One day early," I agreed, panic recedin' slightly as my brain latched on to the plan. "Fine. I'll call Z."

"I'll call Buck."

"No, get yourself and Bat to a fuckin' doctor," I ordered, even though technically Axe-Man had rank over me as the Secretary'a the club.

We had a doctor on call for the club, a new one who worked off the books for us after she got fired from the hospital where Harleigh Rose worked. I didn't know the details, but havin' a doctor who could patch up the serious shit we got into without havin' to go to the hospital was a fuckin' boon.

"I'll have her meet us at the clubhouse. I'm fine. Bat'll be good, too."

Behind Axe-Man, Bat was already on his feet fightin' with Dane, Tempest and Eugene, who were all arguin' with him, probably tryin' to get him to rest.

"I'm comin' with," Bat called to me, hobblin' over relatively well considerin' the bullet hole through his thigh. "You'll need me to clear the way in."

Bat'd won medals in the army for bein' the country's best sharpshooter and truth be told, our plan had hinged on him takin' out the sentries at the property with his sniper rifle.

"You up for it?" I asked, claspin' his shoulder. "Not gonna pretend I don't want you there, brother, but not if you're gonna bleed out in the fuckin' field."

He scoffed, insult written all over his face. "It's a fuckin' bee sting.

Had worse and I'll probably have worse still. I'll get the doc to pack the wound and head out with you when we're ready."

Relief suffused me, leechin' the starch from my muscles. "Means everythin', brother."

He mimicked my grip on his shoulder by squeezing my trap, his dark eyes filled with understandin'. "We lost one Fallen woman and almost lost another last year. There's no fuckin' way we're losin' one on my watch. You get me?"

"Fuck yeah." I knocked my forehead against him.

"Get goin'," Eugene called. "I'll clean this shit up and get rid'a the body--thanks for that, Dane. I doubt anyone called the cops inside, but just in case, fuck off."

I tipped my chin at him in gratitude as we collected ourselves and started to move toward the front'a the bar where our bikes were parked.

"Hey, Boner," Eugene called 'fore I could round the corner.

When I looked back at him, he jerked his head up. "You find our girl and bring her home safe, you hear?"

"Won't come back without her," I swore, filled with the support and conviction'a my brothers, so the panic eased to a dull throb between my temples instead'a an incessant, distracting roar.

No one would take Blue from this earth while I still breathed.

The last'a the doubt squeezed outta my chest on a violent inhale as I swiped my phone open and called my brothers in arms into action.

WE WERE ONLY a day ahead'a schedule, but it still took longer than I could stand to get the brothers into the clubhouse and organized for the assault on the White Raiders farmhouse. The weapons in the bunker out back were distributed by Wrath and Priest while Bat was seen to by the attractive new doctor, and Zeus, King, Buck and Lion pored over the map'a the farmhouse plannin' our approach while everyone else suited up.

Curtains stopped beside me when I struggled with the straps'a my fuckin' bulletproof vest 'cause my hands were uncoordinated with restless energy.

"Here," he muttered, layin' the strap closed.

We stared at each other as words bubbled up my throat, blocked by the fear I couldn't ease from the back'a my mouth.

"We'll get her, brother," Curtains vowed, gently slappin' my cheek and then holdin' the side'a my neck. "Just like we got Elsa out, we'll get Blue. You get me?"

I swallowed convulsively, forcin' the terror down so I could say, "Let's hope for a happier endin' than that one, yeah?"

"Only ever hopin' for happiness for you, brother," he promised, draggin' me into a hug. "No man I know deserves it more than you."

"You do," I returned, thumpin' him on the back as I held him close, takin' comfort from him like a child with a beloved blanket, somethin' well-worn with love. "I'm sorry you didn't get the girl, man."

"Let's focus on yours," he suggested, pullin' away to smile that crooked, freckled smile at me. "I haven't given up hope for mine someday. If Priest can get a happily fuckin' ever after, we sure as fuck can too."

I laughed, chokin' on the end'a it 'cause half'a me was over the highway down in Furry Creek with Blue, hopin' like hell she was okay.

"Let's go get yours," Curtains said, slappin' my shoulder.

"You'll be nice to her, this turns out okay?" I quipped 'cause humour was always my defence. "Save the asshole act for Eugene and Wrath, yeah? It doesn't suit your Archie comic face."

"If I'm Archie, you're fuckin' Jughead," he countered.

"Boys," Zeus said, slottin' two guns into holsters on his belt. "Get that shit outta your system 'fore we ride out, yeah? I wanna come back with every single brother intact."

"Blue told me they've got twenty-four men in the club," Lion said as everyone piled into the main room'a the clubhouse, armed to the teeth and shiftin' on their feet with restless violence. It warmed me to think they were all fired up to help Blue not just 'cause'a me but 'cause they'd fallen for her themselves over beers at Eugene's. "They have loose shifts at the property, six at a time, three in front, two in back and one waitin' at the entrance to the only road in and out. Apparently, they're about to make a deal with some other enemy'a The Fallen to join forces against the club, so look out for more people on the ground than just the Raiders."

"Never a moment's peace," Nova muttered, but there was a curlin' grin at the side'a his mouth.

"You'd get bored otherwise," King said, nudgin' him.

Nova raised his brows. "With a woman like Lila? Yeah, not likely."

"Game faces on, boys," Zeus said, voice low and rumblin' like thunder, shakin' our bones so sombreness settled over the group. "We ride out to getta woman'a The Fallen outta those bastards' hands. She could be hurt, so be careful. You get her, you get out. Leave the others to the rest'a us. Reconvene back 'ere when it's over, and by over, I mean that clubhouse is burnin' to the ground with dozens'a bodies in it, ya hear?"

We roared in tandem, a swell'a savage voices raised in war.

"Let's end this 'fore they get a chance to take anyone else from us," Zeus concluded, harkenin' back to the people we'd lost in the club over the years. "Let's remind them why people don't fuck with The Fallen."

Another roar of brotherhood and bloodlust that filled me with hope.

No matter what, we'd bring Blue back into the fold, and this time, I'd never let her go a-fuckin'-gain.

We rode out in perfect formation, Zeus as our leader at the front'a the pack with King ridin' at the back as Road Captain, our future president.

Curtains at my side keepin' perfect pace with me as we raced down the ribbon'a road toward Blue.

It was almost enough to distract me from the vision'a Blue that kept eruptin' behind my eyes. Broken, battered, even dead, those neon blue eyes dimmed'a their vibrant light forever.

All I could think as we rounded each corner was *no, no, no.*

Please, please, please.

Don't end this 'fore I can give her the happiness she deserves.

Don't end an unhappy story unhappily.

I didn't know who I spoke to, God or the universe as a whole, but I wasn't above beggin' and pleadin' for her safety. I would've fuckin' made a deal with the devil himself for an eternity'a servitude if it meant keepin' her alive.

We split into two factions near Furry Creek, one portion led by Priest takin' the back exit to the roads behind the farmhouse where they'd ditch the bikes and approach by foot through the backwoods.

The other led by Zeus would go round the front, hidin' the bikes in the corn crops 'fore the road split off into dirt and led down to the farmhouse.

I stayed with the former 'cause Blue'd told me her bedroom was at the back'a the house, and I wanted to go straight for it. Curtains was at my side, my twin shadow, as we left the bikes and hiked on foot through the trees for twenty minutes, guided only by small flashlights and the GPS on Curtains phone leadin' us to the heart'a Raiders' territory.

As we got close, gunshots rang out through the still night, stirrin' birds from the trees above us.

My blood froze in my veins, and without sayin' a word, our group shifted to a swift jog, headin' toward the light filterin' dim through the trees ahead. We crouched at the edge'a their cover, usin' a pair'a night-vision goggles to sweep the perimeter.

Three assholes by the barn shootin' bottles and drinkin' swill, another set up at the back'a the house in the shadows near the porch with a rifle in his lap, head leaned back against the house.

Not exactly vigilant, but why the fuck should they be?

They didn't know we were closin' in like a pack'a hounds on the scent'a fresh meat.

The part'a me that rested deep in the pits'a my gut, a darkness without end, unfurled through my blood 'til my tongue and toes tingled with it.

This was the way'a the world I'd chosen to live in. This was how to settle the hearts'a broken men.

With violence and retribution for any wrong.

In my ear, the Bluetooth speaker hissed 'fore Bat's voice came over the line.

"In position, on my mark."

"What the fuck?" Curtains whispered, lookin' through the goggles at the back'a the house.

I snapped my gaze up from checkin' the safety on my gun to see a dark shadow fall outta the second story window to the roof'a the veranda.

"Hold," I snapped quietly to Bat.

A second later, two men came out onto the porch, probably to check out the noise. The man with the rifle at the side'a the house roused and got to his feet, steppin' closer to the forest as he peered into the dark.

I knew Priest was at that side with Wrath, Heckler and Skell only a dozen yards to the left'a them.

He didn't stop walkin', catchin' sight'a somethin' that gave away our men in the shadow'a trees.

"Hey," the White Raider raised his voice to call as the men on the porch disappeared back into the house.

The shape on the porch roof shifted, then paused.

My heart was in my throat, wonderin' if it could be Blue.

The man near the trees turned back to look at the house, probably searchin' for the men who'd been outside. Instead, his head tipped up, and he turned his back on the forest to go toward the porch.

And the shape stickin' up from the flat roof.

"Fuck," I cursed softly. "Priest, straight ahead. Bat, go, go, go."

A moment later, the crack'a a sniper rifle echoed across the flat fields, followed by the sharp fall'a glass in a window. Simultaneously, a dark form separated from the trees and arrowed straight at the Raider with his gun raised to the porch roof.

A garbled cry and then he was down on the ground, the shape I knew was Priest loomin' over him like the shadow'a death.

"Go," I told Curtains, pushin' forward as the person on the roof fell to the other side'a the house and outta sight.

I knew in my fuckin' bones it was Blue and thanked the fuckin' universe that she was well enough to try to escape by herself. Pride undercut the cold sense'a purpose keepin' the hot edge'a panic at bay as I shot forward from the trees. Men poured from the back'a the house, guns raised, eyes set on the trees.

On us as we spilled forth like a dark plague of locusts.

Another boomin' shot from Bat's rifle thundered across the flat lands, but I was too focused on the gunshots pepperin' us from the Raiders crouchin' behind the rails and pillars'a the porch.

"Goin' after Blue," I shouted to Curtains. "Get my back."

"Always," he grunted as he slid to his belly on the ground behind a picnic table in the backyard, shootin' at three men who aimed blindly at us in the dark.

I circled the table and broke toward the right'a the house, firin' off a bullet that caught one'a the Raiders in the throat, takin' him down with a cut-off scream. Another fired back at me, the bullet skimmin' my shoulder with icy fingers, leavin' a brutal burn behind.

Still, I ran, sweat breakin' over my forehead in the sticky summer air. No one lay on the ground around the side'a the house.

The men shootin' beer bottles by the barn were engaged with Zeus and King, father and son workin' in harmony to fight two'a the men hand to hand. The third lay at Z's feet, neck twisted at an unnatural angle.

A scream cut through the night, blood-curdlin' and raw with terror. I'd recognize Blue's voice in any form, even if I'd never had the horror'a hearin' that nightmarish call 'fore.

"HELP!" The word echoed through the clearin' as clear as the bullet from Bat's sniper rifle.

I shot across the packed earth beside the barn, trustin' the Garros to take down their rivals without help.

Blue needed me more than them.

The edge'a the cornfield was a solid wall'a darkness, Blue's voice comin' from somewhere within. I searched the seam methodically for a point'a entry and lost my breath to the relief that surged like bile up my throat when I noticed the broken stalks at the other end'a the barn.

I dove into the narrow gap without hesitation, my heart beatin' hard at the back'a my tongue.

'Cause the screams had stopped.

I refused to think about what that could mean for Blue and sprinted through the stalks, corn slappin' across my face and body as I plunged forward.

"Help me!"

The sound'a the scream was almost sweet to me as it pierced the clouded night sky 'cause it meant she was still alive.

And I was gettin' closer.

Behind me, the sounds'a shoutin' grew near, and the rustle'a stalks echoed my own as someone dove into the dark field behind me.

I didn't focus on that.

Blue's cries grew louder and louder, a beacon for me in the dark.

When I suddenly broke into a small clearin', I immediately noticed the tangle'a two bodies on the ground. Without thought, I shoved the flashlight in my mouth to shine the light on the pair and raised my gun in both hands, steady as a boat keel, not a shake'a a finger.

When I pulled the trigger, the blast reverberated through the clearin', loud as a cannon shot.

A man's head slumped between his shoulders, a neat bullet hole through the base'a his skull, the front'a his face blown out to glisten across the crops like a rural Jackson Pollock paintin'.

No more screams pierced the night.

"Blue!" I shouted as I slid to my knees in the blood-soaked corn and worked to move the dead body'a the Raider off the form pinned beneath it. "Blue, fuck, Blue, baby!"

With one forceful shove, boots slippin' in the bloody stalks, I forced the body to the side.

Revealin' my woman, crushed in the greenery, covered in a man's blood and, maybe, her own. Her closed eyes were caked in blood, chin tipped to the night sky, unresponsive. My hands feathered over her body, checkin' for bullet holes and stab wounds, broken bones and missin' limbs. Her shorts were unbuttoned, but not removed, and I righted them with shaky hands, refusin' to think in what-ifs. I didn't stop murmurin' her name as my fingers pressed to her blood-hot neck, searchin' for a pulse.

It thrummed and thrummed beneath her skin.

"Fuck," I said with an explosive sob just as a shout behind me alerted me to another threat.

I spun, crouchin' over Blue with my gun raised, the flashlight in my other hand keepin' it steadily trained at the parted corn path I'd tunnelled through moments ago.

From the dark maw, an unfamiliar man appeared with a hatchet in his hand, the beam'a the flashlight glintin' off his smile.

Before I could get a shot off, he fell with a surprised grunt to his knees, eyes blown wide a second 'fore a dark shape appeared over him. The sound of a blade slicin' through sinew and muscle hissed slick through the air, openin' a line straight across the Raider's throat.

He fell to the ground at Blue's feet with a gargled cough as he started to choke on his own blood.

In the space where he stood was Curtains, outta breath but grinning maniacally at me in the light'a the flashlight.

"Told you I got your back, brother," he panted 'fore droppin' to Blue's other side. "She's...?"

"Alive," I whispered hoarsely. "I think she's got a broken hand and can't tell what blood's hers or not, but she might be bleedin' from the face or head."

"Fuck," Curtains muttered. "I'm sorry we didn't get to her sooner, man."

"We got to her." My voice was wrecked with relief, cracked and fissured around the consonants so I hardly recognized it. "We got to her. That's what matters."

Carefully, so I didn't hurt her any more than I needed to, I lifted her into my lap and stood with her cradled in my arms.

"Why's she out?" Curtains mumbled, fixin' her hair so it wasn't in her face.

My throat burned. "Don't know. Shock, I hope?"

Without a word, my brother moved in front'a us, leadin' us back outta the field toward the farmhouse. The distant sounds'a warfare were infrequent now, a shout here and there, a last crackin' gunshot, and then silence. By the time we wound our way outta the corn--I decided I'd never eat a fuckin' cob again--the fight was over.

A half-circle'a Fallen men stood at the front'a the house, three Raiders on their knees with their hands behind their heads 'fore them.

"She's okay?" Nova asked, steppin' outta line to go to us.

"'M fine," Blue shocked me by whisperin', blinkin' up at me sluggishly.

I shifted to cover my hand with the sleeve'a my black hoodie and gently cleaned her eyes'a blood so she could see right.

"Bones," she murmured, tears floodin' those pretty blue eyes, vibrant even in the lowlight'a the porch security floodlight. "You came."

"Told you I'd burn down the world for you, Blue," I reminded her, duckin' to press a kiss to her bloody mouth. "Nothin' and no one could keep me from my girl."

She sobbed, clutchin' at my hoodie with her good hand. "God, I was so scared I'd never see you again."

"Even when death comes for us one day, I promise, I'll be waitin' for you on the other side," I whispered just for her, kissin' the tip'a that pierced nose. Love crashed through me with tsunami strength, purgin' my blood'a the violent rage and panic that'd consumed me.

"But first the ever-after shit, right?" she said with a crooked, pained smile.

"Exactly."

Zeus appeared beside me. "Glad we got you home safe, girl."

Blue's smile wobbled, voice thin as she said, "Thanks, Zeus. I-I can't thank you enough."

"Lovin' him," he said, slappin' me on the back. "'S good enough payment for me. But we got a job to finish 'ere. Know you're injured, but you good to wait while we do what Boner promised and burn this shit down?"

I watched her swallow thickly and shift with a wince in my arms.

"Can you put me down?" she asked me, waitin' for me to do so, hand still clutched in my shirt 'fore she faced Z again. "Okay, you can do it. I want to stand on my own two feet as we watch it go down."

"We didn't get Hazard and Rooster," Priest said, appearin' like a wraith over Z's shoulder.

Blue only nodded. "Rooster had to clean up a mess in Alberta, and Hazard was meeting this 'patron' they've been trying to strike a deal with. A guy named Javier Ventura."

Shock reverberated through our group as the familiar name took root.

Javier Ventura.

The same man who'd pitted the Nightstalkers against us years ago. The same man whose wife had nearly got Lila and Honey killed. The current beloved mayor'a Entrance.

He'd been curiously quiet for the past year, but we'd figured it had somethin' to do with Lila. There was an unanswered question'a paternity there, a history between him and Li's mother that made us wonder if he'd stopped targetin' the club and decided to work around it to keep her from harm.

Apparently, that was no longer the case.

"Fuck," I cursed, sharin' a look with Z.

My Prez shook his head, lookin' every one'a his forty-some odd years. "We'll deal with all'a that later. For now, let's end this and get Bat and Blue back to the clubhouse and the Doc."

Wrath, Wiseguy, and Shadow all stepped forward with gallons'a gas, Wrath headin' in to soak the ground floor with the other two takin' a side'a the structure, pourin' as they went.

Axe-Man stepped forward with a bag filled with the same incendiaries we'd brought here 'fore—Molotov cocktails, Firestarters, and flare guns.

"I think Blue should be one'a the ones to do the honours," I suggested, pushin' her forward a little bit. "Blue, Axe-Man, Bat, and Z. You all got beef with this club, and you should be the ones to see it burn."

Blue turned her face to me, eyes shinin', the prettiest thing I'd ever seen even covered in blood, even broken boned and ashen with exhaustion.

"Set the monsters on fire," I said to her, steppin' up against her back to wrap a hand around her belly.

"My monsters are still out there," she confessed.

"Yeah, but today you won a battle. Tomorrow we'll worry about the war. They're not gonna lay a hand on you again, Blue, you hear me? That's a promise I'll die protectin'. You believe me?"

"I believe you," she said instantly, leanin' her weight back against me as Wrath, Wiseguy, and Shadow emerged from the house and took their vigil in our half-moon formation.

Without a word, Axe-Man handed her a flare gun and me a Firestarter stick.

"You'll all die like fuckin' animals for this," one'a the Raiders promised darkly from his place on the ground, kneelin' in surrender. "You got no idea what's planned for you."

Kodiak whipped the butt'a his gun against the man's temple and he folded to the ground like a dropped scarf. Clearly, we were keepin' three'a the Raiders for questionin'. Arguably a worse fate than dyin' on the property, given Priest'd be the one to interrogate them.

"Ready?" I asked Blue, holdin' her to me, wonderin' how I'd ever let her outta my sight again.

"My aunt Rita," she said on a gasp. "She was inside, I think."

"Here, ducky," she muttered from somewhere down the line of Fallen brothers.

A moment later, King helped her forward by the hand so she could smile tremulously at Blue.

"Thank you," my woman whispered to me and King and all'a the brothers. "You'll come with us, right, Auntie?"

Rita sighed, lookin' back at the house for a moment, a strange kinda longin' in her eyes probably 'cause that life was all she'd known.

When she finally turned back to Blue, her mouth was set in a firm, pugnacious line. "Set it ablaze, Faith."

"Ready?" I asked again, squeezin' her hip and givin' her a small, encouragin' smile.

"Ready," she breathed, gaze fixed on the house that symbolized the cage she'd been forced back into by Rooster and Hazard and this fucked-up club.

"Fuck the monsters," she breathed as she raised the flare gun and shot it through the window Bat'd busted open with his gun.

The front room sparkled with light, almost beautiful in the quiet, dark night.

A moment later, I chucked the Firestarter onto the porch, Zeus followin' suit. Axe-Man lit his Molotov cocktail and hurled it through the open front door while Bat shot his flare into a second-story window.

And we stood together, Curtains pressed along one side'a me, Zeus standin' on the other, Blue in my arms, the rest'a my brothers shoulder to shoulder in a line'a family that I knew in my bones could weather any fuckin' storm, as we watched the White Raiders' clubhouse burn to the ground.

CHAPTER NINETEEN

Boner

FOR THE FIRST time since our romance began, Aaron took me to his home.

It was a huge brick building at one end of Main Street where the commercial buildings collapsed into residential houses closer to the ocean. It used to be a post office, and the bronze plaque still remained beside one of the black-painted front doors at the top of a series of short steps flanked by wrought-iron railings.

It wasn't exactly the kind of home I'd have imagined for him if I thought about it.

Especially when he ushered me inside, flicking the lights on to reveal a tastefully restored, open-concept living space. The walls were exposed brick, the kitchen cabinets and appliances a sleek black, the countertop's butcher block gleaming with care under the copper hanging lights above the stove. The furniture was masculine but good-looking, soft black couches, dark wood table and chairs, bookshelves against two walls forming one of two closed rooms on the main floor. Based on the neon sign that read "studio" on the door, I suspected it was where he made his art. Of course that art lit the walls, funny quotes mostly, and a huge, intricate replica of the Hephaestus Auto logo hung above the TV.

It was cool and cozy, somehow perfect for a man who was both a biker and a sweetheart, a funny man and an intensely complicated soul.

I lingered over a collection of framed photos on a long table behind the couch, touching one of Boner and Curtains with their arms wrapped around King at what looked like a wedding in the forest.

Even in his house, Aaron wanted to be surrounded by memories of his found family.

My chest ached as he left me to explore while he went into the kitchen, grabbing water and pain pills from a cabinet.

"I love it here," I told him softly, keeping my head turned away as he approached so he wouldn't be able to see the scar across my face.

Dr. Arora had stitched it closed properly with a delicate hand, promising that the scaring wouldn't be so bad if I took care of it with her detailed instructions. She'd also fitted me with a real brace for my hand, declaring that even without an X-ray, it was clear my pinky, ring, and middle fingers were broken.

Aaron had bracketed my back on the couch the entire time she saw to me, and I'd been grateful he couldn't see the extent of the damage on my face. Even in the car he'd borrowed from the club to take me home, he'd been focused on the road, and it was dark enough to obscure the ugly mark.

But now, in the warm light of his home, there was no avoiding it.

As if sensing my distress, Aaron only placed the glass and pills on the table before kissing my temple and moving back into the kitchen.

I swallowed the lump in my throat, loving him so much it was hard to breathe beyond the swell of it blooming at my centre.

"Gonna make you somethin' to eat," he muttered as he started banging around in the kitchen. "You shouldn't take those meds on an empty stomach. Why don't you take a shower while I fix it?"

He was careful to keep his eyes focused on the pan he was putting on the stove when I turned to look at him, and I felt gratitude warm my chest. "That would be great."

"Up the stairs. Use the one in my en suite at the end'a the hall. Towels on the rack. Call if ya need anythin', yeah?"

"Thank you," I told him as I moved toward the stairs, trying to convey how much it meant that he was giving me space to sort through the complicated feelings rioting through me as adrenaline drained through my pores, leaving me exhausted and bewildered.

Photos lined the stairwell, and everyone in the club was represented in the frames. At the top, I noticed a large canvas depicting Aaron as a little boy. No tattoos or silver jewelry or that distinctive haircut, just a skinny boy with the same eye-crinkling, wide grin and mischief in his eyes. He had his arm slung around a little girl with pale hair and the same dark, wide-set eyes as him.

His sister.

The one who'd been abducted by the Chinese triad because of her skills as a hacker.

He hadn't gone into details yet about the story, but I didn't press. If I knew anything, it was how hard it could be to speak about the pain of loss and wounds that would never heal, no matter how much time passed.

"She would love you."

His voice startled me into springing away from the photo.

I untucked the hair from my ear so it swung over my face as I looked down the stairs at him.

"Yeah?"

"Oh yeah." He leaned against the banister with a soft smile. "You two'd get up to no good, I'm sure. Curtains and I'd be fucked."

"I hope that happens someday," I admitted softly, tentatively, because now that I was *here* with Aaron in his home, with Grouch safe and half our enemy vanquished, our future actually seemed possible in a way that terrified me.

Because I wanted that ever-after shit with Aaron more than I wanted anything else.

There was no remorse in me for the lives of the White Raiders that were no doubt ash in the remnants of the farmhouse. They had shown no kindness in life, and they deserved none in death.

Instead, I was filled with hope, like a new dawn after a violent storm had passed.

"Me too," he said with a little nod, gaze lost to thoughts playing out in his head. "Go wash up, and the food'll be ready when you are."

I turned back around without saying anything, ghosting down the hall to his bedroom.

It felt a little strange to enter it for the first time without him, but it also gave me time to appreciate it.

The first thing I noticed was that the walls were painted cobalt blue.

I didn't have to wonder if they'd always been that colour because there was still tape against the baseboards and an empty can of paint beside the open door.

He'd painted the room he dreamed in the same colour as my eyes and hair.

My heart pounded, tears burning the back of my eyes as I wandered closer to the bed. On the nightstand, tucked into a framed photo of Zeus, Curtains, King and Aaron were two printed-out photos of me. One was the selfie I'd taken in Eugene's Bar bathroom, and the other was a photo he'd taken of us outside Lin's Beauty Emporium. His nails were blue on the hand holding my face, and the shape of his smile was pressed against my cheek as I made a silly face into the camera.

God, we looked happy.

I'd never seen myself look like that.

Not once in my twenty-five years.

I thought of Aunt Rita saying she loved the shape of my smile, and hoped to God Aaron would feel the same when he saw half my face stitched together.

The shower was huge and tiled in glossy black, so it felt like a spa as I cranked the water to scalding and carefully washed without getting my cheek or braced arm wet. Washing my hair took way too long, and my sling ended up wetter than I would have liked, but I got it done.

When I stepped into the bedroom in a towel, Aaron had laid out an old Hephaestus Auto tee and a pair of boxers for me. They smelled like fresh laundry and his cologne, comforting and warm as I pulled them over my pinked skin.

I thought about keeping my wet hair down to shield my face but decided at the last minute to twist it into a bun at the top of my head.

There was no hiding from Aaron, and I didn't want to.

I believed that the kind of love we shared––bone deep, lifelong–– would make me palatable to him no matter what. It was just my own insecurities projecting onto him, and he didn't deserve that. He'd shown me to treat both of us better.

Still, I held my breath as I descended the stairs on bare feet and found Aaron sitting at the round kitchen table doodling in a large sketchbook with coloured pens. He had changed into fresh clothes, his muscle shirt revealing gauze wrapped around a wound he'd taken to his deltoid. He didn't look up immediately, letting me come close enough to peer over his shoulder.

It was the specs for another neon sign. This one said "asking for trouble" in cobalt blue.

When I looked up from the page into his eyes, they were black velvet and a soft place to land. I went easily when he tugged me gently onto his lap, wrapping an arm around my waist so I was pinned facing him, cut cheek on display.

"You gotta know, Blue," he said, so serious every word resonated like a struck church bell, like a holy toll, turning his home into a sacred space and me into a reverent relic. "If I gotta go to hell and back, fight the fuckin' devil himself, sacrifice every one'a my sins or my life itself, I'll do it. You think you're more trouble than you're worth, but you gotta understand, I've always been the kinda man who's not afraid to ask for trouble if it's worth the effort, and there's no doubt in my mind keepin' you safe and loved is worth it all."

"Aaron," I breathed as he reached up to cup my face carefully beneath the stitched skin.

"All my life, I've fought to find beauty in the chaos, to be happy even, and especially, in the hard times 'cause if I waited for the good, I'd be sad most'a the time. I didn't even realize how lonely I still was 'til I saw your colour blue and knew I needed it brightenin' my life."

I cupped his hand to my cheek and dipped my forehead to press against his so all I could see were those warm, dark eyes. "I didn't know what happiness was until I met you."

"Then please," he started, pulling away to bring the bowl of soup waiting beside his sketchbook to the edge of the table before me. He'd made me Alpha-getti. A laughing sob escaped my mouth because I'd told him once how nostalgic I was for it after raising Red and me on the sweet, red soup. "I know it's dangerous to stay here when your piece'a shit for a father and Hazard are still around, but I promised to keep you safe, and I fuckin' meant it. Don't want to live without you, though, so you wanna run, I'm comin' with you." He ignored my gasp of shock and barreled on. "You want that, I'm in, Blue. I swear it. But please, consider stayin'.

Consider trustin' me and my brothers to keep you safe. 'Cause you've been searchin' for home and family your whole life just like me, and I want the chance to make you part'a the one I was lucky enough to find here in Entrance."

Before I could respond, he pushed the bowl a little closer, drawing my attention to the letters carefully arranged in the spoon in the middle of the soup.

Be my Old Lady.

"I belong exactly where you are, wherever that is," I promised him as tears slid past the rims of my lids and wet my cheeks. It was funny that I'd cried more in the last couple of months knowing Aaron than I had the entire time I'd been stuck with Rooster then Hazard growing up. Hope and happiness seemed to have that effect on me. "And I'd never take you from your family."

"So you'll stay," he confirmed, a huge grin splitting his handsome face and shining on me like unfiltered sunlight. "You'll be mine?"

"I already was," I admitted.

He laughed then, bright, bubbling laughter that spoke of relief and hope and joy. It was contagious, and soon I was laughing too, the sound mixing between our mouths as he drew me closer to seal our lips together. He tasted like sweet red sauce, and the familiar burn of his scruff on my chin felt like coming home.

"You should eat," he murmured against my cheek before brushing a tender kiss below my wound.

"Later."

He chuckled again but moved his hand to my hair to gently pull me away, face creased with happiness. "No, Blue. Be a good girl so the meds don't make you sick."

I pouted but lifted the spoon to eat his message off the metal.

He grinned.

I rolled my eyes, but giddiness pushed like a drug through my sluggish bloodstream, reinvigorating me. Combined with the strong pain pills, I barely felt the injury on my cheek, and my left hand was down to a dull throb.

"I'mma drive you to and from work from now on, and you'll live here with me, yeah?" he said, laying out the plan for our life like a kid giving out Christmas presents. "Curtains lives next door, and we share the loft. You okay with that?"

I nodded, hoping that the time together would endear Aaron's best friend to me a little more. Truthfully, I liked the redhead. He was handsome in an approachable kind of way with a crooked grin and bright, clever eyes. I wanted to hear about his history as a red hat hacker and listen to stories about what this terrible twosome had gotten up to over the years.

Plus, he was Aaron's brother in all the ways that mattered. I'd never separate them.

"Good," he continued happily, stroking a hand down my back soothingly as I ate. "I got no doubt Hazard and Rooster'll regroup, but that gives us time to shore our defences against them. They won't catch us off guard."

I believed it.

The operation at the Furry Creek farm that night had been a well-oiled machine like something military. I didn't doubt The Fallen's ability to care for its own and defend its territory. I was just grateful they'd come for me, that they considered me part of that fold.

"You wanna change up the house, just tell me. It's your home now as much as mine, okay?"

I dropped my spoon into the half-empty bowl, too wired to eat any more. I put my hands on Aaron's face, thumbs moving over the sharp, short stubble of his beard.

"There's only one thing I want to add," I confessed. "I want you to teach me how to make one of your neon signs so we can have one together. Maybe even hang it in the bedroom."

Aaron's whole face softened to an expression of love that took my breath straight from my lungs. His hand was tender as he cupped my abused cheek and gently ran his thumb along my jaw.

"Why don't we do that right now? You got the energy?"

A little trill of excitement shivered down my spine.

I was utterly exhausted, and I knew Aaron must've been too, but it felt right to make something with him on this first night of our ever-after together so I nodded, already getting to my feet and collecting his sketchbook.

"Nah," he said, drawing it from my grip and leaving it on the table. "I already got one started in the studio. We can work on that."

He took my hand in his to tug me through the living space to the room he'd created in the corner behind the bookcases. It was dark back there, the windows blocked out. He took a remote from a wooden table strewn with paraphernalia and turned off the lights in the rest of the house so only the ones in this room remained.

"Come here," he said, already pulling me in front of him at the work table.

A large piece of grid paper was laid out in front of us, a design carefully sketched and measured out in precise lines. It took me a moment to look beyond the specs and read the backward letters to discern their meaning.

A heart filled with the words "electric hearts."

"The kinda love I got for you is electric. It lights up my soul and vibrates my bones. I can't fucking live without it. Without you," Aaron whispered in my ear before kissing my neck. "Never wanna know what it's like to go back to a life without your light."

"Same," I whispered, turning my head to kiss him. "I love this. I love you so much it terrifies me."

"Don't be scared, Blue baby."

"Not of you. Never of you. Just of losing you." Fear flickered at the edges of my full heart. Knowing Hazard and Rooster still existed in this world, knowing they'd come for us both with an unceasing determination to end both our lives, wasn't something that could fade until they were both dead and gone.

But Aaron's love was enough to keep the panic at bay.

My faith in him and his family was enough to make me feel safe enough to take a risk on our future together.

"Tell me how it works," I asked, wanting to return to the present moment instead of worrying always about the next.

Aaron reached for a set of protective eyeglasses and fixed them carefully to my face.

"How do you even manage to look cute in nerdy glasses?" he asked incredulously.

A true smile tipped the right side of my mouth, and I knew in my bones that however the wound on my cheek healed, Aaron would find me just as beautiful as he always did.

"So the design is done backwards so the letters will lay flat at the front," he explained, pulling glass tubing in front of us and flicking on a burner that produced a small, powerful flame. "You take every section of glass separately to control the bends."

I watched as he pulled on his own pair of glasses and then lifted the glass over the fire until it glowed. Working quickly, he placed it over the stencil and used an iron tool to lift the soft glass into shape. It was almost hypnotic, listening to him explain the process as he laid out the tricky shape of the heart onto the paper. Fire to paper, sinuous movement against the glass to shape it to his will, and then back to the fire with the next section.

When he finished the heart, he pressed a kiss to my damp neck, sweaty because it was hot near the flame, and asked, "You wanna try?"

I nodded eagerly, accepting the gloves he passed me even though he didn't wear any. The tubing was so delicate in my hands that it was hard to believe it wouldn't shatter under the heat. Aaron carefully guided my hand above the flame, showing me how to properly expose the section to the heat.

When it was soft, I laid it down on the stencil and accepted the metal rod to shape the letter E backward into the glass. Aaron marked off where I should make each bend with a pencil mark, and when the glass threatened to collapse, he taught me how to breathe through a blow hose to bring back its shape. I stuck my tongue between my teeth as I bent over the table, so close to the material, I could smell the heat of it perfume the air.

"Perfect," he murmured as I finished the one letter. "You wanna keep going?"

I did.

He talked me through it, helping me with the end section of the word before I started on "hearts," and then showing me how to press that word over the existing heart shape to get them to fuse. It was way more difficult than I'd imagined even though I was used to working with my hands. Aaron had to file the glass into sections for me and press blocks of wood to the hot material to cool it rapidly enough to handle. There were no visual cues to tell when the glass was molten enough, so I had to rely on feel and Aaron's other hand helping me to balance the tube above the flame, but eventually, I got the hang of it. He only had to correct me a handful of times, which I deemed an accomplishment, mostly because he lavished me with praise the entire time.

When we finished molding the lights, I was a sweaty mess, my right arm oddly tired from the strain, but I felt a blazing sense of accomplishment looking at the complex work of art we'd created together. The paper stencil and table beneath were scorched from our efforts, and I was glad for the glove on my hand because otherwise I'd probably have lost a finger.

There was no colour in it yet. He'd explained to me that the process was even trickier, using electricity to insert and burn off the colours inside the tube because neon gases wouldn't work if exposed to any air. He let me pick out the colours to finish the design later, and he laughed when I didn't choose blue just to be contrary.

It felt good to create something, but even better to be taught by someone who cared about me. I'd never had a loved one take the time and patience to coach me through learning a new skill, and it made me fall even more in love with Aaron, seeing his gentle leadership. It made sense that Zeus had entrusted the prospects to his care.

"Wow," I breathed, looking at the electric heart we'd made, knowing it was the perfect emblem for us, Bones and Blue.

I decided to get it tattooed somewhere as soon as I could.

Aaron laughed. "You should see what Eugene does. He's a proper glass-blower, and I'm just a tube bender. He can make shit so pretty it doesn't look real."

"I can't believe *this* is real," I admitted, touching the cool glass. "I have a whole new appreciation for just how much time it must have taken you to make me these so often."

He shrugged a shoulder. "I can move a lot faster when it's just me, and you were workin' with only one hand. But yeah, I stayed up late workin' on those 'cause I knew I wouldn't sleep thinkin' and worryin' about you."

I sank back into his chest, reaching up to grip his neck so I could bring him close for a kiss. When he pulled away, he gently pulled my protective glasses off and tossed them aside with his own.

"I'm sorry," I offered. "I just couldn't live with myself if something happened to Grouch when he was the only person before you to give me a haven and love."

"Yeah," he said gruffly. "How can I be mad when your big heart is one'a the reasons I love ya?"

I grinned against his mouth. "What're some of the other reasons?"

His grin was devilish. "You sure you feel up to knowin'? I'm more a shower than a teller."

"I'm sure," I said, rocking to my toes to nip at his lower lip.

"Well, then." He lifted me up, walking to the other end of the huge table to set me on the clean surface. "Lie back and close your eyes."

"Um..."

"Just do it, baby," he encouraged, leaning over to kiss me until I closed my eyes for him. "Good girl."

I listened as he moved away and rattled around in some drawers, making a little noise of satisfaction before he came back to my side. Somewhere, music started playing, and "Free" by Ocie Elliott poured through the speakers.

"How's it feel to be free?" he murmured against my stomach as he lifted my shirt slowly up my belly.

"Beautiful." I tangled my hand in his hair as he smoothed his hands over my sides, kissing languidly from between my breasts down to my belly button, dipping his tongue inside, before continuing to the band of the boxers.

I jumped slightly when something cool and damp pressed to my skin and moved in smooth, short strokes.

"What're you doing?" I whispered as I tried not to squirm.

The dual sensation of his warm, open-mouthed kisses and the cool tip of something pressed to my skin made me break into goose bumps.

"I told you, I like to show, not tell," he explained opaquely. "So I'm showin' ya."

I realized as he moved to another section of my torso, the curve beneath my bare breasts, that he was *writing* on me with some kind of pen. I burned to know what he could be inking onto me, but I kept my eyes closed because I loved being his good girl.

He was mostly quiet as he worked, eventually relieving me of my shirt, carefully helping my arm through the sling and then the fabric. Next went my boxers so I was laid out like a naked canvas for his work. I shivered and moaned as he sucked each nipple long and leisurely, the pen constantly moving over my neck and torso. When he moved his mouth down to my mound, I moaned low and long at the first swipe of his tongue through my folds, shocked by how turned-on I was by this experience.

By the sensation of being utterly worshipped.

He held me still with one arm across my hips as he alternated between feasting on my pussy and bending to write more words on my thighs and calves, all the way down to my toes.

When he finished my front, he helped me turn over onto my knees, braced on my elbows so I didn't hurt my left hand, and then he went to work covering me in his love again.

By the time he finished, I was shaking, on the edge of an orgasm that threatened to devour me whole.

"Please, Bones," I begged, head hanging between my shoulders.

Every atom of pain and exhaustion had been swept away by the building tide of pleasure he'd coaxed out of me.

"Hold on a minute, baby," he said as the sounds of photos being taken filled the space. "You look so fuckin' beautiful. Can't wait to see what you look like tomorrow, next year, in a decade. Know you'll just be more and more beautiful to me as I fall deeper in love with ya."

I'd always bear the scars of my past, physical, mental, and emotional, but they seemed so much more bearable under the weight of Aaron's love written on my skin, kissed into my most sensitive places, whispered into my ear.

"No one could ever love someone as much as I love you," I admitted as he helped me turn over and I reached for him blindly, hauling him close when my fingers brushed his shoulders. "I'd take every hardship all over again if I knew I'd end up here with you."

The shape of his smile pressed to my mouth before he whispered, "Open your eyes, love."

I opened them, waiting for them to adjust in the darkness to the sight before me.

He'd propped a frameless mirror against the counter across from me so I could see the way the neon pen strokes glowed against my flesh in the dark. I gasped at the colours, pink and blues and purples, my shadowed flesh brought to life by bright hues the way Aaron told me I'd brought colours to his greyscale world.

The words were backward in the reflection, but I could still pick some of them.

Brave, bold, beautiful, selfless, kind, funny, silly, sweet.

And along my jaw under my wounded cheek: *bone deep.*

I laughed as happiness dissolved the last of my tension, feeling free and beautiful and so in love with the man before me I thought I might cry from the sheer enormity of it.

I fumbled for one of the discarded pens by my hip and pulled off the cap with my teeth so I could write one thing over Aaron's heart.

My love for you is electric.

He grinned down at me as I wrote and then laughed at the design as if he couldn't contain his happiness any more than I could. His hand worked between us for a moment, pulling down his grey sweats so his cock was freed, hard and ready for me. As if the act of loving me was the biggest aphrodisiac.

I clung to him with my right arm around his shoulders and shifted as he pressed his length against my wet pussy, sighing as he slid through my snug channel unerringly until he was fully seated. The stretch and burn of him took my breath away, but he held me close as I adjusted to the sensation, and when he started to move, making love to me in a way I'd never experienced before, I knew this was it.

The ever-after shit he was talking about.

"I love you," I whispered against his mouth. "No matter what comes."

"Love you, my blue-eyed, blue-haired girl," he murmured. "And I'm never lettin' you go again so long as you'll have me."

For all his joking and charm, Boner was serious about *me*. Faith Cavendish, the good-for-nothing daughter of Rooster Cavendish, the asshole set on burning down everything Boner knew. Yet he saw me only as Blue, the girl who loved beauty and fashion magazines, who was low-key addicted to curly fries and chocolate milkshakes, who searched for the fun and loveliness in life with zeal because it distracted from the constant ache of ugly terror I'd lived with at my heart.

He loved my curves and my hard edges. The scars and the soft places.

He loved me enough to burn down the world for me, and I loved him enough to trust he'd keep me safe even when the monsters came back to haunt us.

They would, I knew, but instead of fear, pressed tight to Aaron's strong, sure form, filled with his cum as I called his name like a benediction when my own climax hit seconds later, I knew they could come for us again and again, and we'd survive every time.

We had more to fight for than they could ever know.

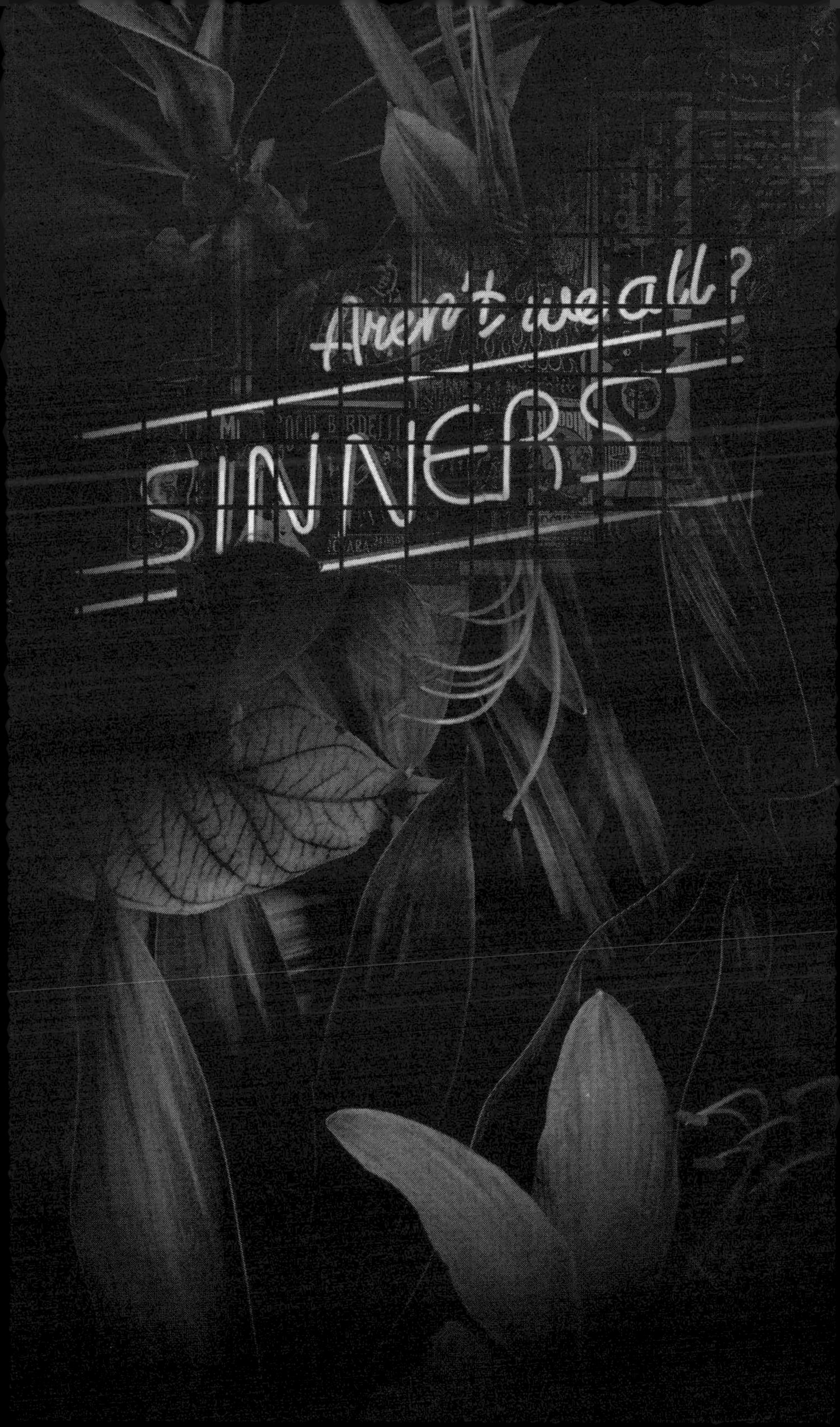
Aren't we all?
SINNERS

EPILOGUE

Blue

I LOVED FEW THINGS more than being on the back of my man's bike. It took me months to get free of my bonds to be able to ride on the back of his blue flaming Harley like a true Old Lady, and from the moment I'd clutched my arms around his narrow waist, I'd known I'd found real peace.

Whenever things got too hard over the few months after that night at the Raiders' farmhouse, we'd slip out into the night on the bike to let the fierce whip of wind and the rumble of the animal engine soothe the jagged edges of our grief and terror.

Because I'd been right, of course.

Rooster and Hazard didn't stop coming for us and the club.

In fact, they hadn't even really begun.

And no matter how prepared we'd thought we were for the onslaught, the ensuing melee brought pain and consequences to The Fallen none of us could have imagined.

Sometimes the guilt got too much for me, dragging my heart down to the depths of that dark place Rooster and Hazard had hollowed out of my gut. In those moments, Aaron and my sisters in The Fallen were there for me, reminding me that I wasn't at all to blame.

There was so much more to the White Raiders' hatred than just the loss of me to Aaron.

A terrifying history of secrets and betrayals.

But we were in the eye of the storm, enjoying the Indian summer weather of early September after spending the last week celebrating a wedding in the family.

Aaron had woken me early the morning after, already dressed in his hoodie and cut, motorcycle boots on his feet and a smile on his gorgeous face.

"Get dressed, Blue," he'd ordered as he stroked the skin of my healed cheek, a habit he'd taken up that made me feel beautiful *because* of the scar and not in spite of it. "We got a date with your birthday present."

It didn't matter that it was my birthday, really. Every single day since I'd moved in with Aaron was a gift I didn't take for granted. I loved our brick house, and I'd even grown to love sharing the loft with Curtains, who turned out to be almost as hilarious as my man and wildly competitive.

The first time I'd beaten him at *Call of Duty*, Aaron bought me a custom trophy. I kept it in the loft so Curtains had to see it every day.

"Where are we going?" I asked Aaron as I applied my make-up, and he waited patiently, used to giving me time to put on my face and choose a cute outfit. I would never be a "wake up and go" girl, and he'd learned to accommodate it without struggle.

"Like the look'a you," he said when I'd questioned his tolerance. "Like the look'a you happy and confident even more. It's no skin off my nose if I gotta factor in some extra time when makin' plans for you to get dolled up the way you like."

The way *you* like.

That was the kind of man Aaron Clare was—selfless and giving and always protective of my mental health and independence.

I was so fucking lucky.

And I couldn't wait to give him the present I'd been waiting two weeks to gift him because I was dramatic enough to want to do it on my birthday.

It was really a gift to both of us, and I couldn't wait, after all this time, to see his face when he opened it. I subtly included the ribbon-wrapped files in my cute sparkly-blue backpack before we left the house and took off into the weak light of the rising morning sun.

We drove the Sea to Sky Highway all the way down to Vancouver to a cemetery of all places.

It was pretty, though, filled with established oak trees and well-tended flower beds. Aaron led me through the tombstones without a word, and I didn't question him.

I'd learned to trust him whatever came, to follow him without doubt, and I was happy to do so now.

Finally, he stopped before a grave at the edge of the cemetery. It had a small plaque placed into the ground, and he had to bend to clear it of debris before I could read what was written there.

Hope Bonham.

I blinked at the name, mouth dropping open as I processed the information.

Aaron started speaking before I could.

"I knew you always wondered what happened to your mum when she left Rooster. Well, after some serious searchin' between the three'a us, Lion, Curtains and I tracked her down. She actually moved to Vancouver, entered a rehab program, and eventually met a man named Sandy. She died five years ago'a heart complications, probably related to her drug problem. But when I got in touch with Sandy, he mentioned she'd set aside shit for you in her will. That she tried to keep tabs on you even though she knew she'd never be able to get you back from Rooster. He'd loved to meet you some day if you're up to it, to talk about your ma."

The pressure of tears in my chest was too much to bear. As if sensing how overwhelmed I was, Aaron stepped closer, taking my left hand, long since healed from Hazard's abuse.

"She loved you to the end," he told me seriously, the lines fanning out beside his eyes pale from being so often crinkled in a grin under the sun. "No one with a heart could know you and remain unmoved by the beauty'a ya."

He pulled something out of his pocket, a little black pouch and set it in my hand. "She left you the only thing'a value she ever had. Sandy said he wasn't even mad when he read the will, only sad he couldn't find you after you ran from Rooster."

My fingers shook as I opened the tiny pouch and upturned its contents into my hand.

Sapphires.

Six stones of various sizes, all glittering in the late-summer sun.

"Apparently, she came from some old mining family out east, and she hid these from Rooster for a rainy day. I guess she sold some over the years to fund her escape, but she kept these for you."

My vision blurred as I stared down at the jewels, feeling the ache of a mystery never answered sew itself shut inside my chest.

"Thank you," I mouthed to my man, my voice lost to the tide of emotion dragging me under.

"Thank you," he told me, cupping my face in both hands, his rings cool against my skin. "For trustin' me when you were terrified to take a chance on anyone. For stayin' by me these past few months even when shit got so bad we thought it wouldn't end. Thank you for bringin' the colour blue into my life."

I reared up, jewels clenched in my fist, to throw my arms around his neck and reel him in for a kiss. He tasted like sunshine and his favourite sugary breakfast cereal. The feel of him, the scent of him, the texture of his love like sunlight against my skin was all so familiar to me now, I'd know him even in the dark.

"Best birthday present ever," I said into his mouth.

He chuckled, palming my ass. "It's not over yet. C'mon, baby Blue, I got more to give you."

OUR NEXT STOP was Hephaestus Auto, which wasn't really surprising because I loved spending time at the garage with Aaron while he worked. There was nothing like the sight of my man streaked in grease bent over an engine. It had ignited a kink I'd never even known I had.

But it was a Sunday, and the shop was empty as he led me through the bays to the fourth one at the end.

"Close your eyes."

I obeyed, already smiling, wondering what could be waiting for me.

"Open," he said a moment later after tugging me through the sliding metal door.

At first, I didn't even recognize it.

But it was still my old beaten-up Mazda, just sparkling with a new paint job.

Cobalt blue, the same colour as my eyes and hair.

"What the hell?" I asked.

Aaron threw back his head and laughed, wiping his eyes when he finally looked back at me. "It was a piece'a shit, and I'm a mechanic. Can't have my Old Lady representin' like that."

"It's beautiful," I crowed, kissing his jaw before moving to the car and checking the paint job in greater detail.

The inside had been reupholstered in baby blue leather and something hung from the rearview mirror.

I opened the door and got into the driver's seat to inspect it closer.

It was a note in Aaron's cramped handwriting.

Look up.

I looked out the windshield to find Aaron gone from the garage, the bay door rumbling open behind me, and a neon sign lit up on the wall across from me.

Come find me baby baby baby.

It perfectly mirrored the one he'd done that still hung up in Honey Bear Café & Bakery.

Laughter spilled out of me as I realized what he'd done.

A scavenger hunt.

Anticipation was sweet on the back of my tongue as I started the car, the engine purring like it never had before, and slowly pulled out of the garage. The door closed after me so someone had to be inside, but I left it alone and pulled out of The Fallen compound to go to Honey Bear Café.

The owner, Lauren, greeted me with a huge smile and handed me a mini cake with a single candle.

"Happy birthday," she yelled even though I was right in front of her.

I laughed as we shared the cake together, looking over at the sign Aaron had added to the wall beside the original.

It was a pretty blue ring.

"Mark's Jewelry?" I guessed around a bite of lemon cake.

Lauren winked at me and sent me on my way with a brief hug.

I had never been to Mark's Jewelry, but Mark himself greeted me at the door and led me inside. His almost wild grin was on his face as he handed me a black shopping bag and gestured over my shoulder.

Where everything is evergreen.

My mouth split wide around the smile that formed at the clue.

I was tempted to open the shopping bag on my way to Evergreen Gas, but I refrained because I knew how much work Aaron had put into this surprise.

It was, by far and away, the best birthday I had ever had.

Grouch had started to include me in his family celebrations and his wife always made a cake for me over the years, but this was different.

This was a celebration of not just me, but us.

It felt good after everything we'd been through, like a victory lap.

When I pulled up to the retro gas station that had been my home for so many years, Grouch stood by the doors with a handful of blue balloons and an enormous smile.

He had only just moved back to town, and it still felt like a treat to see him, so I gave in to temptation and ran to him, flinging my arms around his waist. His laughter rumbled through me as he squeezed me back.

"Happy birthday, Faithy."

He was the only one who still called me by that name, but I loved it. It was the last good tie I had to my past, and I was happy to be reminded of it when he spoke my name like that.

Like something of value.

"Thanks, Grouch. Are you in on this game of Aaron's?"

It was so like my man to make a game out of my birthday. I couldn't believe I hadn't thought he'd do something like this. He was as competitive as Curtains, and I knew he was trying to one-up the surprise party Mei and I had thrown for him at our house, complete with a dunk tank in the backyard we coaxed most of the brothers to take a turn in. He'd laughed so hard that day, I thought he was genuinely going to be sick from it.

In answer, Grouch jerked his head over his shoulder at a new neon sign glowing through the window.

Will you marry me, Blue?

My breath crystallized in my chest, freezing me where I stood.

"Blue."

Aaron's voice, smooth and low and gorgeous as the rest of him.

When I didn't turn immediately, Grouch spun me with both hands on my shoulders.

Aaron stood before me with that charming, devil-may-care grin on his face, the same one that warned me he was trouble the first time I saw him at this very spot months ago.

"I think you got somethin' to give me," he prompted.

I blinked dumbly at the black plastic bag from the jeweller and lifted it toward him.

He accepted it but shook his head, eyes sparkling so bright I had to blink away the sun spots.

"No," he said slowly. "Think there's somethin' else you've been meanin' to give me."

Surprise jolted through me like electricity, setting my heart to racing. My hands were damp with sweat and trembling as I reached for my backpack and unzipped it to reveal the uncontested divorce papers I'd wrapped as a surprise gift.

"You mean these?" I asked, incredulous when he grinned. "But how did you know?"

He shrugged. "Bikers are worse than girls when it comes to gossip, and they absolutely can't be trusted when it comes to romantic gestures. They'll give up everythin' without even the threat'a torture."

I gaped at him as he pulled the papers from my hands, rolled them up, and stuck them in the back of his jeans. When he stepped closer, the amusement was wiped clean from his face, replaced with the vehemence that existed only for me.

The unserious man who took everything about me and our love

seriously.

"You're free'a him. Free'a *them*," he corrected as he took my tingling hands into one of his. "And I knew, the moment we broke the cage that'd bound you for so fuckin' long, I had to make you mine in this last way if you'd have me. You might wanna be untethered for a minute to fly free for the first time ever, and I get that, so I won't be hurt if you're not ready. But the real present I wanted to give ya today was my last name to erase the one *he* gave you. One I think you can be proud'a."

I didn't know when I'd started to cry, but I didn't care. My vision fixed on the beautiful biker before me through the blur of tears. I wasn't even willing to blink and lose a second of this beauty.

A name had never sounded so perfect as Blue Clare did to me.

"Want you to be my wife more than I've ever wanted anythin' else," he admitted. "Not just 'cause you're hot as shit." He grinned when I laughed wetly. "But 'cause you make me feel seen straight through to my bones and the kinda love we share electrifies my life. So, Blue baby..." He dropped to his knee, and I went with him, unwilling to allow the space between us. His smile was brighter than the huge sapphire ring he pulled from the black shopping bag and presented to me. "Will you marry me?"

"Yes," I cried, lunging at him so hard he fell back on his ass on the concrete, one hand braced so we both didn't fall farther and the other wrapping around me instinctively. "Yes, yes, yes!"

He was still laughing when I fixed my mouth to his, but it was okay because the taste of his happiness was the headiest drug, and I was addicted to it.

"Can I put the ring on your finger, baby?" he asked against my eager mouth.

"Later," I offered, climbing more comfortably into his lap.

A chorus of growling motorbikes built like thunder in the air until suddenly, the lot of Evergreen Gas was filled with Fallen men and their women. Horns blared and brothers hollered. Loulou, Lila, Harleigh Rose, Bea, Cressida, Mei, Hanna, Maja, Tempest… all The Fallen women lurched off the back of their men's or friend's bikes and surrounded us, throwing blue confetti by the handfuls out of backpacks.

I tipped my face up into the coloured paper, clutched Aaron tight enough to imprint the shape of me into his bones and laughed with all the happiness in my heart up into the cerulean sky.

Thank you for reading *ASKING FOR TROUBLE*!
If you want to stay in the loop, you can sign up for my newsletter here!

Need to vent?
If you want to stay up to date on news about new releases and bonus content like extended epilogues, join my reader's group, Giana's Darlings on Facebook!

Curious what happens when Rooster and Hazard regroup and come back for revenge against The Fallen MC?
Stay tuned for *Fallen Men #9* coming in 2025.
If you loved Boner and Blue's secret romance, check out Zeus and Loulou's forbidden love story in *Welcome to the Dark Side*.

"Taboo, breathtaking, and scorching hot! I freaking loved WELCOME TO THE DARK SIDE."*-SKYE WARREN, NEW YORK TIMES BESTSELLING AUTHOR*

THANKS ETC.

I still remember the moment Boner appeared in my head. He was cocky and arrogant, but in a fun, almost self-deprecating way that said 'Hey, look at me, I'll make you laugh and charm you until you do what I want, but don't look too closely at what is underneath.' Then, when I wrote Swan Song about Curtains, there Boner was as Aaron, pre-club and sunk deep in his own trauma as his kidnapped sister was found and then lost again within hours. I think we all bear our trauma in different ways, and I was intrigued by Boner's combination of irreverence and bone-deep emotionality and loyalty. As I'm always intrigued by contrasts, I knew I had to explore his story. And this one flew off the tips of my fingers. Blue was ready for me the second I put my hands on the keyboard, driving the narrative with her horrible situation but enlivening it with her love of beauty and everlasting hope. These two reminded me that sometimes you meet people who inexplicably and immediately begin to change your life for the better. And even though it's easy to be suspicious of relationships like that at first, I think life throws us into the deep end sometimes to show us how beautifully we can swim when we thought for sure we'd sink.

As always, I have to start by thanking my beloved assistant, Annette, whose generosity, love, support, and skills keep me going through all the highs and lows of life. You are my sunshine, just as you call me yours, and I am always and forever grateful to know and love you.

Next, my beautiful and incredible agent and publicist, Georgana Grinstead, who not only goes to bat for me as a client but always supports me as a friend. From the moment I met you, I knew you would be a forever presence in my life and I'm lucky to have you as my agent, publicist, and friend.

Jess, you are absolutely heaven-sent. You read my mind and anticipate my goals so beautifully, sometimes I wonder if you have a direct link to my mind. Thank you for always being a sounding board and cheerleader and for making my life so much easier every day. I adore you.

Jenny, I don't even know how many books we've worked on together now, but I am so grateful to you for your editorial skills and friendship!

Sarah Plocher, your support means the world to me. From spreading the love for my books to lending your skills as a proofreader, you are an absolute invaluable member of team Giana and I'm so grateful for you.

Sarah Kleehammer, the HR to my Lila, thank you for being my friend. You enrich my life with your song recs, sweet gifts, constant support, hilarious sense of humour and steadfast love. I'll always be so happy my words brought us together.

Valentine, my Baby Darling, you are like the younger sister I always wanted and as Taylor Swift would say, I love you to the moon and Saturn.

To Najla and Nada at Qamber Designs, who have made my male covers for this series since I first published Lessons in Corruption in 2018, and who always make my visions come to life!

To Cat at TRC Designs, who is not only an incredible talent I am lucky to have create my discreet covers, but also one of my favourite humans (and Canadians).

To my Content team, ARC team, and Street team, I am unutterably grateful for everything you do for me and all the ways you spread love for my books! Without you, no release would be successful so thank you for your constant support.

To Giana's Darlings, my safe, sweet corner of Facebook where we get to talk about all the bookish things. Every single one of you means so much to me. I still remember when I had 400 readers in there and couldn't believe my luck. I hope you know how much I love every single one of you.

For Becca, who is the kind of friend to support you however you need for however long, no matter what is going on in her own life. How lucky I am to know you and love you and have your abundance of love in return.

Brittany, my love, your friendship, laughter, support, and beauty always brightens my day.

Kandi, you are probably sunshine incarnate, and I'm so lucky you shine your light on me.

Emilie, the CEO of Giana Darling fandom, for everything you do to support and uplift me, I love you always.

To my girls, Armie, Madison, Fiona, Lauren, who have taught me the beauty of female friendship. Your support, guidance, and genuine joy for my successes always awes and humbles me. I love you all so much.

My sister, Grace, who is the funniest, wackiest, best sister ever. I don't have one unpleasant memory of you, even when we had to say goodbye to our dad. You are a constant and I feel so lucky to have you as my sister and friend.

To my boys, who always get a little section even though they never read my books! Even though being a girl in a group of guys has its ups and downs, I wouldn't trade our friendships for anything. You taught me so much about loving myself and your unwavering friendships have gotten me through the darkest times.

And finally, last as always because I always want to end on the best note, to my husband. I could write whole essays and epic poems about how deeply I love you, how much it terrifies me sometimes because the feeling is so big and it only continues to grow with every day I spend with you. I met my soulmate at eleven years old and it's the best gift I'll ever receive. Your name was written on my bones at birth and I only had to wait to find you. I'll love you until the end of time.

OTHER BOOKS BY GIANA DARLING

The Fallen Men Series

The Fallen Men are a series of interconnected, standalone, erotic MC romances that each feature age gap love stories between dirty-talking, Alpha males and the strong, sassy women who win their hearts.

Lessons in Corruption
Welcome to the Dark Side
Good Gone Bad
Fallen Son (A Short Story)
After the Fall
Inked in Lies
Fallen King (A Short Story)
Dead Man Walking
Caution to the Wind
Asking for Trouble

A Fallen Men Companion Book of Poetry:
King of Iron Hearts

The Evolution of Sin Trilogy

Giselle Moore is running away from her past in France for a new life in America, but before she moves to New York City, she takes a holiday on the beaches of Mexico and meets a sinful, enigmatic French businessman, Sinclair, who awakens submissive desires and changes her life forever.

The Affair
The Secret
The Consequence
The Evolution Of Sin Trilogy Boxset

The Enslaved Duet

The Enslaved Duet is a dark romance duology about an eighteen-year-old Italian fashion model, Cosima Lombardi, who is sold by her indebted father to a British Earl who's nefarious plans for her include more than just sexual slavery... Their epic tale spans across Italy, England, Scotland, and the USA across a five-year period that sees them endure murder, separation, and a web of infinite lies.

Enthralled (The Enslaved Duet #1)
Enamoured (The Enslaved Duet, #2)

Anti-Heroes in Love Duet

Elena Lombardi is an ice-cold, broken-hearted criminal lawyer with a distaste for anything untoward, but when her sister begs her to represent New York City's most infamous mafioso on trial for murder, she can't refuse and soon, she finds herself unable to resist the dangerous charms of Dante Salvatore.

When Heroes Fall
When Villains Rise

The Dark Dream Duet

The Dark Dream duology is a guardian/ward, enemies to lovers romance about the dangerous, scarred black sheep of the Morelli family, Tiernan, and the innocent Bianca Belcante. After Bianca's mother dies, Tiernan becomes the guardian to both her and her little brother. But Tiernan doesn't do anything out of the goodness of his heart, and soon Bianca is thrust into the wealthy elite of Bishop's Landing and the dark secrets that lurk beneath its glittering surface.

Bad Dream (Dark Dream Duet, #0.5) is FREE
Dangerous Temptation (Dark Dream Duet, #1)
Beautiful Nightmare (Dark Dream Duet, #2)

The Elite Seven Series
Sloth (The Elite Seven Series, #7)

Coming Soon
TBA Sports Romance
Sebastian Lombardi's Trilogy
Fallen Men #8

ABOUT GIANA DARLING

Giana Darling is a USA Today, Wall Street Journal, Top 40 bestselling Canadian romance writer who specializes in the taboo and angsty side of love and romance. She currently lives in beautiful British Columbia where she spends time riding on the back of her husband's bike, baking pies, and reading snuggled up with her cat, Persephone.

Join my Reader's Group

Subscribe to my Newsletter

Follow me on IG

Like me on Facebook

Follow me on Youtube

Follow me on Goodreads

Follow me on BookBub

Follow me on Pinterest

Made in the USA
Las Vegas, NV
04 October 2024

2eea109c-5579-4aff-972b-5247c9bab4d9R01